Narrating Violence, Constructing Collective Identities

Narrating Violence, Constructing Collective Identities

'To Witness These Wrongs Unspeakable'

Giti Chandra

palgrave
macmillan

First published 2009 by
PALGRAVE MACMILLAN

Palgrave Macmillan in the UK is an imprint of Macmillan Publishers Limited, registered in England, company number 785998, of Houndmills, Basingstoke, Hampshire RG21 6XS.

Palgrave Macmillan in the US is a division of St Martin's Press LLC, 175 Fifth Avenue, New York, NY 10010.

Palgrave Macmillan is the global academic imprint of the above companies and has companies and representatives throughout the world.

Palgrave® and Macmillan® are registered trademarks in the United States, the United Kingdom, Europe and other countries.

ISBN-13: 978–0–230–21962–5 hardback
ISBN-10: 0–230–21962–4 hardback

This book is printed on paper suitable for recycling and made from fully managed and sustained forest sources. Logging, pulping and manufacturing processes are expected to conform to the environmental regulations of the country of origin.

A catalogue record for this book is available from the British Library.

Library of Congress Cataloging-in-Publication Data
Chandra, Giti.
 Narrating violence, constructing collective identities : to witness these wrongs unspeakable / Giti Chandra.
  p. cm.
 Includes bibliographical references and index.
 ISBN 978–0–230–21962–5
 1. American literature—Women authors—History and criticism. 2. Violence in literature. 3. Group identity in literature. 4. Women in literature. 5. Morrison, Toni. Beloved. 6. Morrison, Toni. Sula. 7. Kingston, Maxine Hong. Woman warrior. 8. Tan, Amy. Joy Luck Club. 9. Allende, Isabel. Casa de los espiritus. English 10. Chilean literature—Women authors—History and criticism. I. Title.
 PS151.C46 2009
 813'.54093552—dc22   2008030461

10   9   8   7   6   5   4   3   2   1
18   17   16   15   14   13   12   11   10   09

Printed and bound in Great Britain by
CPI Antony Rowe, Chippenham and Eastbourne

For my parents
Kumud and Harish Chandra

Contents

Acknowledgements

I would like to thank Abena P. A. Busia, Marianne DeKoven and Michael McKeon for their guidance, wisdom and warmth; Paula Kennedy, Steven Hall and Jo North for their invaluable expertise and unflagging patience; Larry Steen for giving the book a face; Ariel Dorfman for permission to use the quote 'An invisible country, a true Chile; and my friends across the continents, for preserving my sanity. To my family, as always, gratitude too deep for acknowledgement.

Introduction: Non-realism: the Once and Future Reality *or* Twice Abused Bodies and the Question of Agency

Embedded in the theorisation of violence and its narratives, this study sees Toni Morrison's *Beloved* and *Sula*, Amy Tan's *The Joy Luck Club*, Maxine Hong Kingston's *The Woman Warrior* and Isabel Allende's *The House of Spirits* as being representative of a unique sub-category of the contemporary novel. This sub-category revisits sites of extreme or intense violence in the lives both of its protagonists and of the collective to which they belong in the process of defining the identity of that collective; each of these novels deals with a different historical event of violence.

Beloved returns to slavery in America in its construction of the African American identity, defining its violence as intimate and personal. The violence of the First World War in *Sula* is shown as impersonal and mechanical, while Tan presents the violence of the Second World War from the point of view of a single woman fleeing the Japanese invasion of China. Violence arising from the sexism of patriarchal, feudal China is, perhaps, the only kind in this thesis that is not part of a specific political and historical event, but *The Woman Warrior* includes the Communist revolution. Finally, *The House of Spirits* provides a fictional account of the violence of both feudal Chile as well as state torture.

I will argue that the constructions of individual and collective identities in these texts are deeply embedded in these narratives of violence. Each text interrogates the nature of the collective formed: from the newly freed and escaped slaves of Bluestone, the African American community of the Bottom, the Chinese American immigrant's sense of a heritage from another country and culture and a

1

future in an adopted country to the Chilean rebel and ex-feudal lord. In form and narrative strategies these texts deploy non-real tropes and elements, using these to index realities in registers other than the empirical, to figure forth realities that strain at the limits of human comprehension and endurance and finally, to gesture towards future realities too difficult to imagine.

I want to introduce this area of study by looking at a single incident in one of the novels: the rape of Alba in Isabelle Allende's *House of Spirits* and her decision to give birth to the consequent child. The political implications of literary tropes such as Alba's – the raped and consequently pregnant woman who decides not to abort the child – are important to my study for two reasons. First, in the context of the kind of violence I am interested in examining through the course of this study, the implications of this trope often run counter to the overt intentions of the author. In the case of these highly political works such a contradiction is disquieting and significant. Second, it presents a disturbing aspect of the use of non-realist strategies on which I shall offer a more detailed comment shortly.

The trope is such an ordinary, much-used one, that a reader may well pass over its subtle complexities as being part of its biological (hence 'natural') nature. But it is worth remembering that the peculiar poignancy of this trope derives from its literal facticity: women in ethnic conflicts the world over are raped as much to reap the political capital of the possible child as in violent vengeance to redress perceived grievances. The child, if it is born, is this vengeance made flesh: it derives its power not just from its literal identity (modified/determined by the enemy in racial and religious terms) but perhaps more profoundly, from its symbolic identity. It is this seamlessness that I wish to focus on – a seamlessness that language adopts and reproduces through devices such as symbolism and magic realism. In doing so, I believe, there is a very real danger that it reproduces, also, the social, cultural and political forces that make such a crime possible in the first place. The symbolism that surrounds the woman's body, investing it, against the woman's will and consent, with meaning and value derived from patriarchal social structures and ideologies, is reinvented, reinscribed and perpetuated through these tropes.

Further, the woman's victimhood is ironically twisted to serve the very ideologies that first perpetrated it. The trope works to invest the unborn child with the symbolic power of the future: not, to be sure, necessarily a bright one, but certainly one that bears the responsibility to lay to rest a violent past. In choosing to give birth to the child, the woman is making what is, in essence, a historically compelled choice: to end the cycle of violence by either not accusing the rapist(s) (as in J. M. Coetzee's novel *Grace*) or by not aborting the unborn child, as in *The House of Spirits*. The unborn child (which must remain 'unborn' in order to adequately figure an unseen future) represents a future in which warring factions will be necessarily, even organically, united. Both Allende's context of the state and the rebel and Coetzee's context of racist South Africa demand such a future as the only desirable one. Of course, the power to end such a material thing as state/racial violence lies precisely in acknowledging the symbolic implications of both the crime and the decision to keep the child. (I would like to separate this issue from that of the much debated issue of female agency expressed through the act of suicide. This possibility is raised constantly in both Kingston's and Tan's novels and is pitted against the absolute submission of the woman – even to the death – by patriarchal structures. While I believe that both Kingston and Tan produce these suicides such that the ambiguity regarding the question of agency is left intact, I also believe that Allende skirts wide of the issue, if indeed she recognises it at all. Certainly the text gives no indication of preoccupation with it.)

I think it is important to focus the problems inherent in any trope that seeks to transform victimhood into a species of heroism or agency through the further self-mutilation or destruction of the victim herself. The rhetoric of heroism camouflages all too neatly the fruition of the most destructive form of patriarchy, forcing the woman to shoulder the burden of righting a wrong perpetrated by men and systems beyond her control. Historically, we know this trope to be a completely inaccurate representation of the actual political power or agency allowed/allotted to women not holding political office. The main thrust and efficacy of this trope lies, clearly, in its aesthetic appeal: its ability to play upon or otherwise exploit a symbology that has proved, repeatedly, to be destructive – in the most violent manner – of every conceivable aspect of the woman's being and body.

That these tropes should be used so powerfully in texts that struggle to avoid these very structures and ideologies is, I think, an index to their literal truth: the thousands of women to be thus assaulted, who have no recourse but to bear the resulting child, wield a powerful hold on public emotion – and literary imagination. However, it is, of course, this very 'truth' that needs dismantling and deconstructing; were this symbolism to be stripped from it, the woman's body would be less vulnerable to violence of this kind. Exploiting the trope in the absence of such dismantling amounts to that body being used twice over, both times in the service of an ideology that the authors of these texts most certainly repudiate.

How, then, to account for this fault line the runs between the authors' politics and their aesthetic/literary practices? The structures that magic and other non-realist techniques employ enable, in literary and aesthetic ways, the slippage between the literal and the symbolic. Indeed, the seamlessness with which material reality cohabits the same space as certain symbolic tropes and the ways in which the use of non-realist techniques aids this fluidity is crystallised in this trope. In many ways, of course, this seamlessness is precisely the site that magic and other non-realist techniques seek to inhabit. I do not want to suggest therefore that the use of these techniques is, in itself, undesirable or suspect; but that there is certainly a need for readers and writers alike to be alert and attentive to its vulnerabilities. If I am right, and magic and other non-realist strategies alert and make us attentive to worlds and possibilities otherwise inaccessible through realist techniques, then it is equally true that at least in some cases, these worlds and possibilities are constructed upon and indicated through tropes that subvert and destabilise them. The irony should not be lost upon us: these are tropes that should, themselves, be subverted and destabilised – and indeed would be if they were used in accordance with these authors' political affiliations. Yet, the sheer creative exuberance combined with the literary and political rebelliousness of magic and other non-realistic strategies serve to blind both readers and writers to its vulnerabilities. I believe such blindness is a severe handicap and one that we can ill afford.

While the subsequent chapters will offer detailed studies of the use of magic and non-realist strategies, I would like to include, here, a few observations on the strategic deployment of magic/non-realism and its political and literary implications. Magic/non-realism has been studied in the context of what we understand as the Sublime; most notably, for my purposes, by Madhu Dubey. If, as she observes, the sublime can be defined as the effort to gesture towards something beyond the empirical even while acknowledging the limits/limitations of the empirical, then this is certainly a fundamental enterprise of the novels we are looking at. They each attempt to indicate a level of community, identity and communication beyond that which the authors are able to represent through realist strategies. Some of the texts use allied or alternative strategies such as symbolic representation – as in the women humming in *Beloved* – but the strongest and most effective technique is that of Magic Realism.

Let us set aside, for the moment, the assertions of Morrison, Tan, Kingston and Allende (and those of many other authors like them) that the literary technique of Magic Realism is no more than the more empiricist realism that is familiar to the British novel. It represents 'reality' as faithfully as the more traditional realist novel did – the difference lies, not in the representation, but in the reality being represented: their reality – the African, Chinese, Chilean – is not bound by empirical limits. Thus, they claim, the girl back from the dead and exorcised by the community of women, the ghosts and spirits, legends and myths of China and the proximity of the spirit world to certain women in Chile are no more than the material facts of a culture and heritage that the 'West' cannot understand and does not have. In short, there is an insistence on the truth function of the literary narrative precisely because it is not supported by the more conventional means of realism.

Such an assertion – of 'magic as reality' – has its own significance with regard to studies of the nature of these realities and their narratives. I have no quarrel with such a stance. I wish, however, to separate out this position from the question of narrative strategies which can be fruitfully done without the one issue precluding the other. For the sake of my argument, therefore, I wish to look at magic realism, instead, as a literary device (representative or not of any given reality) that is strategically deployed by the authors in order to achieve certain ends. The question, then, is: what are these ends? From my readings of these novels I think it is fairly evident that the creation of a sphere other than the earthly, a world beyond the material, an aspect of existence transcending the bodily is vital to the worldview of these novelists. Each of these texts contains within itself the tension between the told and the untold, indeed, the tellable and the untellable. That which can be recounted within the accepted boundaries of the novel form and that which strains at these limits is often the focus and subject matter of these novels. Often, this limit or boundary is negotiated through the medium of magic realism or the evocation of a kind of 'reality' that is inaccessible through more conventional narratives. This inaccessible, unrepresentable realm is indicated or gestured towards even as it is constructed by the use of non-realist narrative techniques. I would go so far as to suggest that, given the profoundly political nature of these novels, these non/anti/magic realist strategies are central to their vision of what is a representable, accessible reality and the nature of a reality that may only be represented or accessed through these strategies.

This other reality takes different forms: in the case of Morrison's *Beloved*, for instance, a sort of utopian 'community' of women is evoked in the aural collective created by their humming. Caught within the written, the oral is invoked as a once and future reality, only liminally visible in the present time and 'space' of the novel. The legend of the woman warrior in *The Woman Warrior* embodies both the ancient mythical past of China as well as the 'home' of emancipation and belonging that the protagonist strives for in the course of the narrative. Similarly, the Chile of Rosa and Clara, evoked through their magical powers, resonates in Alba's continuation of her grandmother's habit of writing the past, present and future into being. When Clara returns to Alba and tells her she must stand witness to the suffering she has seen she sets into motion the process of healing and faith that will bring about a future that is a part of the past both in spirit and in body – Alba's child, symbolic of this future, is a direct descendant of Clara.

Most of these novels follow a trajectory of healing and reconstruction: from intense violence and disjunction to hope of forgiveness and suture. It is in this context that a notion of representational responsibility is one of the crucial concerns that animate many of the debates that this book opens and develops. If the critical questions of 'whose' and 'towards whom', cultures and moralities, remain abstract and theoretical, this is, perhaps, one of the necessities of theoretical formulations. It need not, however, blind us to the real and material consequences of literary and popular representations of nations, races, ethnicities and gender already rendered vulnerable by virtue of their historical, economic or other position. The specific context of rape that I have discussed above is a case in point. It is not hard to multiply examples and instances of the nexus between popular images/representation and the matrix of socio-political realities within which they function. The fallout of certain kinds of images and the currency they accumulate in popular imaginations, representations and usages often translate into and encompass everything from the minutiae of the everyday existences of, say, Chinese and African American women to trade embargoes, economic sanctions and foreign policies. In other words, literary texts – especially those that fall within the parameters of the texts I discuss – operate within material matrices quite other than the ones that their authors or their publishers may be concerned with. Thus, whether Kingston or Morrison are writing from within unique and distinct Chinese and African traditions or not, and whether their targeted audiences are Chinese Americans and African Americans or not, their texts circulate within the vast network of social, historical, political and cultural forces cited above and hence, have material consequences for real people.

The parameters that I have chosen to define and select the texts in this study mark them as peculiarly vulnerable and significant in this context. Critics like Caroline Rody have clarified the ways in which traumatic histories are revisited and rewritten by certain literary texts. The texts I have chosen concern histories rendered especially vulnerable by virtue of their nationality, race or gender. Further, these are texts – as I will discuss in more detail later – that are both immensely popular as well as immensely influential. Thus, the implications for questions of identity, especially collective identities, and for the ways in which these collective identities and/or their perceived images function and circulate, are fundamental and acute.

1
The Mystery of Violence

In this chapter I will deal with a fundamental question implicit in much of my discussion of the theorisation of violence in Chapter 2 as well as in the readings of the texts I offer in the succeeding chapters. Elaine Scarry, perhaps, is responsible for the formulation that pain is inarticulable and indeed, for its establishment as a critical assumption. Her groundbreaking work, *The Body in Pain*, establishes this premise so thoroughly and with such power that a whole generation of scholars has drawn upon this foundation. The fundamental question is this: why should pain be a distinct category, with its own unique theorisation, within the more general and fundamental problem of linguistic articulation? And why is it so difficult to begin to address this question? This chapter is concerned with both these issues but further, it is concerned with a specific aspect of how we think of violence itself. What terms, tropes, ideologies and methodologies inform this relatively new area of study? Are they born of this new discipline or do we draw upon other ideas and images embedded in other contexts?

Scarry herself deals with the question of why pain constitutes its own category among inarticulable things briefly and, to my mind, not very satisfyingly.[1] Implicit in her brief comments is, I think, the distinction between the representation of emotion and that of physical sensation which is, perhaps, more useful for our purpose. The distinction between pain and fear strikes me as being fundamental in that it marks the line between the material or physical and the non-material or non-empirical. My own interest in this area is twofold: first, is it possible to identify and understand this gap, this silence within this field, and second, is it possible to voice this silence, to offer some theorisation as to why pain does, indeed, constitute a separate category in the problems of the linguistic articulation of human experience?

Let me begin with the second of my concerns in the belief that it will lead me to a more fruitful formulation of the first. As will be clear from my discussion of the theorisation of violence in Chapter 2, I do not consider pain in all its many contexts, but rather focus on the pain caused by violence. I do this because this is the kind of pain that is not comprehended by an acceptable narrative. So, for instance, I have not concerned myself with the pain of falling and scraping one's knee or even of a headache. Such pain, I would argue, already exists within certain accepted systems within which it is rendered significant; from which, in other words, it draws its 'meaning'. In making this distinction I am, of course, cutting off an entire area of interrogation, but that is a different project. I select the pain resultant from an act of violence because of its profound bond to a context that demands comprehension and language.

Let me outline an argument that I will pursue in more detail in the next chapter (and will continue to pursue in the readings of the texts that I offer in the course of this thesis) to define what I see as a theorisation of the distinctiveness of the inarticulacy of pain. In my formulation of the nature of the energy that ripples out from the act of Titus's cutting off of his own hand I will argue that the terror generated by this act draws much of its energy from the loss of signification consequent upon its severance from Titus's body. The disconnected part becomes disconnected, also, from all the narratives with which the body is surrounded. Thus cast loose, it becomes meaningless – in Stephen Owen's words, a 'thing'. Because one's narrative for one's body is so innate to one's understanding and acceptance of the universe itself, such a severance is a fundamental one. It signifies for us the inherent meaninglessness at the heart of all things (or as Conrad said, the indifference at the heart of the universe). Such a movement away from meaning into meaninglessness becomes the source of fear. If, as I will argue at length in my discussion of *Titus Andronicus*, this is what accounts for the energy that is generated by Titus's cutting off of his hand and the way in which it ripples out into the play, destroying everything, then such a severance signifies, not just the loss of meaning, but 'meaninglessness' itself. (Hence, the little boy is frightened by Lavinia because her violenced body has become, to him, just such a 'thing'. Titus, however, fights to find a system of signification in her gestures; to ascribe, in other words, some *meaning*, some *humanity* to attach to this body/thing.)

In this severance from all known narratives lies the infinity of significations now made possible. That is, once the limits set upon meaning by a particular narrative (or the act of narrativising itself) are removed, an endless multitude of significations is now possible. The unthinkable, unspeakable, unnamable – the unarticulated and inarticulable – is now a possibility – is made manifest. And it is from this possibility that the true terror originates. The infinite multiplicity of meaning made possible by this severance constitutes the other side of this terror in its evocation of the unknown and unspeakable. If this line of argument is carried further, then it is possible to suggest that it is this power of pain and violence – to severe the relationship between signifier and signified – that puts it in an oppositional dynamic with the process of linguistic articulation. This is why pain, specifically that of violence, and violence itself, constitutes a separate category of inarticulacy.

In the theorisation of the distinctive inarticulacy of pain it seems almost counter-intuitive to dismiss the religious narratives and theorisations of pain provided by certain traditions of Christian theology. But if violence and the pain of violence is language-destroying in its ability to negate meaning even while it posits the absence of meaning, then surely its dialectical *opposite* is the religious narrative of faith, which ascribes and invests meaning in objects, events and the universe. Certain acts of violence in the Bible bespeak a complex relationship between the two narratives of violence and Christianity. A reading of the Book of Daniel, specifically the escape of Daniel and Shadrach from Nebuchadnezzar, offers good examples of how faith counters not just violence but *the ability of violence to destroy/negate faith*. From the short extracts I will take from the Book of Daniel (6:18–23 and 3:19–28; King James Bible), the replacement of the narrative of violence with the narrative of faith is clearly traceable.

> 18 Then the king went to his palace, and passed the night fasting: neither were instruments of musick brought before him: and his sleep went from him.

19 Then the king arose very early in the morning, and went in haste unto the den of lions.

20 And when he came to the den, he cried with a lamentable voice unto Daniel: and the king spake and said to Daniel, O Daniel, servant of the living God, is thy God, whom thou servest continually, able to deliver thee from the lions?

21 Then said Daniel unto the king, O king, live for ever.

22 My God hath sent his angel, and hath shut the lions' mouths, that they have not hurt me: forasmuch as before him innocency was found in me; and also before thee, O king, have I done no hurt.

23 Then was the king exceeding glad for him, and commanded that they should take Daniel up out of the den. So Daniel was taken up out of the den, and no manner of hurt was found upon him, because he believed in his God. (Daniel 6:18–23)

Indeed, once Daniel has been cast into the lion's den, the narrative moves away from Daniel altogether and focuses instead on the king. His is the anxiety, the deprivation (of music, food and sleep), the haste and the lament. When Daniel speaks, it is to assure him of his long life, and the succeeding joy is also the king's. Of Daniel and the lion there is no narrative. The event has taken place 'off-stage', as it were, reported and available to us only through the narrative of faith. It is significant, therefore, that the voice of Daniel, affirming the 'angel' of God and his own innocence, should issue out of the very den itself, the site of possible violence, pain and death. It is only after his answer to the king that he is taken out. The replacement of the narrative of violence with that of faith is absolute and all meaning accrues to it from the belief in God. The body of Daniel, possible site of a violent 'manner of hurt', becomes the untouched body, inscribed, instead, in its pristine unbrokenness, by belief.

The account of Shadrach, Meshach and Abednego in the furnace is significant in this context in that it does offer a narrative of the site and period of violence, as well as a more graphic and individuated sense of the body to which violence is to be done. The three men are 'bound in their coats, their hosen, and their hats, and their other garments'. The site of violence, too, is described in more detail, as the 'burning fiery furnace' is heated 'one seven times more than it was wont to be heated'. Indeed, so potent is the description of the site of violence, that it claims its victims even before the event, in the course of the description itself. 'The furnace exceeding hot, the flame of the fire slew those men that took up Shadrach, Meshach and Abednego'.

19 Then was Nebuchadnezzar full of fury, and the form of his visage was changed against Shadrach, Meshach, and Abednego: therefore he spake, and commanded that they should heat the furnace one seven times more than it was wont to be heated.

20 And he commanded the most mighty men that were in his army to bind Shadrach, Meshach, and Abednego, and to cast them into the burning fiery furnace.

21 Then these men were bound in their coats, their hosen, and their hats, and their other garments, and were cast into the midst of the burning fiery furnace.

22 Therefore because the king's commandment was urgent, and the furnace exceeding hot, the flame of the fire slew those men that took up Shadrach, Meshach, and Abednego.

23 And these three men, Shadrach, Meshach, and Abednego, fell down bound into the midst of the burning fiery furnace.

24 Then Nebuchadnezzar the king was astonied, and rose up in haste, and spake, and said unto his counsellors, Did not we cast three men bound into the midst of the fire? They answered and said unto the king, True, O king.

25 He answered and said, Lo, I see four men loose, walking in the midst of the fire, and they have no hurt; and the form of the fourth is like the Son of God.

26 Then Nebuchadnezzar came near to the mouth of the burning fiery furnace, and spake, and said, Shadrach, Meshach, and Abednego, ye servants of the most high God, come forth, and come hither. Then Shadrach, Meshach, and Abednego, came forth of the midst of the fire.

27 And the princes, governors, and captains, and the king's counsellors, being gathered together, saw these men, upon whose bodies the fire had no power, nor was an hair of their head singed, neither were their coats changed, nor the smell of fire had passed on them.

28 Then Nebuchadnezzar spake, and said, Blessed be the God of Shadrach, Meshach, and Abednego, who hath sent his angel, and delivered his servants that trusted in him, and have changed the king's word, and yielded their bodies, that they might not serve nor worship any god, except their own God. (Daniel 3:19–28)

In spite of this production of the site of violence and in direct contrast – almost opposition – to it, the reader's expectations of learning the course of events is deliberately thwarted when the linear narrative jumps to Nebuchadnezzar's reaction to something that has not yet been narrated. When he '[rises] up in haste' 'astonied', the reader is yet to learn why. The suspense is prolonged further when he questions his 'counsellors' and receives their confirmation that the three bound men were, indeed, 'cast ... into the midst of fire'. The substitution of the noun 'furnace' with the more specific and graphic 'into the midst of fire' is intended to convey, not merely the site of violence but the immediate sense of the impending peril of it to the three men. Set up thus, the actual absence of the event of violence and the violenced bodies is highlighted into sharp definition. The erasure becomes the central event.

Once again, it is Nebuchadnezzar upon whom the narrative focuses, his the fury and agitation, the astonishment and transformation. Of the three men, the physical and psychic sites of the violence, there is no narrative, as there is none of their experience in the furnace, the intervention of their God, the effect on their minds or bodies; not even the blessedness when touched by the 'angel of God'. They have no speech where even the king's counsellors are given voice. Thus, the event of their liberty and affirmation of faith is one with the event of the freedom from violence and pain and certain death. When Nebuchadnezzar speaks, it is of 'four men', not three, the fourth being the Son of God who walks with Shadrach, Meshach and Abednego. In the citing of the four men, then, the discourse of violence has already been replaced by the discourse of faith.

As if to reiterate the absence of the violenced body and the event of violence, the details of the physical bodies and their condition is repeated in an almost circular motion that seems to circle around the absence. So, the narrative reminds us again of the untouched bodies, free from violence, over which 'the fire had no power, nor was an hair of their head singed, neither were their coats changed, nor the smell of fire had passed on them'. This cataloguing of the pristine condition of the bodies of the men underlines the erasure of the narrative of violence and its replacement by the narrative of faith. The narrative of faith invests this pristine nature of the bodies with meaning just as the earlier description of the preparation of these bodies for the furnace sought to divest them of it, producing the body merely as a physical entity prepared for its destruction. This is why the three men can have no voice; if they are allowed to speak, the significance of their words will immediately accrue to their bodies, hindering the process of divestment. The body, in other words, is the site of transformation of one narrative to another and indicates the degree to which each narrative is implicated in its anti-narrative.

The meaning ascribed or constructed by faith too, is the unspeakable, the unknowable, but it is absolute. That is, faith is what gives meaning to everything. Thus, the narrative of violence and the narrative of faith (in certain religious discourses) occupy the same narrative space but on opposing sides. They are, in effect, two sides of the same coin. What is significant, for my purposes, is that both inhabit the space (physically, as in the two cases cited above) of the unspeakable, the unknowable and the inarticulable; I would venture to suggest that they are, in fact, identical in that they are equal and opposite.

I will argue that recent discourses of violence and certain religious discourses share many of the same tropes, narratives and even methodologies. I think that it is possible to argue that the narratives that are produced for violence and pain are what may be called the secular version of existing religious narratives. In response to one of the questions I began with, it is even possible to argue that this unacknowledged and undesired use of an ideology and methodology that is drawn from a religious discourse cannot coexist with the rejection of religious discourse as an available mode of theorisation of violence.

That, in fact, this unresolved space can be posited as the site of the silence surrounding the issue.

The impulse behind the rejection of religious discourses for violence lies in Elaine Scarry's idea that the act of describing is often a case of redescribing the event/body of violence, resulting in a disguised erasure. A reading of John Donne's *Good Friday, 1613, Riding Westward* provides a good illustration of how such erasure works. Even as the image of the Crucifixion is broken up into its graphic details,

> . . . those hands, which span the poles
> And tune all spheres at once, pierced with those holes?
> Could I behold that endless height, which is
> Zenith to us and our antipodes,
> Humbled below us? or that blood, which is
> The seat of all our soul's, if not of His,
> Made dirt of dust, or that flesh which was worn
> By God for His apparel, ragg'd and torn?
> (Chambers, 1896, pp. 172–3)

each of those details is reabsorbed into the religious discourse of sacrifice and overpowering divinity. The 'spectacle' (at once act, event and body) is broken down into event and body, in that order. The cataclysmic nature of the event is described first in terms of the effects upon nature (earth, sun, sky) and next, the body is taken separately as hands, blood, 'hole', flesh, height etc. At each turn, each separate segment of the event or body is taken up into the overarching fabric of the religious discourse of sacrifice. (The hands 'span the poles', the blood is 'the seat of our souls' etc.) In effect, the very act of describing in graphic detail serves to reabsorb each part into the discourse of sacrifice, reconstructing the narrative piece by piece. What this reconstruction also serves to accomplish is the construction of the mystery of the crucifixion.

> Yet dare I almost be glad, I do not see
> That spectacle of too much weight for me.
> Who sees Gods face, that is self-life, must die;
> What a death were it then to see God die?

In enfolding each of its component parts into the absolute contexts of Nature and Divinity, the act/event/body of violence becomes as impenetrable and self-referential as these phenomena.

More complex than the process of erasure, however, is the use of what used to be known as the Christian Doctrine of Accommodation. Simply put, the Doctrine posits the simultaneity of the unknowable mystery of God and the expression, articulation and comprehension of this mystery. Thus, Donne accepts the incomprehensibility of the act, event and body of crucifixion even while he seems to describe the act, the event and the body in their minute details. More than this, the essential mystery of this act, event and body, far from being understood or decoded or contained by this dissection, is in fact rein-stated through this very process. I would like to suggest that a similar doctrine can be seen in the work of Scarry, Feldman and Laub or Kleinman and Das. In their work with state torture, Holocaust and ethnic conflict, the materiality of the violence is described in graphic detail. Yet, the inviolability of the essential mystery of the act, the event and the violenced body is maintained; indeed, it is reinforced by the demonstration that it is not merely the sum of its parts. That no matter how minute the detail, how faithful the remembrance and representation of each separate material component, the 'real' act of violence, the 'actual' event, the physical body is somehow beyond our grasp, is incomprehensible, uncontainable, inarticulable.

The Doctrine of Accommodation offers, also, the avenue of indi-rect evocation, such as the allegorical story or the parable. These function as a kind of literary or linguistic burning bush, where the unnameable, the incorporeal, the unknowable, unseeable God may be gestured towards. In an identical fashion, survivors and writers find stories and other representational forms in the acceptance that their experience can only be narrativised, never related. Much of Veena Das's work with survivors of ethnic conflict on the Indian sub-continent is focused around recording and understanding these narratives.

David Tracy puts forward the interesting notion that in the para-bles of Christ, what alerts us to the cosmic dimension in an otherwise familiar and prosaic world is the unexpected moment of extrava-gance, unaccounted for in the normal world conjured up by the parable. For instance, in the parable of the prodigal son, the moment occurs, not in the snubbing of the elder son or even in the return of the younger, but in the excessive and quite literal extravagance of the feast prepared in celebration of his return. Tracy claims that this is the point at which the astonishment of the listeners is transformed into the acknowledgement of another dimension to the tale. I was put in mind of Eli Weisel's account of the moment at which he lost his faith as a young prisoner in Auschwitz. Weisel speaks of the way in which his faith stretches itself to accommodate the inexplicable horror of what he is forced to witness and experience until he sees infants being hurled into the fire at the camp. This is the point at which, he says, his faith snapped, unable to comprehend this fact. It is possible, I think, to see this as the moment of extravagance when the fabric of the familiar – even the traumatised mind's notion of what may still be considered the explicable world – is rent without warning to allow for the intrusion of another dimension. I use this example to indicate the ways in which the theoretical site that Tracy maps out can be occupied by the epiphanic energy of violence or religion.

My reading of the final sections of Isabel Allende's *House of Spirits* offers a formulation of what I call the contract between the state torturer and the militant rebel. While Allende never explicitly uses religious language or even implies its presence as a sub-text, it is not hard to see the common space shared by this secular 'contract' with the more familiar Christian 'covenant'. The deferred signification of the violenced body is fundamentally akin to the notion of deferred revelation in Christian doctrine. The notion of the sacrificial and the scapegoat is common to both discourses and demands the necessity of violence upon the body as an act of materialising/realising the vision/future reality. The subsequent iconic status of the violenced body to which the faithful are drawn and around which they gather establishes its centrality to both Christian doctrine and revolutionary movements. Most powerful, perhaps, is the status of the violenced body as witness to an unutterable event, whose meaning will become clearer at some later time – part of the same narrative that feeds the militant rebel's notion of a deferred reality/vision/dream, so like the coming of the messiah or salvation.

Clear as these convergences between discourses of violence and those of faith are, it is difficult to reach for 'conclusions'. I think that it is imperative that we understand what violence is and what faith – at least Christian faith[2] – is, how they work, and what they destroy.

But it is important, also, to understand how we think about violence and its articulation; to comprehend the words that Titus may have spoken to violence or pain itself – or a martyr of God:

> I am not mad; I know thee well enough:
> Witness these wretched stumps, witness these crimson lines;
> Witness these trenches made by grief and care;
> Witness the tiring day and heavy night;
> Witness all sorrow that I know thee well. (V, ii, 21–5)

2
'To witness . . . these wrongs unspeakable': the Metaphorical, the Material and the Violenced Body

My thesis is founded on the argument that certain kinds of violence demand their own unique narrativisation; thus, Chapter 3 uses Toni Morrison's *Beloved* and *Sula* in order to talk about the differences between the violence of slavery and that of the First World War, and the ways in which they are narrativised. Chapter 4 deals with what I call remembered violence: violence that is both temporally as well as spatially displaced. The texts I have chosen for this investigation are Amy Tan's *The Joy Luck Club* and Maxine Hong Kingston's *The Woman Warrior*, both of which are immigrant narratives. Chapter 5 uses Isabel Allende's *House of Spirits* to study state violence. In each of these studies, I will follow evidence that each form of violence is distinct from the other in its very nature; further, that each kind of violence demands its own unique narrative; and finally, that the collective identity constructed by each of these narratives is unique to that form of violence.

It becomes necessary, then, to provide a few crucial theoretical frameworks with which and within which this study will work. Therefore, this chapter is broadly divided into two main concerns: the first is an investigation of some theories of violence ranging from the socio-anthropological through the linguistic to the psychological/psychoanalytical. The second main concern is the manner and process of the theorising itself. The first concern will include several large issues such as the languaging of violence and the problems of articulation, the reification and inscription of violence and its images, existing narratives of/for violence such as the religious, the social and the political, the connection of certain forms of violence with socio-religious rituals and functions, with language and the body, with politics and the personal, and finally, with the act of collective identity formation. Of course, this is not an attempt to offer a comprehensive, exhaustive or even essential overview of these areas. Each of these will be focused around the central project of understanding the nature of violence that demands narratives and the connection of these narratives to the construction of collective identities. In order to achieve such a focus, I will be using a few key texts in conjunction with the novels I am concerned with, so as to shape/enclose/define these issues. Apart from the novels this study is concerned with, I will use a wider collection of texts that form part of this category in one or more ways. Among these are Edwidge Danticat's *The Farming of Bones*, Alice Walker's *The Color Purple*, Leslie Mormon Silko's *Ceremony*, Laura Esquivel's *Like Water For Chocolate*, and, as a case in point, William Shakespeare's *Titus Andronicus*.

The most primary of the connections I wish to trace is the relationship between violence or pain[1] and language or articulation. What makes this relationship particularly difficult to map in any definitive manner is what I call the double-edged sword model: if pain is 'that which cannot be denied and that which cannot be confirmed' (Scarry, 1985: 4) it is, for that reason, that which demands articulation at the same time at which it resists such objectification. Its lack of what Scarry calls 'referential content' (5) implies that it takes no object. Thus, she argues that 'physical pain does not simply resist language, it actively destroys it' (4) This resistance is not merely an attribute of pain, it is essential to what it is. The struggle to image physical pain or acts of violence in language, then, lies at the heart of the writer's quest for and is essential to the nature of the narrative with which to articulate it. Indeed, much of this struggle demands an evasion of pre-existing narratives which tend to contain the act or the pain through explanation, justification or any other narrative that will serve to 'comprehend' it. (I use the term 'comprehend' in order to indicate the simultaneity of the impulse to understand with the impulse to contain.)

One of the earliest and most detailed significant literary investigations of this double-headed struggle is to be found in Shakespeare's *Titus Andronicus*, where Titus Andronicus battles to the point of insanity to find a means of 'comprehending' the destructive terror generated by the violence done to his daughter Lavinia. I will pursue this struggle in some detail for a number of reasons. Primarily because *Titus Andronicus* is arguably the finest available English text for my purposes: it addresses itself to the nature of violence and the material, metaphorical and metaphysical boundaries created and broken by its comprehension through articulation with a ferocity and honesty that has not, as far as I know, been equalled. Although this study focuses on the novel genre for narratives of violence and the construction of collective identities, I have found it useful to turn to other genres when they facilitate the theorisation necessary for such a study. Using drama at this juncture may, at first, appear unusual, but it allows the exploitation of several interesting and useful conjunctions. First, this play appears at what can be seen as the turning point between the more ritualised phraseology of the representation of violence in the ancient epics and medieval sagas on the one hand and the material and literal representation made available by the flowering of Renaissance drama on the other. Second, Renaissance drama confronts the possibilities as well as conflicts of a form of representation that is simultaneously physical and textual. Thus, in a kind of dramatic doctrine of accommodation, the mystery of the violenced body is maintained in the silent but physical presence of the material body itself even while a narrative is made available in the form of verbal articulation. Third, the emergence of a new genre changes the dynamics of representation, demanding certain energies and suppressing others. The process of negotiating points of incision as well as lines of suture in the symbiotic body of genres and generic contents is one that is, I will argue, revisited at a similar juncture at the appearance of the non- or Magic Realist novel. I will draw upon this reading of *Titus Andronicus* throughout the course of this study in order to theorise relevant aspects of this particular genre of the novel.

Titus, Roman warrior, must abandon the hitherto comfortable narratives of religion and politics with which he has assimilated the fact of the violence of war, the death of his sons in the course of their 'duty' to the state, and the sacrifice of enemy soldiers as the sacred ritual of war. The violated and violenced[2] body of Lavinia remains as a physical presence on stage, rejecting each of these narratives and demanding one that will 'comprehend' the fact of her brutal rape, the cutting off of her hands and the ripping out of her tongue. Her body demands, in other words, that which she, herself, cannot speak and cannot inscribe in any communicable language, written or gestural. The breakdown of the gap between the metaphorical and the material in *Titus Andronicus* extends from the material body to the metaphorical or analogic languaging of it.

In this study of the collapse of the gap between the material and the metaphorical, it is most to our purpose to begin with the question that most demands 'apprehension' (understanding, forceful possession, fearful anticipation) in a reading of *Titus Andronicus*: what accounts for the terror of the cutting off of a hand in a play in which this is possibly the least of the violent acts committed? Like Quintius confronted with the unseen and unknown, we too are 'surprised with an uncouth fear' (II, iii, 211).[3] Much of Quintius's fear derives from the unbridged gap between the body (of Bassianus) and Martius's completely inadequate – and indeed, incongruous – description of it. At no point does Martius describe the body itself:

> Lord Bassianus lies beray'd in blood
> All on a heap, like to a slaughtered lamb,
> In this detested, dark, blood-drinking pit. (II, iii, 222–4)

'Lord Bassianus' is, here, a person – husband of Lavinia, brother of Saturninus – not the body Martius sees before him. Lord Bassianus lies on a heap; he is like a slaughtered lamb; neither fact nor image bears the weight of the horror felt by Quintius. It is the description of the 'detested, dark, blood-drinking pit' which is invested with horror. It is possible to cite this as yet another example of displacement: from the moment when Aaron speaks of 'the loathsome pit' (II, iii, 193), it appears in the text as a 'subtle hole', 'a very fatal place', an 'unhallowed and bloodstained hole', 'this den', 'this fell devouring receptacle', 'Cocytus' misty mouth', until it becomes 'the swallowing womb' itself (II, iii, 192–245). At this point it comes as no surprise when it does, indeed, swallow both Quintius and Martius to their certain doom. But metaphoric multiplicity such as this begs Quintius's question: 'What subtle hole is this?' (II, iii, 198).

Simple displacement seems inadequate, also, in the face of the intensity of Quintius's inexplicable fear, which attaches itself to the narrative complement, not of any description of the dead body of Bassianus, but to the rhetoric of the pit. Even as Aaron mentions the 'loathsome pit', he feels the foreboding of his 'dull sight' – a kind of onset of the darkness of the pit which will not allow him to see its horror. It is 'a very fatal place' to him well before the discovery of Bassianus's body; an 'uncouth fear' has already 'surprised' him into a 'chilling sweat' and 'trembling joints' because '[his] heart suspects more than [his] eye can see' (II, iii, 211–13). That the unseen is more horrible than the seen to him is emphasised a moment later with the actual discovery of the body. Even as Martius invites him to 'see a fearful sight of blood and death', Quintius finds that his 'heart will not permit [his] eyes once to behold *the thing* whereat it trembles by surmise' (II, iii, 216–19; italics mine).

The unseen, thus closely allied with the unknown, produces an affect of horror more intense than any sight or verbal description of the body of Bassianus itself. I would argue, further, that the peculiar fear that so shakes Quintius is an affect, not so much of the unseen and unknown, but of the gap between 'Lord Bassianus' (Martius's answer to Quintius's plea 'O, tell me who it is') and his body, the 'thing' that Quintius refuses to see and trembles even to think of. This gap is evident again from Quintius's inability to put the two together in his mind when Martius identifies Bassianus: 'If it be dark, how dost thou know 'tis he?' (II, iii, 220–5).

Mark Ledbetter begins his book with an epigraph:

> Body is earth, territory of violent metamorphosis and substitution. We are all in peril of becoming thing. The grotesque gap between our humanity and the thing – the body killed, damaged, wounded – is held open by metaphor.[4]

It is this gap which is held open by Martius when, in answer to Quintius's query, he cites the ring which Bassianus wears as identification, rather than 'the dead man' himself ('the ragged entrails', typically, belong to the pit, rather than to the body [II, iii, 225–30]); Martius's citing of Pyramus (II, iii, 231–2) points to the other (than the metaphorical) narrative of violence employed by the play: the mythic narrative. Both are oblique, gesturing towards the violence rather than describing – or, in stage productions, performing – the violence itself. Both (perhaps even all) forms of representation become possible, I would argue, as a result of this gap. The gap separates the 'humanity' which Owen speaks of from the 'thing', even as it separates signifier from signified. Representation and 'humanity' are both brought into being because of this separation. In this gap lies the terror that Quintius feels; in its closing, darkness and the loss of representation and 'humanity'. This is why falling into the pit means silence and certain death for both Quintius and Martius.

A signifier has a unitary relationship with its signified object, especially on stage; but the human person's (whom Owen and Ledbetter identify with 'humanity') unitary relationship with his or her body is snapped when that body is subjected to violence. Thus, 'the body killed, damaged, wounded' signifies nothing other than itself: its signifying relationship with the person it belongs to (or its 'humanity') is irrevocably 'killed, damaged [or] wounded' with it. Once this unitary signification is destroyed and the gap between signifier and signified, human and body collapsed, the violenced body becomes capable both of multiple significations as well as of signifying nothing. It becomes, in Owen's word, 'thing'. It is terrifying in both of these cases: 'nothing' indicates the pit, the abyss, into which all known systems of being, of apprehension and comprehension disappear and become unseen and unknown, and the signifier's ability to signify anything and everything suddenly 'disjoint[s] 'the frame of things' (as Macbeth might have said), opening the portals of the seen and known to a multiplicity of unseeable and unknowable significations. There is nothing that such a sign may not signify; nothing, as Titus's sanity, stretched to its limits, understands, that the human mind may not be forced to comprehend.

In his anthropological study of torture in the initiatory rites of tribal societies, Pierre Clastres writes:

> The body mediates the acquisition of a knowledge; that knowledge is inscribed on the body...An initiated man is a marked man. The purpose of the initiation, in its torturing phase, is to mark the body: in the initiatory rite, society imprints its mark on the body...The mark is a hindrance to forgetting; the body itself bears the memory traces imprinted on it; the body is a memory. (Clastres, 1987: 80–4)

I would argue further that the violenced body, in its performativity, becomes the event: not merely its inscription or memory. As such, it produces a rupture in time that creates a history by keeping always in the present the apocalyptic event. If the apocalyptic event questions, in Walter Benjamin's framework, whether 'history' was what took place before or after the event, then 'history' is in a constant state of becoming in the presence of the violenced body.

The 'acquisition of knowledge' which the violenced body 'mediates', then, encompasses in its locus a vast field of knowledge; of the selfhood of the individual, as well as of the nature of the collective identity to which the individual affiliates himself/herself. Further, it throws into relief the systems by which this knowledge is or was acquired (prior to the violenced body).

Thus, the Titus we see coming home bloodily victorious from the wars, bearing the bodies of his two dead sons, ordering the killing of Tamora's eldest son and killing his own 'rebellious' son, is a man who comprehends this violence largely through the systems of patriotism and religion. Within these systems, the 'mourning weeds' of Rome become 'victorious'; Titus can re-salute his country with his tears because these are subsumed by the fact that he comes 'bound with laurel boughs'; the 'rites' for his 'five and twenty valiant sons' are 'gracious' even as the 'poor remains [of his twenty-five sons] alive and dead' are likened to 'King Priam['s]'. The 'dreadful shore of Styx' is a mere passage to the 'sacred receptacle of [his] joys, [the] sweet cell of virtue and nobility' where his sons will 'sleep in peace' because they have been 'slain in [the] . . . war [of Rome]' (I, i, 70–93).

So enclosed is Titus within this system that the dramatically physical rhetoric of his son Lucius does not seem to impinge upon his consciousness as being any different from his own. To Lucius's disturbingly enthusiastic

> Give us the proudest prisoner of the Goths,
> That we may hew his limbs, and on a pile
> Ad manes fratrum sacrifice his flesh
> Before this earthly prison of their bones,

Titus replies, with all the dignity of the rhetoric of the patriotic warrior:

> I give him you, the noblest that survives,
> The eldest son of this distressed queen. (I, i, 96–103)

That the said queen refuses to be part of this system – rhetorically or materially – and that she and her sons denounce as barbaric,

'cruel [and] irreligious' a system which kills a man because he is
the 'noblest' and 'eldest' does not, again, seem to come under the
purview of Titus's understanding of the violence he is sanctioning.
His language ('religiously they ask a sacrifice; to this your son is
mark'd, and die he must') is vehemently opposed both by Lucius
(who responds to this grave speech with 'Away with him, and make
a fire straight, / and with our swords, upon a pile of wood, / Let's hew
his limbs till they be clean consum'd') and by Tamora and Chiron
('O cruel, irreligious piety!'; 'Was never Scythia half so barbarous!'
[I, i, 124–31]).

The system of religion through which Titus alternatively understands violence is emphasised in the ritualistic, liturgical nature of the
language with which he and Lavinia receive the sacrifice of Alarbus
moments later. Although the stage directions make no mention of
it, one wonders whether the dismembered body of Alarbus is actually
brought onto the stage in full view of the audience, or whether Lucius
is merely gesturing towards his bloody sword or hands as he says:

> See, lord and father, how we have perform'd
> Our Roman rites: Alarbus' limbs are lopp'd
> And entrails feed the sacrificing fire. (I, i, 142–4)

Titus's 'Let it be so' not only suggests the tone and manner of the
liturgical 'amen', it is the literal translation of it. He then delivers
the equivalent of the priest's funeral oration, the lines suggesting the
incantatory cadences of the liturgy not only in their metre, but in
the repetition of the first and last lines: 'In peace and honour rest
you here, my sons'. Lavinia's echoing 'In peace and honour live Lord
Titus long' then comes like the liturgical response of the congregation
to the priest (I, i, 148–57). Hence, in Lavinia's little speech steeped in
the rhetoric of patriotism and religion, Titus's hand appears as the
sacred extension of the loyal warrior and the priest ('O, bless me
here with thy victorious hand, / Whose fortunes Rome's best citizens
applaud' [I, i, 162–3]).

Titus's (and, in this instance, Lavinia's) inability to see the
(violenced) body in itself, and his dependence on oblique systems
of the knowledge of violence such as those set up by religion and
patriotism keep him bound to the metaphorical apprehension of violence, maintaining always the gap between the signifying language of

Church[5] and State and the violenced body itself. It is this metaphorical realm which is shattered and rendered redundant by the presence of the body of the raped and mutilated Lavinia from Act II Scene iv onwards. Lavinia's is the 'marked' body, beyond language (it transcends even the mythic narrative – of Philomel – which would otherwise contain it) or individuality. It is transformed by its markedness into a terrifying signifier which signifies both the 'thing' which all humans are in danger of becoming – a kind of 'nothing' – as well as the multitude of unseeable, unknowable, unthinkable significations which it makes possible. It is this changed world which Titus must now contend with.

The brutally physical language of Chiron and Demetrius casts into lurid contrast the excessively – almost ridiculously – metaphorical language with which Marcus responds to the sight of Lavinia's body. While the metaphorical system within which Marcus understands her body enables him to infer her rape (Philomel, too, had her tongue cut out, therefore Lavinia must have been raped as Philomel was), the utter incongruity of his reaction is the most striking aspect of it. Unable to comprehend the body as it is, in trying to find language that will signify it he takes constant recourse to descriptions of her body before it was thus changed. Thus, her dismembered arms are 'those sweet ornaments, / whose encircling shadows kings have sought to sleep in, / and might not gain so great a happiness as half [her] love'. The blood from her mutilated mouth is 'like to a bubbling fountain stirr'd with wind, / [rising] and [falling] between [her] rosy lips'. Marcus's language undergoes these complex contortions so that it may eventually indicate the violenced body as what it was, and now is not. He has no language with which to signify the violenced body in itself. In a sense, his language is rendered as 'blind' as he says Titus will become at the sight of this body.

Act III opens with the ironically fruitless eloquence of Titus's speech pleading for the lives of his sons. His speech is an example of metaphorical language's ability to be moving, its ability to articulate and communicate deep human emotion. With the entrance of Marcus with Lavinia, however, the limits of such language are reached. 'This was thy daughter', Marcus says, implying that what 'this' now is, is merely her body. This sense of Lavinia becoming 'thing' is underlined by Lucius's referring to her as an 'object': 'Ay me, this object kills me' (III, i, 63–5). Titus's eloquence directs itself now to the subject of his grief, but now the metaphorical sits disturbingly next to the materiality of the body before him: 'My grief was at the height before thou cam'st, / And now like Nilus it disdaineth bounds. / *Give me a sword, I'll chop off my hands too*' (III, i, 70–2, italics mine).

Even while the uselessness of his hands offers an ironic complement to the futility of his earlier eloquent language (they have fought 'in vain', been raised in 'bootless prayer', served him in 'effectless use'), the question that Titus raises is a tragically material one: 'What shall I do / now I behold thy lively body so?' (III, i, 73–105). The very picture of this body, Titus says, would have been enough to make him mad: the gap between the body in itself and a representation of it, then, has been collapsed to the point where representation is no longer possible or valid. No distancing device remains available to Titus, for whom the question now translates itself into action; direct, immediate, *the thing in itself*, beyond metaphor and representation, or systems of knowledge within which to place this body. It is in this changed context that Titus hopelessly suggests that they sit and gaze at their grief-stricken and tearful faces in a pool of water, or that they make a 'legend' of their sorrow. Both attempts to provide distance through an objective representation made possible by independent systems within which the violenced body may be understood and contained are mentioned by Titus with the knowledge that they are no longer available to him.

The only other option Titus can conceive of at this moment is to succumb to the collapse of this gap and the impossibility of representation. (Thus, their tears will change the very nature of the reflecting pool of water, making it another pool of tears.) 'Shall we cut away our hands like thine? / Or shall we bite our tongues, and in dumb shows / pass the rest of our hateful days?' (III, i, 130–2). If, as Clastres says, 'the body mediates the acquisition of a knowledge [and that] that knowledge is inscribed on the body' then this is the alternative 'system' of knowledge which Titus is positing. Indeed, it seems to be the only alternative to the surrender to the 'pit' (represented by Quintius and Martius), the voiceless 'womb', in his struggle to retain a language capable of such signification. Will cutting off of his own hands and tongue be a sufficient objective correlative to Lavinia's body? The question itself is suspect in that it circumvents signification altogether; it is at this point of impasse that Aaron arrives with his 'message' of hands and heads.

In the ensuing forty lines, the gap between metaphor and materiality collapses irrevocably, culminating in the act of Titus's cutting off his own hand. In his discussion of the penal colonies of Moldavia, Clastres speaks of the practice of forcing the prisoner to inflict physical punishment upon himself. '*The prisoner* himself . . . *is transformed into a machine for writing the law* and who inscribes it on his own body . . . The law fixes upon the very hand, the very body of the delinquent victim for its declaration. The limit is reached; the prisoner is *utterly outlawed*: his body writes the decree' (179, original emphasis). If Titus has been the 'prisoner' of systems of knowledge imposed by State and Church (even as he has been the stereotypically loyal subject of both), then this is the point at which these systems seek to subjugate him completely. The word 'outlaw', however, has, in our context, another implication as well: that is, in his complete subjugation, Titus 'outlaw[s]' himself from them by taking things, as it were, into his own hands. His 'body' does, indeed, '[write] the decree', but the nature of the decree is no longer under the control of the system which decreed it. Ledbetter also speaks of the peculiar power of the act of violence perpetrated on oneself, putting forth the idea that it is through this act that the victim 'others' himself or herself most conclusively. Ledbetter's context of slavery is not altogether removed from that of *Titus Andronicus* and it is possible to understand Titus's situation in the context of Clastres's notion of a 'limit' which defines the boundaries between the prisoner and law enforcer, and in Ledbetter's notion of the 'other' in its racial and historical parameters. The othering of Titus is, at this point, necessary to both his sanity and his survival. He must break out of the systems within which he has always existed and *only within which* he is able to comprehend himself and the world if he is to find ways of comprehending the body before him.

The notion of the limit, then, would seem to imply the possibility of new modes of existence and comprehension; but this would be to overlook the sense in which the limit functions as the point at which the subject is wholly taken over by the systems within which he has existed until this point. This paradox, which was first presented in the double possibility posited by Quintius's efforts to pull Martius out of the pit (and thus return him to the world of signification/representation) and the possibility that Martius may drag Quintius into the pit after him, thus rendering them both mute, underlines the double nature of the pit as 'womb' as well as tomb.

The act of cutting off of his own hand makes Titus both the creator of new modes of comprehension as well as wholly subject to those which made such an act inevitable.

This fraught space includes both what Clastres speaks of as society's inscription on the body of its adherents of its 'law' and its 'identity', as well as the quiescence of its members in this process (185). Such quiescence as Titus's marks him, in this framework, as accepting his place within that community as a 'full member... *Nothing more, nothing less*' (186, original emphasis). But in the case of Titus, the act of doing violence to his own body makes him both 'more' as well as 'less' than the system which forces him to perform such an act. Less, insofar as he reduces himself to the mere 'thing' that his body signifies, and more in that such an act, in Ledbetter's framework, creates an unbridgeable space between himself and that system. Thus, the 'othering' of himself casts Titus beyond the pale of both social and representational systems.

Such a casting out, stepping beyond the 'limit', renders systems of signification vulnerable and volatile. To address the question I began with, this 'limit', reached and breached by Titus's cutting off of his own hand, accounts for some of the terror generated by an act which becomes *unsignifiable*. This space beyond the signifiable is marked by the playwright in the decision to perform the act on the stage itself, rather than taking recourse to the classical convention of reporting violence that has occurred offstage. As a 'dramatic' decision, then, it recognises this space beyond referentiality in order to capture and generate the terror that Quintius felt, at the unseen and unknown, now become the *unnameable*. Titus struggles with this new non-referentiality, unable to see his dismembered hand as either 'thing' (mere material body) or a part of his 'humanity' (the 'lively body' that is no longer Lavinia, a body with a metaphorical life received from its significatory relationship with its owner).

> Good Aaron, give his majesty my hand:
> Tell him it was a hand that warded him
> From thousand dangers, bid him bury it;
> More hath it merited; that let it have. (III, i, 193–6)

The status of Titus's hand in these lines shares the inhumanity of the 'it' that is repeatedly used for it, signifying its 'thingness', with the humanity contingent upon his insistence upon the hand as part of his own 'lively body' that defended the king and merits burial. For a while, also, Titus wallows in the limitlessness of his sorrows: in so doing, there is still a remnant of the notion of limits. His language still spills over into the deeply metaphorical when he speaks of his sorrows. To Marcus's remonstrance 'Speak with possibility, / Do not break into these deep extremes', Titus justifiably claims that his sorrow is beyond the realm of 'possibility'. 'If there were reason to these miseries, / then into limits could I bind my woes', he says, where 'reason' must be read as connoting 'limit' rather than 'cause'. But he sees himself as beyond such 'reason': 'I am the sea...I the earth' (III, i, 214–26). In other words, Titus still exists within some marginal system of referentiality where no matter how 'bitter [the] tongue' it still has some connection with the 'stomach' (of grief) and can 'ease it' by containing it within the limits and reason that language functions by (III, i, 233). He is still able to find metaphorical analogues for his suffering.

The entry at this point of the Messenger 'with two heads and a hand' marks the limit of even this limitlessness. Titus, finally beyond language itself, says nothing until he is able to vow revenge. The recourse to revenge is significant because of its status as unthinking action, loyal and unquestioning adherence to its codes.[6] Hence, it is a possible variation on Titus's earlier attempt to find adequate signification for Lavinia's violenced body by doing similar violence to himself. Revenge has the advantage of righting a wrong, closing, in so doing, the rupture made by violence in the moral and emotional fabric of its victims.

The plea that his family 'circle [him] about' as he takes the vow of revenge becomes significant then to his vow to 'never come to bliss / Till all these mischiefs be return'd again / Even in their throats that hath committed them' (III, i, 272–6). This realm of action and non-referentiality is immediately audible in Titus's language. His insistence on the strictly material is heralded by the macabre allotting of sundry heads and hand to Marcus, Lavinia and himself.

> Come, brother, take a head;
> And in this hand the other will I bear.
> And Lavinia, thou shalt be employed in these arms:
> Bear thou my hand, sweet wench, between thy teeth.
>   (III, i, 279–82)

Act III Scene ii opens, then, with a speech in which the materiality of Titus's own and Lavinia's violenced bodies has overtaken the metaphorical functions of language. Their bodies, themselves, are not to be allowed to signify anything more than themselves: instruments of action and revenge. The grotesqueness of his advice to Lavinia is a function of the literalness of what used to be metaphorical: 'wound it with sighing, girl, kill it with groans' he tells Lavinia as means of subduing her heart. This clichéd usage of metaphor for the heart is, however, immediately rendered material when Titus continues:

> Or get some little knife between thy teeth,
> And just against thy heart make a hole,
> That all the tears that thy poor eyes let fall
> May run into that sink, and soaking in,
> Drown the lamenting fool in salt tears. (III, ii, 19–23)

This dramatic rejection of the common metaphorical nature of such language draws forth shocked reproach from Marcus who seems almost comically unable to break free of it himself. But Marcus's ability to continue to use such language ('Teach her not to lay such violent hands upon her tender life!') in the presence of violenced bodies is even more shocking to Titus who urges its material incongruity and linguistic non-referentiality.

> What violent hands can she lay on her life?
> Ah, wherefore dost thou urge *the name of hands,*
> ...O, handle not the *theme,* to *talk of hands,*
> Lest we remember still that we have none.
> Fie, Fie, how franticly I square my talk,
> As if we should forget we had no hands,
> If Marcus did not *name the word of hands!* (III, ii, 25–33;
>   italics mine)

Marcus's ability to 'name the word of hands' as if the gap between this metaphor and the material reality of hands still existed as a valid form of linguistic referentiality[7] is opposed by Titus's attempts to learn a new system of signification without the metaphoric referentiality of verbal language. 'I can interpret all her signs', he tells Marcus. Lavinia 'shall not sigh...nor make a sign, but [he] of these will wrest an alphabet, and by still practice learn to know [her] meaning' (III, i, 36–45). The violenced body, therefore, is not devoid of meaning; it requires its own system of knowledge with which it may be comprehended. The lack of such a system renders it a fearfully meaningless object. Hence the need for the opening scene of Act IV, in which the young Lucius's fear of Lavinia stems from his regarding her as mad, not because of her disfigured body, but because he cannot understand her gestures and takes them to be meaningless. Titus's reproach, 'Fear her not, Lucius: somewhat doth she mean', signifies not only his ability to understand Lavinia's signs, but his struggle to comprehend the violenced body itself. For this sequence leads to the revelation of the perpetrators of the crime, and from this point onwards, the violence generated by such a body on the fabric which attempts to contain it and within which it is forced to exist is brought into the open. Its disruptive energy ripples out until the body of Rome itself 'by [these] uproars sever'd'; only then can Marcus 'teach' 'the people and sons of Rome . . . to knit again . . . these broken limbs again into one body' (V, iii, 67–72).

Titus's understanding of the violenced body is complete when he is able to see his own body as violenced. Free of the perils of the pit, he is then able to tell Tamora:

> I am not mad; I know thee well enough:
> Witness this wretched stump, witness these crimson lines;
> Witness these trenches made by grief and care;
> Witness the tiring day and heavy night;
> Witness all sorrow that I know thee well. (V, ii, 21–5)

The repetition of the word 'witness' indicates its multiple meanings: Titus not only asks Tamora to 'see' his body (the 'stump', 'trenches' etc.); not only that the day is tiring and the night heavy as functions of his body, but also that his body *is itself witness*, just as 'all sorrow' will stand witness to his not being mad. Perhaps the real power of the violenced body lies in its ability to stand witness to the horror committed upon it and to the horror that it has become. Marcus, denied this comprehension because his body remains whole, may call attention to his 'frosty signs and chaps of old age [as being] grave witness to true experience', but immediately senses that his 'words' (about the violence committed upon the Andronici) do not accord with his body, and takes recourse to the mythic narrative (of Dido, Priam, Sinon, Troy). Titus's last long speech (V, ii, 166–205), on the other hand, is a simple and stark recital of the violence committed and that which he is about to commit.

Impatient of all 'speech', and careful of his own speech as 'witness' (to his actions, his experience, his body), Titus's pronouncement 'Let them not speak to me / But let them hear what fearful words I utter' (V, ii, 167–8) reverberates through the play with the resonance of language which draws its power from the material rather than the metaphorical. If fear is the affect of the unspeakable implying the unthinkable, then Titus's words are 'fearful' – terrifying as well as awe-inspiring – because they recognise the unseen and unthinkable in the violenced body and articulate it without the palliative of metaphor. In his essay, 'Political Poetry', Michael McKeon has called such language 'radically purified, stripped down to the brutal, empirical truth of things, with an outrage whetted by being unspoken, the prohibition against saying more' (26).

The recourse offered by drama in the form of physical action unmediated by metaphorical language is not one that is open to the novel, where all speech and action alike is transcribed onto the written page. When even 'pure' description is, by virtue of the medium, less than pure, the abandoning of analogy often transforms itself into what Lawrence L. Langer calls 'the quest for analogy'. 'The quest for analogy,' he says, 'whether by literary artist or historian, is the task that bedevils anyone aiming to initiate the imagination of an audience into the singular realm of the unthinkable' (in Kleinman et al., 1997: 51). I would like to argue that when that artist and audience are in the symbiotic relationship that the non- or Magic Realist novel situates them within, then the 'intitiat[ion]' of the literary 'imagination' is achieved through precisely non-, or Magic Realist tropes. Eschewing the literal and material transcription of violence into literary text becomes a necessity rather than an option because of the inarticulable nature of pain:

> The moment it is lifted out of its ironclad privacy of the body into speech, it immediately falls back in; nothing alerts us to the place it has vacated...Invisible in part because of its resistance to language, it is also invisible because its own powerfulness ensures its isolation, ensures that it will not be seen in the context

of other events, that it will fall back from its new arrival into language and remain devastating. Its absolute claim for acknowledgment contributes to its being ultimately unacknowledged. (Scarry, 1985: 60–1)

When cast into language, or otherwise narrativised, Scarry claims, the invisibility of pain is wrought first by omission and again by its active rediscription. The analogic language found for events of violence, as can be seen in my reading of *Titus Andronicus*, transfers the reality of pain and violence onto another reality, erasing the event rather than bringing it into being in language. I would argue further that, therefore, redescription can be seen as a more active form of omission and omission as an extreme form of redescription where the fact of violence is so enfolded into the language that its presence cannot even be sensed beneath it.

Veena Das suggests that it is 'in the register of the imaginary' that we can 'recover the narratives of violence'. Here, the seemingly unnegotiable schism between the (material) body and the (metaphorical/analogic) text can be bridged because it responds to 'the pain of the other [which] not only asks for a home in language, but also seeks a home in the body' (in Kleinman et al., 1997: 88) The relationship between the real and the imaginary evolves, Das says, from the 'relationship between speaking and hearing, and between building a world that the living can inhabit with their loss and building a world in which the dead can find a home' (88). I will argue (briefly, here, and through a detailed study of the texts I have chosen, in the course of the thesis) that it is in this 'register of the imaginary' that Morrison, Allende, Tan, Kingston and other novelists situate their narratives of violence; that they employ non-realist or Magic Realist tropes in order to generate the same energy of signification that the cutting off of the hand generates in Shakespeare's play; and finally, that the terror that is the affect of this energy is harnessed in the construction, rather than the destruction, of identity formation, collective and individual.

The inability of violence to find articulation in language is countered by what is seen as its self-referentiality. Veena Das remarks that 'violence, at the height of the crisis, [becomes] the subject, the object, the instrument and purpose of the action' (Das, 1986: 187). It may not be contained, in other words, even by other acts or events. I would like to extend this notion to the idea that such self-referentiality allows the violenced body to function as 'object as well as witness to violence'; it becomes the medium through which 'the pact of violence' is 'concretised' (189). The violenced body, thus, retains the memory as well as the marks of violence of which it becomes both literal and symbolic object. Important as this function is in the course of recovering signification for the violenced body, it denies agency in any form to the body itself, as well as its owner who is erased out of the equation by the act of violence which transforms the 'person' into 'thing' – an object inseparable from the body. In this lack of agency, both as literal object and as symbol of violence, articulation of and for the violenced body becomes an impossibility; the body, only, may signify itself, and it may signify nothing other than itself.

The terror that emanates from the act of violence (the cutting off of Titus's hand on stage, or Pedro Tercero's fingers in *House of Spirits*) or the violenced body (Lavinia's, or Sethe's) finds a boundless source of energy in the silence that surrounds it. Marcus's inability to speak of Lavinia's body as it is, the reader's lack of knowledge as to the violence responsible for the tree on Sethe's back, Sethe's ignorance of Halle's condition, are functions of the unsignifiablity of violence, and the terror ripples outward into the text as the writer struggles to find a system of signification and the reader's desire for referentiality becomes desperate.

It is a peculiarity of academic research in the past half century in India that the actual violence of the Partition has rarely been researched, recounted or retold.[8] Historians have stayed away from it as have writers and film makers. In the wake of the celebrations surrounding India's fiftieth year of Independence, however, much thought and research has concerned itself with the silence surrounding the Partition which many saw as the event being commemorated, rather than the achievement of Independence itself. Other than Kushwant Singh's *Train to Pakistan,* Sadat Hussein Manto's short stories remain almost the only fiction to deal directly with the violence of the Partition. Asis Nandy, pioneering the documentation of survivor narratives from the Partition, in a newspaper article published in *The Times of India* in the anniversary month of August, 1997, offered several reasons that help explain this silence, among them the fact that most survivors needed to forget in order to rebuild lost lives and regain control over old ones. Many pointed to the desire to shelter and protect their families and children from the horrors that they had seen or committed. In the extensive interviews conducted with survivors, Nandy also came across the belief, earlier related only to the realm of the supernatural, that speaking of, or articulating an evil thing brought it into being. The resistance to providing 'the horror' with a body, if only in language, spoken or written, may well be considered, subconsciously, as a kind of re-production of the violenced body itself. Many of the interviewees were reluctant to speak and unable to explain their silence. This, in itself, is not surprising, considering the lack of referentiality of such violence. Presumably, fiction, functioning 'on the register of the imaginary', is able to provide more indirect and thus less horrifying systems of signification in that it does not re-produce the violence/violenced body in as literal a fashion as survivor narratives.

Manto acknowledges the inarticulacy inherent in such violence, claiming that his stories struggle with, even as they illustrate, the manner in which bodily mutilation results in the permanent mutilation of language. However, Manto looks forward to a time when 'the capacity to signify will be recovered' (1997: 194). In her reading of survivor narratives of riots and ethnic violence, Das (1990) unearths the notion put forward by several women that they remained silent in an effort to contain the terror of the violence they had witnessed and been subject to. The metaphor used is an interesting one: the women speak of themselves as vessels which remain filled with a poison they have drunk and which they dare not let escape. They see themselves as being pregnant with this terrible knowledge but never allowed to release this knowledge into the world. Interestingly, for my purposes, this reluctance to 'give birth' or bring into being a knowledge which will then acquire a horrifying, destructive life of its own, is closely akin to the belief cited by some of Nandy's interviewees that the act of languaging violence is also an act of bringing it into physical being. The idea is intriguing for many reasons. Apart from the connection it draws between articulation and literal being, it seems to suggest that the violenced body or the act of violence itself is always already in existence. That is, for both the female survivors who see themselves as harbouring it as a living body within their bodies as well as for the – now elderly and largely well-settled – survivors of the Partition, the event and body exist in Lawrence L. Langer's idea of Durational Time. Langer's notion of Durational Time is formulated specifically with reference to Holocaust survivors, although I have extended its use. The term refers to the unique sense of time experienced by survivors of such events whereby a linear understanding of time is disrupted by the event of violence. Thus, the event exists within a frame of temporal referentiality of its own – it does not exist in the past against which a sense of present or future can be postulated. The survivor exists within this Durational Time even as she simultaneously exists within a traditional system of linear time. Thus, the violence (event or body) is always there, always alive. Hence the fear that the act of speech will render it physically forth and, perhaps, unleash the same forces again.

When Sethe's long-dead daughter Beloved reappears, Morrison is at pains to specify her physical existence. I believe that in Beloved's 'pregnancy' which saps Sethe's life and is eventually exorcised, destroying Beloved and releasing Sethe from her hold, the metaphor is given a literal life and functions in a manner similar to that narrated by Das's survivors. Manto's hope that 'the capacity to signify will be recovered at some future time', then, can be understood within the parameters of the temporary need for containment and the historic urgency to regain signification and thus, meaning. The violenced body and the event of violence can be seen, then, as the site of a deferred signification. The 'meaning' of the tree on Sethe's back, the knowledge within Beloved's womb, the three fingers of Pedro Tercero and Alba in Allende's *House of Spirits*, the drowned 'no-name aunt' of *The Woman Warrior*, the death of Chicken Little in *Sula*, is always a deferred revelation. It is true that it is revealed, but this revelation is always partial, contingent, specific to the person to whom it is revealed. Thus, the significatory power of each of these bodies and events is neither curtailed nor exhausted by the revelation of its meaning for any person or at any single moment in time.

This limitless and inexhaustible reserve of signification is partially explained by David B. Morris when he refers to the insurmountable and absolute otherness at the heart of the structure of suffering (in Kleinman et al., 1997: 29). Morris uses Auden's 'Musée des Beaux Art' and Brueghel's *Fall of Icarus* as his case in point, and although the structure of both poem and painting is such that they emphasise the ironic marginality of the suffering of Icarus, each of the instances of suffering I have mentioned above gestures towards the same sense of complete alienation from the essence of pain that violence produces. It is possible to argue, then, that, just as Titus Andronicus captures this union with pain/violence in the very act of othering himself and the violence absolutely, so violence itself can be seen as being committed in order to recapture a sense of individual subjectivity for the perpetrator. Veena Das, in her reading of Rabindranath Tagore's short stories, points to the loss of self of the terrorist in his dedication of his body and soul to the cause. The terrorist seeks legitimation and subjectivity through the structure of self-sacrifice (violence to the self) or sacrifice (of the victim). However, as René Girard has also pointed out, this legitimation can only be fulfilled with the consent of the victim to function as sacrificee. The process, Das writes, 'loses its sanctity if the subjectivity of those who are compelled to be victims and the identification with them is lost to consciousness' (in Kleinman et al., 1997: 187). In other words, the structure is one of what I will call contractual violence: as my reading of Allende's *House of Spirits* shows, the reality at stake for both rebel/terrorist and state includes the sense of self that both bring to the act of violence. This understanding can be extended to the contract between slave and master in Morrison's *Beloved*, as I will show in Chapter 3.

Halle's loss of subjectivity, memory, articulation – or its surrender to Schoolteacher – and his inability to speak[9] (he cannot reply to Paul D.'s entreaties that he follow them) is mirrored in Lavinia's loss of speech/articulation, and the silence of Sakina,[10] the no-name aunt and the thousands of violenced bodies for whom Alba bears written testimony. The silence which surrounds the violenced body is constructed, as has been suggested earlier, in its active erasure through the generalised, metaphorical language that is used to refer to it rather than to describe the graphic specificity or the particularity of the experience or body itself. Often, the events and circumstances surrounding the event or body are delineated instead, leaving the body/event, itself, unrepresented. Veena Das points out that 'none of the metaphors used to describe the self that had become the repository of poisonous knowledge emphasised the need to give expression to this hidden knowledge' (84). In part, this code of silence protected the women who returned, or were recovered by the state, to their homes after the Partition. Their 'honour', so closely interwoven with the honour of the family, was thus kept intact. Not bearing witness to the violence perpetrated upon them also enabled the women to prevent the release of the disorder that the poison represented and memorialised. Such a consensual, indeed, necessary silence, Das points out, converts the passivity and loss of subjectivity of the women into agency through the metaphor of pregnancy. 'Just as the relation between speech and silence is reversed here, so is the relation between the surface and the depth of the body' (84). Pain becomes the child that the woman harbours within her body, thus displacing the memory from the surface to the depth of her body. Since the woman will never allow this birth to take place, the movement in the woman's language for or narrative of herself from surface to depth transforms her from a passive being into an active agent: she is able to recover her body in her mind.

This recovery of the violenced body from its 'thingness' into the mind, and from there into a system of signification and agency is, in other instances, a movement that occurs along with, or is facilitated by, the agency of speech. Indeed, as Dori Laub says of his own experience as a child survivor of the Holocaust, 'testimony is ... the process by which the narrator (the survivor) reclaims his position as a witness: reconstitutes the internal "thou," and thus the possibility of a witness or listener inside himself ... Repossessing one's life story through giving testimony is itself a form of action' (85). Repossession of one's body and life is, then, contingent upon the recovery of subjectivity from the absolute othering which the violenced body undergoes in the process of being reduced to object as well as the maintenance of the necessary distance – or gap – between signifier and signified consequent upon the othering which the body experiences as it finds adequate referentiality or signification. Thus, the stories which Sethe tells and for which Beloved hungers, the articulation of Sakina's life and subjectivity in her father's pronouncement, Alba's testimony, the recounting of the no-name aunt's suffering and Titus's decoding of the meaning of Lavinia's gestures are all movements towards a recovery of signification, meaning and subjectivity through speech.

It is important, at this point, to differentiate certain kinds of violence: the violence which this thesis deals with is specifically racial, national, ethnic – intimately connected with the human, social and political process of the defining of collectivity. In the process of articulating such violence, 'a mimesis', Das claims, 'is certainly established between body and language, but it is through the work of the collectivity that this happens, rather than at the level of the individual symptom... it is the objectification of grief on the body taken as both surface and depth, as well as in language, that bears witness to the loss that death has inflicted' (Das, 1996: 80). Das takes as her case in point the tribe of women in Rajasthan whose traditional function it is to mourn. 'In the course of everyday life, men dominate the public domain in terms of the control over speech, but in the case of death they become mute' (80–1), she says, and this is one of the senses of articulation in and for the public domain in which suffering and violence finds its expression in and through the collective. At a more fundamental level, the gendering of racial, national and ethnic violence, recorded and theorised in various forums is more to my purpose.

While I do not wish to repeat the painstaking and suggestive theorisation of woman as culture bearer and her body as territory, I do wish to particularise my discussion in specific ways. First, I would like to emphasise the difference between the metaphoric displacement of the woman's body as 'territory' and the site inhabited by the woman's body in the political and violent struggle for possession of actual land. It is in this sense that the Partition is unique in 'the metamorphosis it achieved between the idea of appropriating territory as nation and appropriating the body of the women as territory' (Das, 1996: 83).[11] Second, it is a fact of such conflict that the violence perpetrated upon men is significantly different from that perpetrated upon women. Racial, national and ethnic violence targets men as enemy to be killed: the object of the violence is death and erasure. However, the violence visited upon women is calculated to mark their bodies with the ownership or desecration of the perpetrator. The body is designed to live and carry the memory, literally as well as spiritually, of the destruction wreaked upon it, even as land and buildings are appropriated or defaced. The raping of women is, ironically, as much a symbolic act as it is one of lust: the planting of a literal poison in the womb of the enemy. Finally, because of this distinction, survivor narratives consist largely of women's voices: they are the only ones, other than very young children, to survive such conflict. Thus, the burden of memory, of memorialising the community as it existed prior to the violence as well as the violence itself as event, and of envisioning a future, falls upon the surviving women. (In this sense, of course, the Holocaust is an exception in that everyone was targeted equally: it may even be that, for reasons of physical endurance, more men survived the camps than did women or children.) Making pain, violence and death public and utterable, articulating absence and loss and transforming silence into speech becomes, then, not just a means of recovering self and subjectivity, it is also – and perhaps is seen as the primary obligation by the women themselves – the means of representing, healing and giving a new life to the collective.

For Langer, however, 'the tentative world of duration' outside the 'security of chronology' forces us to revise our assumptions about 'shareable memory' and the 'collective unconscious' leaving only a 'form of private and communal endurance, based on mutual toleration rather than mutual love' (63). Langer's research centres almost exclusively on survivor narratives of the Holocaust and indicates, I think, the unique lack of referentiality that this event has when compared with the violence of slavery, the Partition, the First World War, the Pinochet regime, or even of the massacres along the river boundaries of Haiti and the Dominican Republic in Edwidge Danticat's *The Farming of Bones*. The difference, as we have seen, lies at least partially in the peculiar genderisation of the ethnic, racial and national conflicts with which these texts deal. In her essay 'Language and the Body: Transactions in the Construction of Pain', Veena Das points to the genre of lamentation which, she says, gives women

> control both through bodies and through their language – grief is articulated through the body, for instance, by infliction of grievous hurt on oneself, 'objectifying' and making present the inner state, and is finally given a home in language. Thus, the transactions between body and language lead to an articulation of the world in which the strangeness of the world revealed by death, by its non-inhabitability, can be transformed into a world in which one can dwell again, in full awareness of a life that has to be lived in loss. (68–9)

The process of witnessing or testimony is similar in structure to the process of lamentation and, indeed, is a form of lamentation itself. While the forms and traditions of the act of witnessing or bearing testimony may not be as ritualised as are the traditional forms of lamentation in many cultures, it does acquire and establish acts and gestures through which it is articulated, as my reading of Morrison's and Allende's texts will show.

In her novel, *The Farming of Bones*, Edwidge Danticat devotes entire sections only to the stories of individuals told either by themselves or by surviving witnesses. What is emphasised in these sections is not only the need to hear every individual story, but the need for each of these individuals to testify to their own experiences to a community of like sufferers and willing listeners. Many invoke their violenced bodies as witness to their narratives in a manner akin to Titus's calling witness to his wounds, dismemberment and evidence of grief. In a dialectical movement, these narrators testify to what they see as a collective that is formed in the act of witnessing such testimony. In the following chapters the transformation of these communities of sufferers into ethnic, racial or national collectives has been traced. Indeed, Langer feels that in order to understand suffering on a communal or collective level, it must be approached individual by individual. Scarry also, in distinguishing the violence of torture from that of war, makes the distinction that although violence can be multiplied numerically in order to be applicable to the thousands injured in war, pain must be understood individually. While my argument so far and in the following chapters will make clear that I do not believe that the 'multiplicity' of war can be 'replaced by the close proximity' of torture (Scarry, 1985: 65) I do feel that her notion of pain, here, may be conflated with the kind of suffering and violence which I have instanced above.

Das's assertion that it 'worries' her that she has been 'unable to name that which died when autonomous citizens of India were simultaneously born as monsters' (Das, 1996: 89) gestures towards a vital obstacle to the construction of narratives which succeed the simplicity of those narratives which bear witness. Those who tried to name the unnameable, Das claims, either suffered insanity themselves, or spoke glibly of national honour. The process following testimony is one in which justificatory narratives, analogues, meta-narratives and systems of referentiality are sought. The 'register of the imaginary' which is suggested by Manto functions, I believe, on two levels: first, as the necessity for fictionalisation, and second, as the necessity for a non-realist system of representation. Of the few fictional narratives of the Partition which exist, Das uses the idea of the register of the imaginary in this first sense: it is in fiction, she believes, rather than in non-fictional narrative, that 'the question of what could constitute the passion of those who occupied this unspeakable and unhearable zone was given shape' (Das, 1996: 87).

Dori Laub points out, also, that non-articulation of trauma causes the memory to become suppressed and, sometimes, distorted. Over time, the survivor extends this distortion into her sense of herself, seeing herself as the product of that distorted memory or event.[12] Thus, in the case of a Holocaust survivor who had come to see herself as someone with 'a heart of stone' due to her no longer authentic memory of her experiences, began, as a result, to live her life differently. Laub says that 'her previous inability to tell her story had marred her perception of herself . . . In other words, in her memory of her Holocaust experience, as well as in the distorted way in which her present life proceeded from this memory, she failed to be an authentic witness to herself' (80). The inauthentic narrator, not a new device in itself, certainly has, it seems to me, been used as effectively as it has in these novels as an articulation of this displacement or unreliability of the survivor's memory/self. Within this framework, the survivor's very life can be seen by the survivor as being inauthentic – something it would not otherwise have been, if the memory had been articulated fully earlier. The insanity that threatens many of the protagonists can also, therefore, be seen as an extension of this inauthenticity.

That this threat is a constant presence in the text is, thus, not surprising. The insanity which dogs the heels of those who try to name the unnameable, for instance – the case of Titus Andronicus serves, almost, as an archetype – is a function of the insanity of the event or experience itself. Indeed, I would extend this idea to conflate the distortion of the memory/body with that of its articulation, resulting in the sense that many of us have of survivor narratives expressing pain as a kind of hysteria or insanity. Langer's notion of Durational Time helps focus the specific kinds of 'insanity' that such narratives evince. Since the survivor does not exist in a normal system of chronological time, her narrative for her experiences often has no beginning or end: its non-linearity suggesting the survivor's sense that the event of violence is always already present. Thus, even realist fictional accounts often find it necessary to follow what seems to us to be an arbitrary structure.

The break from realist narrativisation comes, perhaps, from the need to find new modes of signification to account for experiences that have no precedent. Arthur and Joan Kleinman point out that 'we live in an age haunted not by the kind of suffering that religion and literature have taught us to accept, but by a spectacle of atrocity, on smaller and larger scales, that no past traditions have prepared us to absorb' (in Kleinman et al., 1997: 63). In the absence of analogy, and unable to comprehend or imagine a world with no referent in the past, these writers take recourse to non-realist modes of representation. Magic or anti-realist strategies and the narrativisation of certain kinds of violence come together, then, in a unique genre of our time.

Isabel Allende takes this idea further: Chilean reality is, for her, out of the ordinary, unbelievably arbitrary and violent. When Western critics, she says, ask her how Latin authors 'dare to invent those incredible lies' (referring both to the Magic Realism as well as to what they see as excesses and extremes of violence), she insists that these are not pathological ravings. 'They are written in our history; we can find them every day in our newspapers; we hear them in the streets; we suffer them frequently in our lives' (quoted in Zinsser, 1989: 9–10). 'A land of crazy, illuminated people' can only be harnessed through stories. Similarly, what appears in her novels as rupture is also, for her, directly consequent upon the fact that 'the military coup in Chile changed everything and [she felt] that [her] life had been cut into pieces' (Allende, 1985: 4–5). For Allende, then, Magic Realism is, in itself, a kind of realism: it is the only credible objective correlative to a disordered – or unordered – reality. 'The most extravagant evil. Obscene, incredible or magnificent facts . . . in Latin America, are not hyperbole, because that is the dimension of our reality' (quoted in Zinsser, 1989: 45). Indeed, implicit in her description of her fiction is the idea that the stories are often far more ordered than the reality they represent. 'In a novel,' she says, 'we can give illusory order to chaos' (Allende, 1985: 10).

It is possible to argue, in fact, that the 'order' given to the 'chaos' is sometimes difficult to sustain in certain historical contexts. Morrison's insistence, for instance, on the unique 'Blackness' of her themes and narrative strategies is a proposition that I will be invested in destabilising throughout this book. The appearance and use of violence for the specific purpose of constructing collective identities can be seen as a means of countering the undesirability of an essentialising view of the collective on the one hand, and a recourse to constructions of hybridity and mobility on the other. The events of violence chosen by these authors offer, instead, a foundation fundamentally absolute in its very nature. The multiplicity of narratives violence demands notwithstanding, the collective that is constructed upon it draws some of its absoluteness from the event. Thus, while these novels are carried forward by the powerful energies of the act/body of violence, the endings are often weaker, unsatisfactory, relying more on overt 'illus[ion]' and artifice, and lack the force of the rest of the novel.

For many of these novelists, the act or process of writing is, itself, a powerful force. It is interesting, for instance, to see how the metaphor of violence functions in Allende's narrative for the creation of *House of Spirits*. Inspired, she says, by the image and memory of her grandfather starving himself to death ('calling for Death'[13]), she uses an extended metaphor of violence to describe the act of writing itself. 'Words came out like a violent torrent. I had thousands of untold words stuck in my chest, threatening to choke me. The long silence of exile was turning me to stone; I needed to open a valve and let the river of secret words find a way out' (1985: 42). Not only are the inspiration for and act of writing, in themselves, violent, they are like violence itself: arbitrary, necessary, destructive as well as cathartic, apocalyptic in their need and ability to forge order through destruction. Significantly, these are also, perhaps necessarily, physical, empirical, material, real.

Hence, once the deed is done and the novel written, the flood of words abated, Allende's metaphors change into those of transcendence, spiritual peace and order – in one sense, non-real. When she is done, Allende writes, 'I just organised it a little bit, tied the manuscript with a pink ribbon for luck...the spirit of my grandmother was protecting the book from the very beginning so it was refused in Venezuela' (Allende, 1985: 43). This non-realism is intimately tied to her notion of writing as an 'act of hope': it can be seen, in that context, as a function of the necessity of stretching the imagination in order to construct the possibilities for the kind of extension of the human spirit required to break free of oppression and build a new future. There is, therefore, a great deal of the same impetus that impels the utopian or post-apocalyptic vision into finding articulation in largely empirical terms. The requisite idealism can often conflict with the compulsions of art or aesthetics: political optimism almost always carries the danger of verging on sentimentality.

Because the utopian vision is so often a large part of the compulsion behind political writing, the desire or temptation to write what one believes rather than what one knows, the tendency towards propaganda, wish fulfilment and fantasy is a dangerous terrain that must be negotiated carefully. This negotiation can also be seen as the interface between realism and non-realism that such novels so often produce as a narrative strategy for the envisioning of the collective.[14]

I will not spend much more time here on the nature of these negotiations and connections that are exhaustively dealt with in their several specific aspects in the following chapters. I would, however, like to touch briefly upon the phenomenon of the popularity of the novels under consideration. All of them, without exception, are on bestseller lists in America and, in Allende's case, in their home countries. This confluence of 'high' literature – Morrison is a Nobel Laureate, and most of these writers are institutionalised as contemporary, canonical works – with widespread and broad-based popularity is often seen within the context of postmodernism's conflation and collapse of such categories as 'high' and 'low' art. Clearly, this is the case on two counts, at least: one, the narrative strategies and techniques employed by these writers recognise these boundaries only to cross them; two, if sales are any indication, a readership has developed, over the last thirty-odd years, that, also, is prepared to cross these boundaries and read Walker or Danticat, as it were, on the train.

The popularity of and fascination with the image of violence, verbal or visual, has been explained in different ways at different times and I will not repeat much of that work here. Suffice it to add to this discussion the idea that the human mind is drawn to images of violence as a source of pleasure, or *jouissance* in the instant that the shock of recognition attracts even as the perception of otherness repels. It is in the very nature of violence to render itself other to anyone who has not experienced the kind of violence being narrated. In that sense, regardless of place and time, all violence is marked as 'exotic' to all but those who have shared in it.

I would like to conclude this chapter with a brief discussion which I hope will help focus some key issues regarding the act of theorising violence that the critic, artist or listener necessarily performs. I have touched, in passing, on the dangers that dog the footsteps of the person who attempts to articulate the experience of violence; one of the most significant aspects of theorising violence is that it necessarily makes of the critic a sharer. In his chapter titled 'Bearing Witness or the Vicissitudes of Listening', Dori Laub refers to this situating of the critic as sharer as the 'contract of testifying' and the process as a 'journey' (in Felman and Laub, 1992: 72). Reciting the trauma which attaches to such a positioning, the reasons which explain it and the reactions which accompany it, Laub makes clear, it seems to me, the primary fact that governs such an undertaking: the critic is, first and foremost, a listener.

The act or process of theorising for the literary critic clearly demands some degree of sympathy, even empathy in several contexts other than that of violence: the difference, I think, is both one of degree as well as one of kind. The thin line that the critic of narratives of violence must define is one that runs between the complete and absolute surrender that such narratives demand by virtue of their magnitude, and the distance necessary for the act of theorising. In other words, the surrender of one's defences, the voluntary immersion in a trauma that threatens to 'drown' or 'flood' (Laub, in Felman and Laub, 1992: 72–3) one's consciousness must learn to coexist with the objectivity required for such a task. Stanley Cavell remarks, in this context, that 'a society may be allowed some degree of unconsciousness of itself, to disguise itself from itself. But a science can make no allowance for itself of such a kind' (in Kleinman et al., 1997: 95). To my mind, there is no substitute for the act of 'listening', no alternative to becoming a sharer and, in Cavell's rigorous framework, no protection or allowances to be made towards the 'science' which is the only means of processing the violence. Indeed, to extend Laub's framework, the proper functioning of this 'science' is, in fact, the critic's end of the 'contract'.

It is not surprising, then, that the critical texts I found most useful in my own research were almost exclusively responses to survivor narratives or anthropological studies of penal colonies and actual social practices, other than my own readings of the novels and texts such as *Titus Andronicus*. This is not to say that less context-specific texts were not useful, of course, but that, given the vast complexity and the sometimes fundamental differences between kinds of violence and narratives, and given, also, the relative paucity of critical work available, the activity of the listener seems best suited to being adapted as praxis. Veena Das raises the issue of whether the claim to objectivity in the description of a culture must come from a stance inside or outside it; Laub battles with the problem of whether the listener can ever fulfil his contract as narrator and translator: neither question can arise, I think, without first assuming the role and responsibility of sharer.

In my own work I have tried to negotiate these minute divisions in as dialectical a manner as possible, allowing my own understanding of survivor narratives to inform my readings of literary texts and both, in turn, to qualify and be qualified by critical and theoretical texts and the provisional theorisation stemming from survivor narratives.

3
Remembering and Dismembering: Toni Morrison's *Beloved* and *Sula*

1 The poison in the womb: dis/placing the violenced body in Toni Morrison's *Beloved*

The understanding of the reciprocal relationship between sacrificer and sacrifice as outlined in Chapter 1 can be extended to the contract between slave and master where Schoolteacher, in Morrison's *Beloved*, documents the absolute otherness of Sethe as she is being assaulted by his sons. Parasitically connected to his definition of Sethe is, of course, Schoolteacher's own defining of himself: not simply in the sense in which the slave or colonised person is rendered other by the master or coloniser, but more intimately, in that the perpetrator wrests from this violence a sense of self and subjectivity. While Sethe herself survives the ordeal as violenced body, realising the significance of the tree of welts on her back over time, I will argue that Halle, witness to the violence but denied the bodily witness and marking which contains the horror, is Schoolteacher's true sacrificee.

As Paul D tells Sethe, 'You said they stole your milk. It was that messed him up. That was it, I guess. All I knew was that something broke him. Not one of them years of Saturdays, Sundays, nighttime extra never touched him. But whatever he saw go on in that barn broke him like a twig' (68). The distinction between the physical violence perpetrated upon a slave and the taking of Sethe's milk is crucial. As Paul D points out, it is the taking of the milk, rather than the brutal beating, which breaks Halle. Intimately associated with the sexual assault is the idea of Sethe as animal, whose milk can be taken at will. This act is, therefore, set apart from the more familiar physical or sexual violence of whipping and rape, both of which are forms of subjugation which recognise the humanity of the slave in the very attempt to suppress the rebellion. The taking of milk, however, is a qualitatively different form of othering whereby the polarisation is not one of master–slave but the far more radical one of human–animal. In whipping her, Schoolmaster has merely asserted his authority over Sethe: in allowing his boys to take her milk, he has authored/authorised her status as animal, and his own as human.

Submitting to the dehumanisation integral to such a contract, Halle is reduced to the 'animal' devoid of reason and dignity that Schoolteacher sees the slave as being. 'You may as well know it all,' Paul D tells Sethe. 'Last time I saw he was sitting by the churn. He had butter all over his face.' If Sethe's real triumph has been able to wrest herself out of the contract etched by Schoolteacher by refusing to accept its terms, then Halle's surrender to it must be the true horror, the real annihilation. Internalising the animalisation that Schoolteacher seeks to impose upon Sethe, reduced to the pre-speech, pre-rational stage that characterises the animal state as defined by Schoolteacher, he is Schoolteacher's true sacrificee.

Although Paul D escapes and lives to relate Halle's story to Sethe, he, too, is implicated in Halle's sacrifice and his survival and sanity are not without their own price. When Sethe asks Paul D why he did not speak with Halle and try to bring him along, Paul D reveals the degree to which his sanity and soul are implicated in Halle's. He does not speak with Halle because he is as incapable of speech as Halle is, although for a different reason. His announcement – 'I had a bit in my mouth' (69) – is as terrifying in its dehumanised ferocity as his account of Halle. Paul D, too, has participated in the dehumanising of Halle, and is also, at the same time, made beastlike – like a horse, with a bit, hobbled – even though he has not been part of the contractual ritual with Schoolteacher. Like Halle, therefore, he is unable to speak, indicating a reduction to the animal state. But unlike Halle, his inability to speak is not a function of an entirely internalised animality; it is forced upon him by the bit in his mouth which both confers as well as signifies his status as animal. This distinction is crucial because, in retaining his sanity, Paul D is able to distance himself enough from his experiences to put them away into the 'tobacco tin'. Thus, even though Paul D is not reduced entirely to the animal state in spite of being treated like one, he has been forced to set aside a critical part of his humanity, locked away in his tobacco tin.

The tobacco tin functions as a survival strategy insofar as it allows Paul D to retain some semblance of sanity and humanity, as long as he does not have to confront the experiences locked in it. Thus, when Sethe hears of the bit in his mouth, she observes: 'People I see as a child, who'd had the bit always looked wild after that. Whatever they used it on them for, it couldn't have worked, because it put a wildness where before there wasn't any. When I look at you I don't see it. There ain't no wildness in your eye nowhere.' Paul D has been able to reclaim himself from the 'wildness' that would mark the memory of his 'animalisation'. But as he points out to Sethe, like her 'journey', it, too, has come at a price. 'There's a way to put it there,' he says, 'and there's a way to take it out and I haven't figured out yet which is worse' (71).

Hence, the true significance of Sethe's violenced body is not fully revealed even in the telling of the event of violence to which it is witness: the hidden knowledge that Paul D, witness to Halle's dehumanisation, harbours within himself is not yet released, and will not be until it finds a physical home/body in Beloved's womb. In order to trace this process, I will provide a reading of the episode in which Paul D and Beloved share some version of sexual intercourse in the shed outside Sethe's house. I will do this in the context of Veena Das's discovery, while recording survivor narratives, of the metaphor of pregnancy employed by women survivors who chose to remain silent discussed in Chapter 1.

The tobacco pouch (so closely associated with the metaphorical 'tobacco tin' of his heart but literally softer, more permeable) is almost the only material object associated with Paul D and it appears the first time Sethe begins to introduce the narrative of the tree on her back, so central to the novel. ' "I got a tree on my back and a haint in my house, and nothing in between but the daughter I am holding in my arms. No more running – from nothing... I took one journey and I paid for the ticket and... it cost too much!"... Paul D fished in his vest for a little pouch of tobacco.... "What tree on your back?" ' (15).

The next time the account of this critical episode of the past is raised, we see, not the tobacco pouch, but the tin. It appears in the context of the dehumanising experience of being saddled and bound by the bit in the mouth as Paul D tries to explain to Sethe the depths of his dehumanisation and the degree of his implication in the sacrifice of Halle. '"Mister [the rooster] was allowed to be and stay what he was. But I wasn't allowed to be and stay what I was...wasn't no way I'd ever be Paul D again. Schoolteacher changed me. I was something else and that something else was less than a chicken sitting in the sun on a tub"' (72). Paul D wants to tell Sethe more but '[she]...stop[s] him. Just as well...Saying more might push them both to a place they couldn't get back from. He would keep the rest where it belonged: in that tobacco tin buried in his chest where a red heart used to be. Its lid rusted shut. He would not pry it loose now in front of this sweet, sturdy woman, for if she got a whiff of the contents it would shame him. And it would hurt her to know that there was no red heart bright as Mister's comb beating in him' (72–3). The tobacco tin, then, is what allows Paul D to distance and displace the experiences of dehumanisation that threaten his sanity and humanity, his soul and self-worth. He, too, like Sethe, has 'paid a price for it' and for him, too, it has been 'too high'. It is clear that the tobacco pouch is merely the material signifier of the metaphorical tin which is central to the encounter with Beloved.

The sexual intercourse between Paul D and Beloved becomes deeply symbolic when considered in this context, the manner in which Beloved sees the meaning of her own name and the way in which her wound and genitalia are introduced into the narrative. 'Beloved let her head fall back on the edge of the bed while she found her breath and Denver saw the tip of the thing that she always saw in its entirety when Beloved undressed to sleep. Looking straight at it she whispered, "Why you call yourself Beloved?" Beloved closed her eyes. "In the dark my name is Beloved"' (74–5). The wound at her throat which is the fatal mark of her mother's love, also marks Beloved as representative of the 'sixty million and more' to whom Morrison dedicates her book. But the scar of the open gash becomes, in the encounter with Paul D, emblematic of her genitalia, enabling Paul D to get to his own 'inside part' by touching hers.

When Beloved comes to Paul D in the shed, this is the connection she makes over and over. 'I want you to touch me on the inside part and call my name' (117). Morrison recalls the tobacco tin: 'Paul D never worried about his little tobacco tin anymore. It was rusted shut' (118). The unspoken mirroring of the closed gash in her throat in that of her genitalia, opened/touched by Paul D is mirrored again in the opening of the shut tobacco tin of Paul D's 'red heart' as each seeks healing in the other.

> 'Call me my name.' 'No.' 'Please call it. I'll go if you call it.' 'Beloved.' He said it but she did not go. She moved closer with a footfall he didn't hear and he didn't hear the whisper that the flakes of rust made either as they fell away from the seams of his tobacco tin. So when the lid gave way he didn't know it. What he knew was that when he reached the inside part he was saying 'Red heart. Red heart. Red heart', over and over again. Softly and then so loud that it woke Denver, then Paul D himself. 'Red heart. Red heart. Red heart.' (118)

Beloved has taken Paul D's tobacco tin into herself – into her 'inside part' – and thus returned to him his 'red heart'. The poison that Beloved has internalised and which her womb contains is, in this context and sense, the knowledge of Schoolteacher's contract successfully completed. That this knowledge is seen as a sort of pregnancy is evident in Beloved's reaction to the prospect of Sethe's and Paul D's child. She begins, literally, to disintegrate, to fall apart. She pulls out a back tooth and thinks: 'this is it. Next would be her arm, her hand, a toe. Pieces of her would drop maybe one at a time, maybe all at once...She would fly apart' (133). Such a child would herald the beginning of the process of healing for which Paul D is now ready, having had his 'red heart' restored to him, and for which Sethe is ready, having placed her tree in Paul D's hands. Such a healing would neutralise the poison in Beloved's womb, rendering her existence unnecessary. That Beloved is a fierce love that harbours the debilitating hatred, grief and anger of the 'sixty million and more' becomes evident as her pregnancy progresses and she becomes a life-denying force, sucking the vitality out of Sethe and literally starving her as she herself grows bigger and bigger.

But the whole truth has not yet been revealed and the healing process cannot therefore be completed. As Sethe affirms the killing of Beloved, she is met by Paul D's incomprehension; a lack of understanding that consigns her to the very animal status that Schoolteacher reduced Halle to and which Sethe has spent the rest of her life resisting. ' "You got two feet, Sethe, not four" ' (165) he tells

her as he leaves, and it is evident that the process of healing and comprehension – both understanding as well as containment – is as yet
incomplete. There is, therefore, no longer any means of Sethe and
Paul D producing the child that would have heralded the beginning
of the time of healing, of replacing Beloved who would have flown
apart (as she does at the end) – destroyed, exorcised – at this birth.
The bitterness and the despair over the seemingly final end to any
such hope for healing becomes the baby in Beloved's body instead.
The tobacco tin will not re-form in Paul D's chest but it will take
a new life in Beloved's womb and another exorcism will be needed
before she will fly apart, taking the poison with her.

2   Narrating collectivity from violence: the case of slavery and World War One in Morrison's *Beloved* and *Sula*

It may be most feasible to unravel the intricately woven fabric of the
interlacing narratives of violence and identities in these two novels
by tugging at one thread: the Pauls and the deweys. Paul D carries the
weight of the history of Sweet Home, and in his consciousness are
preserved the lives and pain of the Pauls who did not survive. This
burden and the shouldering of it with the responsibility that Paul D
brings to it invests his 'identity' with stature and significance. Differentiated only by their second initial, the Pauls focus a shared past and
an intense bond in their common name, a 'commonality' which then
is capable of extending to a 'community' of all those who are such
sharers – Sethe, Sixo, Baby Suggs and the other residents of Bluestone.

Whether their common name is coincidental, or whether it was
given to them by their owner eventually becomes irrelevant in a way
in which it can never be to the question of the deweys. Renamed
dewey by Eva, these three boys of different ages, races, sizes, colours
and names, 'slowly . . . accepted Eva's view, becoming in fact as well
as in name a dewey – joining with the other two to become a trin-
ity with a plural name' (38). Coming from separate histories, the
deweys not only forge an identical 'present', they eventually share
the same future fate. In other words, the deweys seem to exemplify
the very opposite of 'identity': 'identicalness'. It is hardly surprising,
then, that while the deweys literally stop growing in mind and in
body and are marginal in the narrative, the fracturing, healing and
unifying growth of Paul D forms a distinct strand in the pattern of

the narrative of *Beloved*. This chapter will trace these patterns in the narratives of *Beloved* and *Sula* in order to explore the ways in which a violent past is narrativised, and how that past participates in the construction of the collective identities of those people who have suffered it.

Slavery in the antebellum South of America and World War One in the global arena are the two framing experiences in these novels; while *Beloved* is set in the post-abolition years of the Reconstruction, *Sula* inhabits – with the exception of the first and last chapters – the decades between the two World Wars. Compared to *Beloved*, *Sula* seems neatly linear: indeed, its chapters are headed by the year in which the events take place, and they follow in a clean chronological fashion, from year to year with few breaks. This chronological linearity most significantly departs from that of *Beloved* in that the experience of violence is also narrated in its appointed place in the sequence of events. Thus, Shadrack's experience of World War One occupies the first terse one and a half pages following the opening prefatorial section of the book.

As intensely narrated as it is – in its single incident, its one death that stood for the millions similarly dismembered – the violence Shadrack witnesses is so vast in its reach, so alienating in its impersonality, so cosmic in its disruption, that the only 'identity' left to the shattered survivor is the black face staring out of the chamber pot: single, individual, signifying nothing more than its own presence. The only reality left to Shadrack is that of the horror of death: the only response – to kill, in mercy, both oneself and those one loved.[1]

The structure of *Beloved*, on the other hand, is such that the past is always a mystery, a secret, encoded in the 'rememory' of the present. It functions as a kind of cryptic centre around which the narrative circles, swooping closer in narrowing rings of revelations until it is laid bare in all its horror. In this manner, the entire book is constructed in sections in which a significant part of the past is revealed, and around which the narrative revolves. Thus, the narrative structure integrates the experiences of the past with those of the present, making the past an ever-present part of the consciousnesses of the people who suffered it. This integrative enterprise then, seeks wholeness and assimilation, seeing Time and Consciousness as being tortured out of their proper continuum by the extremity of the violence perpetrated upon them.

Shadrack's institution of National Suicide Day, however, is founded on the notion of containment: 'that if one day in the year were devoted to it, everybody could get it out of the way and the rest of the year would be safe and free' (13). People react to Shadrack in similar fashion: 'once the people understood the boundaries and nature of his madness, they could fit him, so to speak, into the scheme of things' (15). 'The scheme of things' consists, then, of many distinct, independent, even contradictory pieces that can be fitted together into a whole that does not require the 'wholeness' of integration and assimilation.

It is perhaps too easy (ahistorical though it is) to see *Beloved* as being, in this sense, 'modern' and *Sula* 'postmodern', but these frameworks allow the differences in the patterning of collectivity to appear. The Shadrack who awakens in the hospital who 'didn't even know who or what he was' not only has 'no past, no language, no tribe, no source', but, of equal significance, 'no comb, no pencil, no clock, no pocket handkerchief, no rug, no bed, no can opener, no faded postcard, no soap, no key, no tobacco pouch, no soiled underwear' (12). The 'epic list' of minutiae participates in the scattered and independent pieces that go to make up the postmodern sense of 'identity', cut loose from the past, language, tribe and source that are considered the roots of one's identity in a classicist sense. The violence that Shadrack experiences – so universally destructive, and so destructive of the universe – leaves him in a world where 'anything could be anywhere' (8). He reacts by demarcating his life and himself into sections like those of his hospital food tray, whose 'neat balance' of three triangles gives him a sense of 'equilibrium': so that things do not 'explode or burst forth from their restricted zones' (8).

When Sethe arrives at Baby Suggs's door, she carries nothing with her except the baby and her wounds; yet, it is in these that the violence she has experienced is both literally and symbolically articulated. The intensely symbolic narrative of *Beloved* connects and integrates time, events, consciousnesses and people that the largely realistic representations of *Sula* make separate, fragmented and fractured. While the structure of *Beloved* focuses different aspects of life around and into a single violent event, the narrative of any one incident in *Sula* ripples out into the multifarious minutiae of living. Thus, Jude's marriage to Nel spirals out, beginning with an account of waiters and their salaries at a time of 'fake prosperity', and, like the road that was to 'wind through Medallion' to the river, to the 'great bridge' which would then 'connect to Porter's Landing', the telling of Jude's marriage encircles in its narrative the 'Council of Founders', trade with 'cross-river towns', 'house rafts', the naming of roads, the war and the overt racism of post-Abolition America (81). The coming together of Paul D and Sethe, on the other hand, crystallises in their relationship the separate strands of the text, paring away anything that might distract from or diffuse its intense symbolic and human significance.

Of the sparingly used symbols in *Sula*, the most significant in this context is the birthmark over Sula's eye. Variously interpreted as a rose, a snake and a tadpole, the symbolic nature of the mark seems to underline its invitation to interpretations. It is different things to different people, as is Sula herself: she rarely exists outside of this realm of 'interpretability' – of someone's perception of her. Thus, the depth, intensity and inclusiveness made available by a symbolic representation, here function in the opposite capacity of a destabilising, fracturing and widening, rather than deepening of the sphere of the symbol.

Morrison's characterisation of the men in these two novels is also telling in the context of their relationships with women. Both Paul D and Ajax are wanderers in a certain sense; Paul D, like the peripatetic Odysseus, is travelling away from the site of a violence so extreme that the coherence and cohesiveness of consciousness required for the formation – or recognition – of a space called 'home' takes years to reconstruct. After eighteen years, however, Paul D does reach such a stasis. His history of suffering has created a man in whose presence women feel they can weep. The strength which supports Sethe finds its narrativisation in the chain gang's collective survival: 'one lost, all lost' (110). But each of the chain gang must thereafter survive alone as well, and with Sethe, Paul D shares both experiences of survival: they can both 'put their stories next to each other'.

For Ajax, in whose narratives there is no such violent destabilising of the consciousness, there is not only no such movement 'towards', there is constantly a 'moving away from': away from the grounding, infantilising love for his mother, impelled by the rootless, untethered freedom of his love for airplanes. Sula exists for Ajax insofar as she relates to this movement away from 'home'. Their relationship is constructed from disparate, arbitrary objects that they both delight in, from milk bottles which charm because they don't belong to them, to the butterflies that he sets free in her room. There is an aesthetic pleasure that both responds to and is expressed in these objects that find no 'source' in or connections with any conscious 'self' or racial/cultural context: it is self-delighting and self-sufficient. If Jude feels Nel will complete *him* (with no thought as to whether she even needs to feel 'complete', much less if he can complete her), Ajax represents a movement away from the ideology of 'completion' itself. Indeed, Sula's feeling of possessiveness – or her 'desire' for it (131) – are seen as an incipient surrender to the bourgeois ideologies that she sees Nel as having succumbed to.

Sula's very postmodern 'experimental life', her amorality and her artist's consciousness are most vividly articulated in the deaths that she witnesses: the death of Chicken Little, the burning of Hannah and her own; Plum's is perhaps the only death 'in the family' which she does not witness – which, 'belongs', in a sense, to Eva. If responsibility is the one overriding factor in Sethe's and Eva's relationship with their children, and the one lesson Stamp Paid learns from his experience of violence, then it is equally true that Sula's 'one major feeling of responsibility [is] exorcised on the bank of the river with a closed place in the middle of it' (118). Indeed, the act itself is not represented as an action: the construction of 'when he slipped from her hands' so deftly 'exorcise[s]' the 'responsibility' of Chicken Little's death from Sula (65).

In this, she is clearly set against her grandmother, Eva, whose epiphany in the shed with her child is so akin to Sethe's. The emphatic 'no' which is wrenched from both is an index to the acts of violence it connects; the making of the 'tree' on Sethe's back and the taking of her nurturing milk, with the attempt to kill all of her four children (resulting in the death of one), and the poverty and desertion of Eva with her dismemberment in exchange for financial security. The responsibility which Hannah cannot comprehend as 'love' propels Eva through the window in a futile bid to save her burning daughter.

That such responsibility is a crippling thing is inscribed on Eva's and Sethe's bodies. But violence to one's own body becomes counterproductive if such responsibility is also crippling for the child. Hence, Eva may even consider the forceful re-entry of Plum into her womb, but for the fact that that is not the place for a grown man. Her immolation of Plum is described, therefore, in terms of freedom and sublimation, while the prospect of his re-entry into her womb is a graphic act of violence. For Shadrack, too, the ringing of his bell of suicide and murder is the call of love and the feeling of responsibility that it engenders. When the death of Sula makes him realise the absence of an absolute 'always', he rings his bell again, but 'it [is] not heartfelt this time, not loving this time, for he no longer care[s] whether he help[s] them or not' (158).

It is the shattering of this last remnant of the feeling of responsibility that breaks the fragile bonds of the 'community' of the Bottom, leading to the death of many and the scattering of the rest. In a book that begins with the end of World War One, the chapter heading '1941' – the year in which the United States of America joined World War Two – indicates, perhaps, that it is time for another cataclysmic event, apocalyptic in its violence, to give birth to such feelings of responsibility again. The death of Sula, however, represents also the loss of that enigmatic but exciting 'something' that postmodern notions of identity revolve around. Amoral and unconventional in itself, the image of Sula (true to her artist's consciousness, she exists only in the image she generates in the minds of others) helps define the morality and conventions by which the people of the Bottom live. In this sense, at least, she does produce a kind of 'collectivity' in the Bottom.

When contrasted with the sense of community and positive collective identity that centres around Baby Suggs, the absence of the need for the 'rememory' that functions almost like a Jungian *anima mundi* binding a group of people is evident. 'Rememory' functions like an organic connective tissue, connecting people's memories, their experiences, their moralities, even the colour of their skins, so that neither time nor space can break it.[2] The narration of the meeting of Paul D and Sethe after eighteen years has only to be juxtaposed with the meeting of Eva with Sula after ten years to make evident the seamless community of one and the fracturedness of the other. Violence is thus continuously narrativised in the form of 'rememory', while in its absence, the fragmentation inherent in the differences of time and place results in a multitude of scattered narratives.

Morrison's construction of these narratives of violence do not, of course, create any hierarchy within violent events, but certainly the historical differences between slavery in America and America's experience of World War One contribute to different narratives. Race and personal experience of violence born of hatred are primary for the narrativisation of the violence of slavery and give rise to formations of identities that construct themselves within these frameworks. The racism in *Sula*, however, is not tied to the narrative of slavery; it becomes one among many factors of post-war living. The impersonality of the weaponry and scale on which the war was waged produce, rather, the narratives of a more Existential sense of the destruction of the Self.

Thus, if the 'tree' on Sethe's back is a symbol of a violence that is an organic, living and interconnecting history, it is also a 'tree of life' in that it binds, in this sense, the people of Bluestone and other communities like it into a collective identity. The corresponding symbol in *Sula* is the little grey ball of string and fur that is constantly with Nel. If Nel's life is typical of those of the women in the Bottom, then this thing without colour, form or life is its defining symbol, reminiscent of the imagery of the Existentialists. This influence is felt in Sula's life of 'experimentation' and aesthetic amorality also, and it is significant that it is the boarded-up window that symbolises to her the fact that she has 'sung all the songs there are' and this, to the artist and experimentalist, is death (137). (That all songs, have, indeed, been sung also predicates the fact that Sula does not so much 'die' as witness her own death – with as much interest as she had earlier witnessed her mother's.) Sula will be 'beloved' only when, as she tells Nel, everyone has done everything, good and bad, right and wrong, conventional and unconventional. Only then will Sula be a symbol that unites a collectivity of people.

That these people may be of what race and colour they choose is implicit in this novel that includes images – howsoever minor – of the Irish who can only be seen as 'white' in their expressed hatred of the 'blacks'; of Tar Baby who is white and despised by his own race; of the red-haired dewey, and the Mexican dewey. The war did not create for America a sense of collectivity in terms of 'race' or 'country' that included these people. Just as the narrative of oppression embraces the dispossessed Cherokee and the white Amy Denver in *Beloved*, the war engenders narratives of alienation and disconnectedness that span genders and races.

The final disintegration of the community of the Bottom, then, is as much a sign of its times as an index to the lost bonds of responsibility springing from Shadrack's ability to see all peoples as a collective created by the violence of the war. Significantly, those who do not die in the tunnel, who refrain from following Shadrack, are the ones 'who understood the Spirit's touch which made them dance, who understood whole families bending in a field while singing as from one throat, who understood the ecstasy of river baptisms under suns just like this one' (160). In other words, the singing and dancing of these people's understanding (and not necessarily of their memory) were narratives for a shared oppression become a 'baptism' of a whole people; the singing and dancing that follow Shadrack are, in contrast, articulations of a 'curious disorder', a 'headless display' (160).

Meanwhile, the 'old and young, women and children, lame and hearty, they killed as best as they could, the tunnel they were forbidden to build...In their need to kill it all, kill all of it...they went too deep, too far' (161–2). This stream of revellers is also a 'collective' formed from the shared experience of oppression; but just as Beloved eventually becomes a life-denying force, so does this righteous vengeance become self-destructive. Morrison creates little 'collective identities' such as the deweys to demarcate the limits of such identities: the deweys do not grow, and while they may be as 'inseparable' as the chain gang of which Paul D was a part (it becomes, for the deweys, a game that they often play), they also 'lov[e] nothing and no-one but themselves' (38). This is the limit of Baby Suggs's injunction to her people to love themselves.

Love of oneself, within a certain history, is inseparable from a love of one's place, of 'land'. 'In all of [Paul D's] escapes, he could not help being astonished by the beauty of this land that was not his...Anything could stir him and he tried not to love it' (268). In other words, there is never an escape from violence: it disrupts and disjoins the man from the land. In *Sula*, this rupture is effected, not by violence (although the people of the Bottom react to their dispossession with a self-destructive violence) but by financial and social forces. In 1965, there aren't 'any places left, just separate houses with separate televisions and separate telephones' (166).

Within the context of this genre, it is the mythic, the oral and the folk which focuses this love for and the connection with *land*, while the realist novel, when it emerged in Europe, took upon itself the task of delineating the minutiae of the everyday effects of specific social and economic forces on the lives of the people of a *nation or country*. This distinction between *land* and *nation/country* has been a crucial one in the narrative of collectivity; that it remains one for Morrison's purposes as well will be argued in the next section.

3   The voice and the book: collectivity, orality and novelistic discourse

Morrison's construction of collective identities depends largely on two modes of narrative: that taken from oral traditions and that from novelistic discourse. The oral tradition – or 'orality' – is organically a part of the 'village' identity that Morrison has so painstakingly set up in her non-fictional writing. The 'tradition', not meticulously defined or traced, is placed loosely within the oral practices of pre-Abolition African Americans of the rural South. Since it is seen, at the same time, as being preserved in its 'African' purity, it simultaneously invokes the existence of an ancient and timeless ritual which constructs, even as it is constructed by, the collective.

For Morrison, it is also vitally connected to the speaker, the initiator as well as the keeper of the tradition, the 'ancestor' figure who is the narrator of the identity of the 'tribe' and the keeper of its wisdom and lore. The collective crystallises around this figure who provides not only the connection between the individuals in the collective, but also their connection with their common past, heritage and history. Of course, this history is both narrated by the ancestor as well as narrated *into being*, thus making the oral narrative both the history as well as the construction of collectivity in itself.

Sula and *Beloved* constitute two distinct ways in which contemporary fiction establishes and uses the relationship between past, socially constitutive events of violence and the present experience of collective identity. In *Beloved* the relationship is symbiotic and reciprocal because narration works so as to make the 'rememory' of the original event a means of reconstituting some sense of the original collective in the present. The novelistic mode of narration becomes significant in that the narrator uses internal monologue that is necessarily dialectical so as to connect different states of mind but register, at the same time, the distance between them. Morrison herself, therefore, I see as attempting to narrate orality to a tribe that no longer has access to it. I think that despite the seeming paradox involved here, this mode (oral/novel) does succeed in building the bridge between the utopian orality of the past and the present collective.

In its structure, orality depends on the 'call and response' system, the assumption of a listening 'tribe' – i.e. a homogeneous collective of people for and of whom the narrator speaks – and uses the first person in the sense that it is an immediate and autobiographical mode of communication with an immediate audience. In other words, the oral narrative functions practically as a ritual of and for the collective: in Morrison's hands, it becomes more than an oral narrative – her fiction is an attempt to narrate orality to a tribe which no longer has access to it.

It is possible to read Morrison's use of the oral tradition and novelistic discourse as marking the imaginary utopia of Morrison's 'village' and the fragmented, material realities of contemporary African Americans respectively. The ending of *Beloved* can be seen as a crystallising of Morrison's use of novelistic discourse in the internal monologues of the three main women characters, Sethe, Denver and Beloved herself; the internal monologues representing the novelistic inscribing of 'unspeakable things unspoken'. The complex status of Beloved the character as real/unreal can then be read in terms of the narrative's straddling of oral and novelistic discourses. Beloved's indeterminate status between real and unreal can be seen as an index of Morrison's moving through and from the oral tradition to the novelistic (the last passages can be seen as novelistic discourse also in their foregrounding of the fact of the narrative as cast in the novel form). This technique is also uniquely novelistic in that it invokes the imaginary utopia of oral tradition even as it inscribes its impossibility. Not only is this position historically peculiarly that of the novel, but Morrison goes to great pains, in foregrounding the form of the novel, to show that the three interior monologues can merge only in the form of the novel – a reminder that emphasises both the imaginary status of the utopia of the oral tradition as well as the impossibility of such a collective in the present historical context. Thus, Morrison's reading of history recognises the utopia of the oral tradition as imaginary and no longer possible, even as she replaces it with the utopia-under-erasure of postmodernism, and inscribes in the only way she knows how – through the medium and discourse of the novel.[3]

I would like to argue, further, that Morrison's use of novelistic discourse emphasises, in this context, the distance between the narrator and the ancestor figure. The foregrounding of the form of the novel claims for the novel the status of narrator: fallible, incomplete, human in a way in which the living ancestor-narrator never was or could afford to be. This novel-narrator does not claim for itself the status of the ancestor-narrator: it is neither the giver of wisdom nor the memorialiser of history, neither the symbol nor the narrator of the identity of the tribe. Indeed, it recognises, also, the distance between itself and its audience, in that the audience is geographically dispersed and thus removed from the novel-narrator both in space as well as in shared identity. Thus, this distance translates into the rupture between the call and the response of the oral tradition, recognises the loss of this connection and inscribes the disruption of the tribe's ability to narrate itself through the ancestor.

Finally, the ending of *Beloved* forces upon us the recognition that the novel itself is both the physical as well as the metaphorical mode of communication between the narrator and new audience which is now the reader – that certain thoughts which are not speakable (insofar as they would not be comprehended by the tribe audience) can be *written* – to no one, no audience, as it were. Thus, the internal monologue which establishes the interiority of the narrator also separates her from the collective, and can only be narrated in the discourse of the novel; similarly, even as the interior monologue establishes the interiority of the characters, it separates them from each other as well as from the collective, and, as such, their union into a collective can only be inscribed by and within novelistic discourse – an inscription which is, as has been seen, constantly under erasure.

This argument can be developed further. The structure of *Beloved* departs from the oral tradition in that it, also, can only exist within the novel: it is circular, symbolic, polyphonic and fragmented, relying heavily upon interior monologue. Much of the compulsion behind this structure comes from the peculiar demands of narrativising the violent event and the violenced body, as my reading of *Beloved* (in this chapter as well as the preceding one) shows. The status of the 'real', then, would signify the place of the oral tradition within the context of the mythic, the folk and the non-real – associated with narratives of the imagination and the symbolic. The discourse of the novel would fall, on the other hand, within the context of the real, the material, the empirical.[4] As such, the construction of the collective can be seen as moving from that of the tribal/village one to the more fragmented, dispersed black community. The narrator, then, must move from the oral to the novelistic mode in order to narrate an identity which has also moved from the (pre-Abolition Southern, rural) village to the (contemporary) dispersed, urban one.[5]

It is interesting that nevertheless, the lush, luxuriating language of the oral narrative indicates a nostalgia for this primal, utopian village. More than this, it is conjured forth by this language as an essence, a core around which the dispersed and fragmented community can crystallise itself, and as such, it is not surprising that this language is used primarily in the narrativisation of the events of violence and those of utopian community experience (such as the meetings in the clearing presided over by Baby Suggs, Holy). Morrison uses the novel form with its discursive strengths to recall and reconstruct this identity and this allows it to move – but not seamlessly – into the more contemporary, material reality of the urban black community.

This seemingly neat division between the 'real' and the non-real is problematised by placing it within the context of the oral tradition with its utopian collective identity constructed upon the events of violence surrounding slavery. The status of violence as both graphically immediate in its reality as well as mythic in its proportions and signification thus finds articulation in the oral tradition because of its complex structure of both immediacy as well as symbolic reverberation. At the same time, in its irrefutable physical presence, in its continued survival in and as the violenced body, the violence committed seeps, as event, into the realist discourse of the novel. The event of violence becomes the necessary connective tissue between the imaginary utopia of the oral tradition and the fragmented reality of novelistic discourse. The oral tradition, then, is able to serve its function as the necessary bridge between a physically violent but otherwise imaginary utopian past and the materially non- (or less/differently) violent present which needs this 'past' in order to construct/crystallise a contemporary collective around it.

In my reading of *Sula* the violence itself is used more as an analogical narrative to the disruption and dispersion of the collective of the Bottom. The violence of World War One is described right at the beginning of the novel and, as such, functions as a determining factor in the construction of the collective identity throughout the novel. It is, thus, both symptomatic of as well as conducive towards the fragmented identity that is set up. Unlike *Beloved*, the violence is not only not shared by the collective but it remains invisible to most of the community throughout the text. The collective remains ignorant of it, even as they remain untouched by Shadrack until the end – he remains on the fringes of their lives and consciousnesses Thus, the violence functions more as a narrative trope than as a shared past – in other words, it serves more to image the dispersion of the collective rather than its cohesion.

Significantly, Morrison chooses not to recount the violence of lynchings and other violence against African Americans during this time. This would have been akin to the violence of slavery and the narrative would have constructed a similar community identity out of the collective. Instead she chooses to focus on the economic and social opportunities that opened up with increasing urbanisation and industrialisation in terms of construction jobs and the like. These forces share with the violence of the war its impersonal, rippling out nature, its disregard for the race, class and nationality of the individual – unlike the more intimate, passionate violence of slavery which derived its intensity from the individual, one on one, personalised violence based exclusively on race and class.

It is also true that women and men experienced the war differently in significant ways. By and large women were not seen as having participated in the war and its violence and suffering, even though large numbers of women did work at the front. Moreover, the war was, in some ways, a period of economic liberation for women and, as such, their experience was not necessarily so much one of loss of Self as of the discovery of economic and social independence. It is hardly surprising, therefore, if the violence of World War One is experienced and remembered by, and affects only, the male – Shadrack – in *Sula*; the community of women remains untouched by the self-destroying violence, their minds and bodies entirely free of such memory.

As Marianne DeKoven argues in her essay 'Postmodernism and Post-Utopian Desire in Toni Morrison and E. L. Doctorow' (in Peterson, 111), Morrison's utopias are maternal ones; as such they are also incomplete and transient (DeKoven points to the exclusion of Stamp Paid and Paul D from the union of the three women at 124). I would like to suggest that this maternal union is predicated, in large part, upon the violence which binds these women together. As my readings of *Beloved* and *Sula* show, while this union is valorised (if not vindicated) in *Beloved*, in *Sula*, Eva's epiphany and sacrifice, so akin to Sethe's, does not establish a similar bond between herself and her daughter or grand-daughter. Eva's compulsion is poverty rather than racist violence, and Hannah and Sula are caught up in the same forces of socio-economic compulsion which whirls them out of Eva's orbit and sphere; a movement captured so beautifully in the outward spiralling movement of the narrative itself.

This outward spiralling movement can be seen as heralding the breaking up of the village identity/community which Morrison sets up in *Beloved*. Indeed, Sula actively negates the female ancestor figure in the character of Eva – thus putting the village behind her – and heads for the city. She chooses an education rather than the wisdom of the ancestor, and takes upon herself the task of inventing herself – as an artist – rather than be invented by the ancestor in her own image. Thus Sula comes to represent the self-imaging, self-making Self, functioning within a contingent and changing environment rather than a cohesive identity which founds itself upon and within a collective.

It becomes increasingly significant, then, that not only does the physical killing of half of the residents of the community of the Bottom signify this actual breaking up of the village community, but that, in fact, the only people who do not follow Shadrack to their deaths are the ones who 'remember' the 'village' life of the rural South. All those, that is, who share a collective past of shared violence and labour – as well as the gladness of community living which was so central a part of the village utopia which Morrison invokes – and thus have access to a collective identity prior to the Bottom and the war, survive *as a collective*: those who die, die individually, a fragmented, motley crowd of people joined only by their common isolation.

Thus, even as Morrison seems to be suggesting on the one hand that the village is an anachronism and that strength lies in the independence of a Sula who takes on the changing world by adapting herself continuously to its demands and compulsions, on the other hand, it is also fatal: the ones who survive are the ones who are rooted in the village past. Thus, in Marianne DeKoven's definition of the post-utopian, the impossibility as well as the undesirability of a utopia – maternal or otherwise – is inscribed by the postmodern novel even as the desire for it is registered as a historically specific and tempered one, a realistically modified enterprise charged by the desires and limitations of its place and time. I would add that the unanchored and core-less 'community' united in its destruction at the end of *Sula* is, in large measure, a lack of cohesion consequent upon the absence of a defining violent event or violenced body. Shadrack carries his violence in his mind rather than on his body; Chicken Little disappears, enabling the violent 'act' of his death to disappear with him; Eva is made to disappear by Sula, as Plum's body is by Eva. Even the death of Chicken Little survives as a 'secret' in the minds of Sula and Nel, rather than as a physical event – indeed, as Marianne DeKoven has shown, the 'event' itself is all but written out *as event*.

The presence of violence in the mind rather than on the body is distinct, in *Sula*, from the trauma exorcised by the survivors of violence in *Beloved*. The externalisation of the violent event for Sethe, Paul D and the community of Bluestone enables, as I have tried to show, the 'healing' process of the split between mind and body. The internalisation of the violence of World War One by Shadrack, on the other hand, finds its articulation in the Existential destabilising of the Self – a framework which precludes the construction of a unitary, cohesive Self. Where the narrative of *Beloved* sees the division of mind and body as an artificial splitting of a unitary whole, *Sula* posits the linear and hierarchical system of an 'Existence [which] precedes Essence' – a formulation which makes possible only contingent and temporary constructions of individual selfhood.

As much of this discussion will have made clear, the symbolic, sometimes mythic reverberations of the violent event and the violenced body force the narrative into strategies of representation which depart from the empirically, materially understood sense of realism. The status of Beloved as real, symbolic or mythic has, as we have seen, significant implications for Morrison's understanding of the collective and her reading of history: that Morrison does not allow the reader the luxury of reducing Beloved to either of these – real, symbolic or mythic – is an index to the complexity of her vision. The compulsion towards the non-real is also, however, a function of the violence which is an integral part of Beloved the character as well as *Beloved* the text.

The intensity of the violence inflicted upon Sethe as well as Beloved, its continuance in the minds and memories of its victims – all of them – over time and space, and its deep significance for the understanding of the individuals of themselves and the collective of itself, gives to both event and body a magnitude not readily contained by narratives bound within the empirical, material real. It demands, in other words, narrative boundaries extended into the non-real even as the violence itself seeps out of its physical manifestations into the minds and memories of all the survivors as they define and redefine their Selves and their collectives. More than this, it functions as a surviving core around which a fragmented consciousness or community can crystallise and re-form. As such, it exists, in a sense, almost as an essence – necessarily beyond the empirical.

In its function as a surviving core, this 'essence' invokes a utopian community seemingly caught forever in an ancient timelessness: an idealised collectivity outside the corrosions of time and space, suffering and material change; a reservoir which the community can take recourse to in its fragmentation and dispersion. In other words, it is constructed to serve as a non-empirical, non-material core that remains eternal and unchanged even as political and material realities are in a constant state of flux. Hence, this core demands a non-real representation which combines with the real to reconstitute the collective.

In the final description, then, of the community of women humming in an empathetic circle about Sethe, Morrison can be seen as constructing such a core of communal 'harmony': a music that predates language and which communicates without words and dissonances. It is an attempt to 'realise' an ideal vision of collectivity, and functions, in the novel, as a 'resolution', if not a 'conclusion'. It can be argued that, as such, it remains an artistic resolution rather than a real alternative or construction of a social possibility. It may be relevant to ask how this vision translates into a political entity. The answer might well be that it doesn't: that in fact, it seeks rather to recapture a moment out of historical time, not in real space, independent of social or political probability. In other words, this final vision of utopian collectivity is 'realised' by the sheer effort of imaginative will, and occupies, therefore, the stratum of the non-real that runs constantly within the real in the novel. Indeed, if the 'orality' of this community is placed, as it is no doubt intended to be, within the oral tradition as constructed by Morrison, the materiality of this community is necessarily compromised by the register of the non-real invoked by that tradition.

In the case of *Sula*, however, the event of violence, as we have seen, seems to act more as a trope and catalyst of dispersion rather than community. Perhaps it is for this reason that its narration takes little from the non-real; indeed, the account of Shadrack's experiences in the war remains firmly embedded in its historical and physical specificities. *Sula*, as is evident from its distinctly linear narrative, narrates a past (recounted realistically, in the beginning) that does not penetrate into the present, but remains separate from it. Consequently, the originary event of violence figures forth not collectivity but dispersion and bespeaks the inability of this event to survive over time as a means of binding the collective together. Individual identity, as with Sula herself, along with collective identity is equally fragmented. Non-realist and realist modes are not combined through symbolism; rather, the non-realist element is separated out and isolated within the voice of Shadrack and thus remains unintegrated with the rest of the narrative. The notion of individual identity, here, I see as not so much opposed to the construction of collectivity, as a vibrant aspect of the more Existential sense of dispersion and fragmentation which is consequent upon the narratives emanating from the unique nature of the violence of World War One.

Thus, even as Morrison confines her description of the violence to chapter 1, relating it in realist, even graphic terms and leaving the rest of the novel free of any further narration of this violence, Shadrack carries the violence in his mind/memory as a continuous presence. Unlike Morrison's realistic account of the war, Shadrack's articulation of the violence finds – if not non-real – non-rational expression: from his hallucinatory experience of his body and surroundings, to his formulation of a national holiday when people are called upon to kill themselves. National Suicide Day is seen to be as insane a notion as Shadrack himself: indeed, it is largely why the people of the Bottom regard him as insane.

In other words, both the authorial narrative and Shadrack attempt to contain the violence in different, even opposing ways. Just as the ignorance and indifference of the community of the Bottom threatens the memories which the hermetic and isolated Shadrack carries within himself with denial, its symbolic, authorial articulation is also constructed as one that is continually under erasure. Not only does the novel not rely on symbolism, save for the mark and the grey ball, as I have tried to show, but even these symbols are either constantly being either destabilised by reinterpretation and recontextualisation (as with the mark above Sula's eye), or exist precariously on the edges of consciousness, on the verge of disappearance – as with Nel's grey ball. It is never really possible, therefore, for this symbol to evolve into the kind of central core around which a stable collective identity can crystallise: the tension between Morrison's authorial 'realism' and Shadrack's non-realism serves to keep this core unstable in its signifying agency.

In *Beloved*, however, the non-realist narrative that Morrison generates embraces both her own creation of Beloved as well as Sethe's understanding of her non-real status – an understanding she shares with the community of Bluestone. That the community shares also her memories of violence in their shared history and experiences, allows Morrison to weight the central symbol/character of Beloved with the signifying agency needed to function as the stable core around/upon which a collective identity may be constructed. The real and the non-real are combined in the voice of the narrator and Morrison is able to use an intensely symbolic weave to bridge the (oral) past myth/experience of collectivity and the present effort to understand it.

The narratives of violence in Morrison's novels are intricately involved, then, with not just the collective identities that are constructed from and upon them, but through strategies of the non-real. Amy Tan and Maxine Hong Kingston, too, construct collective identities from narratives of violence, but do so in very different ways and with radically divergent results.

4
Immigration and Identity: Maxine Hong Kingston's *The Woman Warrior* and Amy Tan's *The Joy Luck Club*

1   *The Woman Warrior: Memoirs of a Girlhood Among Ghosts*

'Those of us in the first American generations have had to figure out how the invisible world the emigrants built around our childhoods fits in solid America' (5). Kingston's production of this 'invisible world' is most 'solid', perhaps, in the person of her mother: the 'emigrant'. I believe that the character of the young Maxine's mother is the key to an understanding of the nature of this 'invisible world'.[1] At first reading, what most strikes one about Maxine's mother are the unresolved contradictions of her character. On the one hand, she is the young rebel who defies convention and goes away from home to earn a medical degree. In her two years at medical school, she lives a 'daydream of a carefree life' (62). She takes pride in her brains and her ability to study hard and make accurate diagnoses on the basis of an excellent memory (64). She exorcises the ghost that haunts the medical school building alone – ' "You have no power over a strong woman"' she taunts it, while insulting the ghost as being 'lame and lazy' with a 'hairy butt' (70) – when all the other women are paralysed with fear. She leaves China and moves to America where her flourishing career as a midwife is brutally replaced by that of tomato picker. Her life of privilege gives way to one of gruelling labour. She is one of the adults who teach their girls that '[they] failed if they grew up to be but wives or slaves. [They] could be heroines, swordswomen...Her voice [is] the voice of the heroines in [Maxine's] sleep' (19). Indeed, she is the one who first tells her daughter about Fa Mu Lan, 'the two of [them] singing about how Fa Mu Lan fought gloriously and returned alive from war to settle in the village' (20).

On the other hand, this is the mother who instils in her daughter the fear that unless she did 'something big and fine... [her] parents would sell [her] when [they] made [their] way back to China. In China there were solutions for what to do with little girls who ate up food and threw tantrums' (46). This is the mother who teaches her daughter that when she announces that she has earned straight A's in school she should understand that girls consumed precious food, and that 'you can't eat straight A's' (46). 'When one of [her] parents... [undifferentiated from] the immigrant villagers said, "Feeding girls is feeding cowbirds" [Maxine] would thrash on the floor and scream.' This is the mother who would respond to the question of what was wrong with her daughter with 'I don't know. Bad, I guess. You know how girls are. "There's no profit in raising girls. Better to raise geese than girls."' ' "Stop that crying!" my mother would yell. "I'm going to hit you if you don't stop. Bad girl! Stop!"' (46).

Thus begins the litany of oppression Maxine faces at the hands of her mother. As this first instance shows, her mother remains largely undifferentiated from the other Chinese immigrants or the rest of Maxine's family itself. What is also evident from the many Chinese proverbs interspersed in their speech is that these 'villagers' along with her mother remain undifferentiated, also, from any notion of 'Chinese'. 'There is a word in Chinese for the female *I* – which is "slave". Break the women with their own tongues!' (47). Maxine's rage against this sexism is mixed with her anger at the 'tyrants who for whatever reason can deny [her] family food and work' and the 'stupid racists' she must confront in America (49). Although the reference to the racism in America is fleeting and restricted to this reference, the class oppression is traced back to the 'Communists' from whom she would have to go back to 'China to take back [their] farm' (49). But the overwhelming sense of victimisation derives its emotional and material source and power from the sexism and feudalism that are defined as Chinese.

In the face of this sense of victimisation (which centres around the mother) there is no sense of empowerment that may be traced back to the stories that her mother told her. 'No bird called me, no wise old people tutored me [as in the myth of Fa Mu Lan]. I have no magic beads, no water gourd sight, no rabbit that will jump in the fire when I'm hungry' (49). The chapter 'White Tigers' concludes with a description of the brutality and injustice of the Communist revolution. Kingston catalogues the oppression of the already poor Chinese farmers and villagers – her extended family. 'It is confusing that my family were not the poor to be championed. They were executed like the barons in the stories when they were not barons' (51). With absolutely no historical bracketing to mark this as a unique political event (it is the single reference to 'the Communists' that alerts us to the historical nature of the event), this description is almost indistinguishable in its details from the feudalism of the Fa Mu Lan chapter earlier.

What these two opening chapters produce, therefore, is a 'China' that is transportable in both space and time: it remains, in essence, the same in its terms of oppression, forming a single monolith. This 'China', in its feudalism and sexism can be seen as being typified in the story of the 'no-name aunt' whose village hounds her and her newborn baby to death because of the aunt's unexplained pregnancy. Its materialisation in America in the person of Maxine's mother is significant also because her mother brings with her the stories of support and empowerment – typified in the story of Fa Mu Lan – that form the other axis of Maxine's 'Chinese' inheritance. I suggest that the contradictions within the mother's character (or characterisation) can be seen as being symptomatic of a similar schism in the construction of 'China'. As in the characterisation of the mother, the two aspects of 'China', too, remain unresolved. In other words, what I see as contradictions within the character of the mother remain, for me, unmediated by the author. Similarly, the two aspects of 'China' remain, throughout the novel,[2] isolated from each other in a very essential sense. As I will show, they are never brought into dialogue with each other so as to produce a unified, complex and dynamic vision of 'China'.

Part of this isolation is effected, knowingly or unknowingly, by the vision of 'China' that does not allow for movement within or out of it. Quite apart from the images of unmitigated oppression that proliferate through the novel, Maxine makes it clear that 'China' as she knows it or conceives of it means certain death for her spiritual life, her independence and everything of value in her life. It is the 'China' that reminds her that she is 'useless. One more girl who couldn't be sold' (52). Indeed, when she must confront her 'China' in the form of visits to her family, she 'wrap[s] [her] American successes around [her] like a private shawl' (52). So unrelieved is this vision of oppression that Maxine's only response is 'to get out of hating range' of her parents' 'ink drawing of poor people snagging their neighbors' flotage with long flood hooks and pushing the girls on down the river' – proof of their belief that ' "when fishing for treasures in the flood, be careful not to pull in girls"' (52).

Thus, 'China' is constructed as a place defined almost solely by its violence, a place where life of any value is not, has not been and can never be supported. As the 'Shaman' chapter opens, it is also produced as a place of stasis, unchanging in its ancientness. In the extended description of Maxine's mother's medical degree can and its contents, especially the graduation photograph, that takes up the first few pages of this chapter, this notion of 'China' is deepened and intensified. 'When I open [the can], the smell of China flies out, a thousand-year-old bat flying heavy-headed out of Chinese caverns where bats are as white as dust, a smell that comes from long ago, far back in the brain. Crates from Canton, Hong Kong, Singapore, and Taiwan have that smell too, only stronger because they are more recently come from the Chinese' (57). The three scrolls inside are depicted as similarly archaic, drawing attention to the capitalised words, the misspellings and the affectedly inflated terminology and areas of expertise acquired in just two years: 'Midwifery, Pediatrics, Gynecology, "Medecine," "Surgary," Therapeutics, Opthalmology, Bacteriology, Dermatology, Nursing, and Bandage' (57).

Finally, Maxine sees her mother in her graduation photograph as 'intelligent, alert, pretty' but 'can't tell if she's happy' (59). 'My mother is not smiling; Chinese do not smile for photographs. Their faces command relatives in foreign lands – "Send money"' (58). Her mother looks towards 'foreign lands' in other ways as well. 'She has spacy eyes, as all people recently from Asia have...My mother's eyes are big with what they held – reaches of oceans beyond China' (58–9). Contingent upon such an essentialist construction of China (as, indeed, of 'Asia') is its fundamental dehistoricisation. I will argue this point at length later: for the moment, I wish to focus on the manner in which this dehistoricisation results in the complete objectification of 'China' and the 'Chinese' (inflated into and conflated with 'all people from Asia'). Such is the impetus of this movement that it projects itself into the past, projecting the immigrant experience backwards even on to non- or pre-immigrant Chinese. In effect, no other reality exists: before the immigrant immigrates, she exists only in the future. Any subject position she may have had independent of this (future) experience is appropriated by the immigrant (Maxine, in this case, in her position as a Chinese American: a first-generation immigrant) so that it exists only in the stasis of a now dehistoricised and essentialised 'past'.

Johannes Fabian's notion of Allochronism is useful in understanding how this 'past' is constructed. Anthropological in its original usage, this idea is taken up by Rey Chow in her study of literary and historical narratives of Chinese women, with special attention to the question of Chinese modernity. Simply put, Allochronism refers to the variations in time lines and attitudes in the study of tribal cultures. Fabian points to the empathy with which such cultures are understood while the anthropologist shares this existence. In this way, the anthropologist sees his own existence and understanding as being coexistent with that of the tribals and their culture. However, Fabian claims, when the anthropologist leaves this existence and reverts back to his or her own culture and space, these same tribals and their culture are now seen as existing within a chronological framework which allows the anthropologist to see them as being 'behind' his own culture and position in the time line. Such a positioning consequently marks this culture and people as 'backward', even 'primitive' when seen in relation to the anthropologist's positing his or her own time frame as the norm – one that is shared, of course, with the audience for whom the study is intended. Such an Allochronistic framework positions the culture under investigation – in this case, Maxine's understanding of 'China' – as alien, exotic, other: existing out of 'normal' space and historical time. From the many instances of such a framework in this novel, I will take one example.[3]

Maxine's story of how her mother, Brave Orchid, left her village to go to medical school, lived every woman's dream of an independent existence there, exorcised the local ghost, was given a hero's welcome when she returned to her village and had a busy and fruitful medical career ends with a lengthy description of her mother's purchase of a young slave girl from the local market. Given the pejorative images surrounding the notion of the female/slave in the novel up to this point, this scene is rendered in a remarkably judgement-free, sympathetic and even humorous manner. The reader is encouraged to fall in with the adroitness with which Brave Orchid evaluates the worthiness of the slave (examining her teeth and nails along with her intelligence and willingness to work) and the market savvy with which she forces the parents to accept her price rather than the one they quote. The parents of such girls are similarly rendered in sympathetic fashion, eager to hear details of a chair in the kitchens so that they may console themselves that even now their daughter is resting in it. As Brave Orchid walks away with her slave she comments on the cleverness with which she managed to buy the slave for the price she had wanted: 'we fooled him [the slave's father] very well' (82), voicing the complicity of the reader and the slave in her triumph.

> The unsold slaves must have watched them with envy. I watched them with envy. My mother's enthusiasm for me is duller than for the slave girl; nor did I replace the brother and sister who died while they were still cuddly. Throughout my childhood my younger sister said, 'When I grow up I want to be a slave,' and my parents laughed, encouraging her. At department stores I angered my mother when I could not bargain without shame, poor people's shame. She stood in back of me and prodded and pinched, forcing me to translate her bargaining, word for word.

This paragraph, following immediately upon the mother's inclusion of the reader and the slave in her satisfaction, serves as the other end of the bracket opened in the beginning of the chapter when the story of this part of Brave Orchid's life begins. That bracket, it is worth remembering, took the form of the 'thousand-year-old bats'. Fabian's notion of the Allochronistic framework allows us to see the manner in which the 'China' of ghosts and slaves can be represented with sympathy, even empathy, and without judgement – only until the presenter returns to the normative home-base in which she herself (and, by extension, her audience/reader) is located. Consequently, regardless of how sympathetically or with what attention to detail and facticity this picture of 'China' is presented, bracketed thus, it remains trapped in the narrator's overarching construction of stasis.

The process renders 'China' and the past – good and bad – inaccessible to the modern person. In other words, there can be no dynamic relationship established with such a construction. Wendy Ho (1999), writing of her experiences living with her grandmother ('Popo') and mother, compiles a kind of anthropological file documenting a culture and language that she had access to through her grandmother. 'We still keep Popo's memories of a place called China as a symbolic geopolitical ancestral homeplace even as we live our lives dispersed throughout other homeplaces', she writes (17). Kingston provides such an access for the young Maxine, but, unlike Ho, brackets it off within an Allochronistic framework that makes it narratively or emotionally impossible (as I have illustrated earlier) for Maxine to establish any kind of complex relationship with it.[4] The only evident 'relationship' formed is that of the desire of the 'Chinese' (in the photographs, in the letters) for the 'distant lands beyond China' – in this case, America. It is a desire of the 'past' for the future/present, looking to it for fulfilment and completion. Also unlike Ho, Kingston provides, as we have seen, an almost exclusively negative and violent picture of the past and China. The positive aspects, largely in the form of stories that her mother tells her, are cast in the form of myths and legends (as in the legend of Fa Mu Lan) or deal with non-real aspects such as the exorcism of ghosts. Ho's construction, which is almost a kind of documentation, registers both the nostalgia for a past that, in its acceptance of and dealings with the non-real, is not an alternative for the quite different 'homeplaces' (such as America, in Ho's case) that the modern person inhabits as well as its inaccessibility.

Kingston's construction of China, however, selectively conceived as it is, is never put in perspective as 'a place called China...a symbolic geopolitical ancestral homeplace'. Subjectively narrated through its first-person persona of the young author, this text can, in fact be seen as exemplifying the modernist novel that, according to Lukács, accedes dominance to subjectivity. 'The insistence upon a faithful representation of a "slice of life"...is historically determined; it is the result of an incapacity to conceive reality as a unity in motion. The more true to life the "slice of life," the more fortuitous, barren, static and single dimensional compared to reality will this "reality" be' (180).[5] In his stringent critique of Naturalism, Lukács points to the necessarily static and sterile nature of any selectively chosen representation of a larger 'reality'. (While it is clear that the nature of this 'reality' in its 'objectivity' is open to debate, I do not think that the outcome of that debate will affect the focus of this critique.) The notion of historical determination is particularly interesting here: clearly no two historical moments could be less comparable than the Naturalists of post-1848 France and Kingston in the mid-1970s in America. I wish to focus, however, on the similarity of what Lukács sees as a certain rupture between writer and history. To adapt Lukács's criticism of the French Naturalists as being divorced from the history of their times, I think it is possible to see, in the dehistoricisation of her construction of China, a similar kind of severance between Kingston and the dynamism of vision offered by a fuller engagement with a historical past. Several scholars have taken up the task of historicising Kingston's 'China', providing social and political contextualisation that works to put it in perspective and their work is, of course, extremely useful for readers less aware of China's socio-political history. I am not suggesting, of course, that Kingston – or any novelist seeking to represent such a totality – should have taken this course of action or any other. I do wish to emphasise, however, how such information helps provide a perspective that is prominent in its absence from Kingston's novel. For an enquiry such as mine that attempts to interrogate the narrative and political fabric of the construction of collective identities and events of violence, this absence becomes crucial to an understanding of the foundations for the protagonist's eventual rejection of any possible collective identity that she can participate in and the production of the 'identity' of one as 'forever wandering'.

It is in this context that Lukács's injunction to the writer engaged in constructing such representations is germane. In demanding that 'the work of art must...reflect correctly and in proper proportion all important factors objectively determining the area of life it represents' (1978: 38) he seems to be asking for a certain degree of representational responsibility to a larger historical reality. Problematic as terms such as 'reality' and 'life' are in our post-structuralist vocabularies, and archaic as notions of 'correct[ness]' and 'prop[riety]' are in such critiques, I will argue that both sets of terminology continue to have a bearing on my enquiry. Realism, differentiated from Naturalism and Modernism by Lukács, 'with [its] critical detachment, places what is significant, specifically modern experience in a wider context, giving it only the emphasis it deserves as part of a greater, objective whole' (51). Of course, the realist is not, therefore, required to represent 'reality' in its vast infinitude, but, as I have shown above, Kingston goes to certain lengths to emphasise the general and universal nature of her 'China', particularly in its complete dehistoricisation.[6] I believe that the two aspects of 'China' that she offers remain 'slices of life' that masquerade as a whole, failing, at every step, to establish any relationship of dialogue or dialectic; never, indeed, engaging each other to create any kind of dynamic whole. Kingston provides no overarching perspective that would place this fragment within the context of a larger frame; there is little to distance the reader from any viewpoint or vision of the narrator. Thus, even though more than one kind of information about 'China' does, indeed, exist, this potential is never exploited in order to place any one aspect of it in perspective with another. In effect, the narrative does not acquire a sense of totality or give the reader a sense of the whole, substituting for these, instead, an essentialised generalisation constructed upon the part, standing for the whole.

Such 'single dimensional[ity]', then, constructs, in its turn, the state of stasis that I have been at pains to focus: Lukács takes this notion further by noting the 'barren[ness]' of such a construction. This formulation is instrumental to my understanding of the final position of the narrator as a person 'forever wandering'. I suggest that no other position is possible from a space of stasis that will not allow for the development of individual or collective identity from or upon it. In such a representation of reality, the modern person is, almost by definition, 'an ahistorical being . . . without personal history' (Lukács, 1978: 20) or collective identity. While it may appear, at first glance, that a text presenting itself as a 'memoir' consists of nothing but a personal history, I wish to argue that this is the position towards which the narrator moves and wishes to establish for herself by the end of the novel.

As I have argued earlier, Maxine's single most powerful response to her construction of 'China' is one of hatred and rejection. Such a response is, of course, consistent with the unidimensional vision of it as a place of violence that will mean certain death to any valuable sense of identity she may want or have. Indeed, the greater the degree of oppression represented, the more the individual is cast in the role of victim. Such a position increasingly excludes the possibility of agency of any kind, especially that required for the construction of any sense of selfhood or autonomy necessary for forging an 'identity'.

There is, indeed, a fleeting reference to the 'no-name aunt' who is feared by the villagers after her death because hers is a drowning suicide and she has poisoned the family well by committing suicide in it. The villagers believe that such suicides return after their deaths and wait by the wells to lure substitutes to their death. The question of the victim wresting agency from the very contingencies of her victimisation is an interesting and highly debated one, perhaps most famously formulated in the question 'can the subaltern speak?' It is not a debate I wish to enter at this point in my enquiry: suffice it to say that even if such degree of agency is granted to the victim, it is not enough to contribute significantly to the kind of identity formation I am concerned with here. Further, as I have argued more fully in the Introduction, I find such tropes extremely problematic in the manner in which the violence against these women is redeemed by a literary symbolism that bears no relation to the political reality of the powerlessness of such victims.

The stories of ghost eaters and exorcists are more significant to the question of whether this 'China' allows the protagonist enough agency/empowerment from or upon which to found an identity of any sort. As I have argued earlier, there are several reasons why this does not happen. First, the casting of these stories *as* stories (told, read, inferred) serves to distance them from the realities of the everyday persecutions that Maxine faces at the hands of her mother and her environment. This distance is especially significant when placed next to the immediacy of the narratives of oppression that, for all their occupying a similar status of story or legend, are distinguished from the empowering stories by their lack of the non-real elements such as ghosts and supernatural powers. Second, as I have shown, the Allochronistic framework within which they are presented cordons them off, as it were, and Maxine's own sense of the norm (against which these stories appear bizarre and alien) prevents her from gaining the necessary access to them that would make them a dynamic force in her life. Finally, the association of these stories and legends with the images of ancientness and death that Maxine surrounds her sense of 'China' with results, in conjunction with these other factors, to sap these stories of any transformative energy they may have had.

It is evident that for the purposes of my enquiry I have positioned *The Woman Warrior* as a novel which I consider both realist and modernist in very specific ways. Given the quite different positioning that Kingston herself demands for this work, perhaps some clarification is prudent here. As a text of the late 1970s this novel clearly lays some claim to being postmodern rather than modernist. In many of its structural features this certainly seems to be a viable definition: the dominance of the subjective, the use of folk and mythic material and the blending and effusion of several generic categories are all markers that postmodernism appropriates to itself. In my understanding of the history of the novel, however, none of these is peculiar or unique to postmodernism: indeed, these are the very features that first characterised the emergence of the novel form. In its ideology of identity, also, *The Woman Warrior* cannot be equated, to my mind, with the notion of the contingent self peculiar to postmodernism that controverts the very possibility of a 'self'. I suggest that the novel is closer to the more modernist notion of the divided or fragmented self in need of healing and the sense of alienation that is so characteristic of modernist fiction. In my discussion of the identity that the protagonist finally chooses I will clarify the differences between the modernist notion of alienation and Maxine's own notion of the eternal wanderer. At this point I wish merely to point to the factors that allow me to fruitfully apply Lukács's formulation of certain aspects of the modern and realist novels to this text.

The question of the realism of this novel is less complicated – at least for the present purpose. Again, I do not wish to enter the debate about the differences in the apprehension of 'reality'. I want to focus, instead, on the issue of the representation of national, social or cultural identity which has long been the domain of the realist novel. Although the non-real elements such as ghosts and supernaturally gifted humans mark this novel as being non-realist in the most obvious sense, I believe that the issue at stake is not the nature of 'reality' itself (that is, whether ghosts are 'real' or not) but rather the fidelity with which this reality is represented. Thus, the narrative still lays claim to faithfully representing the material circumstances of a particular existence. Kingston's text, beginning with its title, posits these non-real elements as very much a part of her world, as real as anything more solid; the narrative claims a truth function in its representation of this reality. In this very specific sense, I do not see this text as any less realist – in its form or its concerns – than the texts that Lukács studies.

Indeed, making a distinction between accepted, expected and familiar reality and an unusual or abnormal reality, Lukács observes that it is 'necessary that within this richness and subtlety [of the familiar] the artist introduce a new order of things which displaces or modifies the old abstractions. This is also a reflection of objective reality' (1978: 39). If we can see the non-realist elements of Kingston's novel as constituting this 'new order of things which displaces or modifies the old abstractions', then it is clear that in its conception of 'reality' and the complexity of its representation, realism as Lukács understands it is very close to Kingston's own positioning of her text.[7] Lukács's unusual but, I think, astute, critique of Naturalistic selectivity can thus be seen as the fatal flaw in Kingston's realism.

What kinds of identities, individual or collective, are possible, then, from such a narrative? Kingston navigates her way through the alternatives that 'China' offers, making her way to the final formulation of the eternal wanderer. The dominant trope is that of the ghost: a state of not-being, the opposite of identity. The image of the ghost is pervasive; Kingston has been taken to task for translating the Chinese *kuei* as ghost rather than 'demon' which is the more accepted translation.[8] A generic word used for foreigners, the generation of immigrants use this word for all non-Chinese American people, registering their complete alienness for the Chinese immigrant. For the first-generation immigrant protagonist, however, these Americans eventually become the norm against which her family and China-town appear bizarre and grotesque. After a lengthy description of the various ghosts in America ('Jesus ghosts', 'Hobo ghosts' and 'Wino ghosts', 'Grocery ghosts' and 'Teacher ghosts') Maxine turns to the evils that awaited her if she went to China. 'I did not want to go to China. My father would marry two or three more wives, who would spatter cooking oil on our bare toes and lie that we were crying for naughtiness. They would give food to their own children and rocks to us. I did not want to go where ghosts took shapes nothing like our own' (98–9). Although Kingston retains the translation 'ghost' rather than 'demon', it is clear that the American 'ghosts' are merely alien and incomprehensible – insubstantial – while the 'ghosts' of 'China' and the 'Chinese' are the demons, the malevolent forces of violence and oppression. Other than the actual ghosts, then, the term refers to the ghosts among whom the protagonist's girlhood is spent. The title of the novel alerts the reader to the centrality of this notion and one can safely infer, therefore, that this notion of ghosts refers to the horrors and violence, the oppression and persecution that the young Maxine lived with and which she chronicles.

The ghostliness of the Americans wears off, as we have seen, as Maxine grows to adulthood and learns to see them as the norm. The 'Chinese' remain demonic and when, a couple of lines later, Maxine speaks of her nightmares of violence she adds: 'the trains sounded deeper and deeper into the night. They had not reached the end of the world before I stopped hearing them, the last long moan diminishing toward China' (99). It is clear that 'go[ing] to' 'China' is an option that cannot be escaped merely by remaining in America. 'China' has finally been constructed as a demonic space, 'the end of the world': almost, a 'heart of darkness'. This is the alternative that the protagonist rejects.

A variation of the trope of the 'Chinese' ghost can be seen in the quiet descent into insanity that makes a 'ghost' of Brave Orchid's sister, Moon Orchid. In her complete inability to acclimatise herself to an alien landscape and people, Moon Orchid forfeits her husband and her Chinese life when she comes to America. This insanity, closely allied to the loss of self that makes a ghost of her aunt, is the other alternative that Kingston offers her protagonist. The figure of the insane woman is, perhaps, the single most recurring image of Chinese women in the text. Through the course of the novel it attaches itself almost seamlessly to the image of the slave or the wife – two alternatives constantly flung in Maxine's face. The 'crazy lady' of Brave Orchid's village, stoned and vilified, is eventually lynched by a crowd of Chinese villagers who believe that she is a spy. This woman and her fate recur in the text until the trope proliferates into a catalogue in the final twenty pages of the novel. 'Insane people were the ones who couldn't explain themselves,' Maxine says, beginning the catalogue of the 'half a dozen crazy women and girls, all belonging to village families' (186). In the context of a chapter called 'A Song For A Barbarian Reed Pipe' dealing with the protagonist's discovery of her own voice, such a definition can be taken as a kind of rudimentary definition of identity: to be able to 'explain yourself'. Thus, the cataloguing of 'the woman next door' and 'Crazy Mary' (186), the 'witchwoman' and 'Pee-A-Nah...the village idiot' ends with the protagonist thinking that 'every house had to have its crazy woman' (189).

At the end of a narrative that seeks to 'explain' herself, then, Maxine asks herself 'who would be It at our house? Probably me' (189). She sees herself as a likely candidate because in her fantasies she is 'frivolous and violent, orphaned'. 'I was white with red hair, and I rode a white horse ... I hunted humans down in the long woods and shadowed them with my blackness. Tears dripped from my eyes, but blood dripped from my fangs, blood of the people I was supposed to love' (190). At the end of the narrative, the tropes of crazy woman, slave and wife come together to form a single, ugly identity. She 'did not want to be [the] crazy one', but the alternative seems to be that of slave, a fate reserved for her sister. ' "Now when you sell this one, I'd like to buy her to be my maid,"' the neighbours would joke with Brave Orchid. Maxine makes it a point to exhibit her incapacity at housework so that they would not consider her good slave material, but reminds herself that 'if I made myself unsellable here, my parents would only wait until China, and there, where anything happens, they would be able to unload us, even me – sellable, marriageable' (190).

This passage is followed by a detailed account of the protagonist's grandfather who would shout, 'his neck tendons stretched out. "Maggots! ... Maggots! Where are my grandsons? I want grandsons! Give me grandsons! Maggot! Maggot! Maggot! Maggot! Maggot! Maggot!"' (191). The last ten pages of the novel seem to intensify, to the point of grotesqueness, the litany of sexist oppression that the rest of the text has been cataloguing. The narrative strategy becomes clearer when Maxine reveals her fear – without available evidence – of being forcibly married off to the local 'mentally retarded boy', a large 'frankenstein ... mummy ... zombie' (195). Convinced that her parents would get her married to 'this monster, this birth defect' – the personification, it would seem of Maxine's recurring nightmares about deformed babies with birth defects – she stores up the fear and hatred within her until she begins to shout at her mother. This building up of the fear and hatred is merely the climactic surging of a powerful emotional charge that the text has been accumulating from its first account of the suicide of the no-name aunt. The seemingly repetitive, unnecessary and unnecessarily grotesque descriptions of the 'Maggot!'-shouting grandfather and the selling/marrying off to the 'monster' serve, I think, the sole purpose of architecting this concentration of fury with its powerful emotional impact. As a confrontation, however, this climactic episode with her mother is hardly the denouement that such climactic energy portends. In response to Maxine's furious litany of grievances her mother snaps: ' "I cut [your tongue] to make you talk more, not less, you dummy. [A revelation that has already been made earlier: 164)] You're still stupid. You can't listen right. I didn't say I was going to marry you off. Did I ever say that?...Who said we could sell you? We can't sell people. Can't you take a joke? You can't even tell a joke from real life. You're not so smart. Can't even tell real from false"' (202). In response to Maxine's threats that she will go to college and study mathematics, her mother retorts that she should be a doctor, why just study mathematics?

In a similar manner, Maxine inserts other bits of information such as the fact that the Communists are supportive of women's rights. The pattern of information in isolation – two separate aspects of or pieces of information about 'China' unable to engage with each other to provide crucial perspective – culminates here in this intensely prepared for yet anti-climactic episode. Thus, after her 'confrontation' with her mother Maxine's account seems almost to erase the event from the narrative. There is no evidence that her mother's revelation that her basic fears are and have always been unfounded modifies her consciousness in any way. Set against the emotional power of this (narratively reignited) fear and hatred, Maxine's own revelation that '[she] know[s] now that they don't sell girls [in China] or kill each other for no reason' (205) has little or no narrative impact. 'What I'll inherit someday is a green address book full of names. I'll send the relatives money, and they'll write me stories about their hunger' (206). This final formulation of the nature of her inheritance (embellished with details of the poverty-stricken family and starving children of the relative requesting $50.00 for a new bicycle) is bracketed by the decision to go to 'China' to 'find out what's a cheat story and what's not' (206). The disclaimer about the nature of 'China', however, fades in the face of the emotionally laden and evocative details of the poor relative.

This, then, is the point to which the narrative has led: the construction of a 'China' that can only be exorcised (and is, in fact, almost inseparable from the images of exorcism that pervade the text); a 'China' so irredeemable that the protagonist can only flee from it; so static and essentialised that no identity, individual or collective, can be constructed from, upon or through it. Clearly, such a construction produces no real alternatives in terms of identities. The only irrefutable and acceptable site that Maxine claims as her own is that of her marginally mentioned 'American successes', made explicit only once in her statement 'my job is my only land'. Although Kingston has said in several interviews that she wrote the book in order to 'claim America', 'America' is made available to the reader largely indirectly, through the gaze directed at 'China'.

In the next chapter titled 'At The Western Palace', the account of their aunt's view of the children as 'barbaric' and 'savage' carries with it the inference that the American-born generation to which Maxine belongs is under the scrutiny of the 'Chinese' gaze. However, as I will argue, the orientation of the narrative towards the clearly American audience results in the gaze reverting to the 'Chinese' aunt. This chapter functions, seemingly, as a complementary narrative which reverses the gaze, seeing 'the American' through the eyes of 'the Chinese'. At its most effective, this strategy is capable of providing the necessary double perspective, giving both gazes equal space and showing them to be the mutually exclusive boundaries between which the protagonist is supposedly caught. I am going to argue, however, that what Kingston succeeds in setting up instead, is a 'Chinese' subject position so uncomprehending that the protagonist's subject position – which, in its exclusion of the Chinese presents the American as the norm – becomes unpersuasive, even somewhat grotesque. The aunt's (Moon Orchid) view of the children as 'wild, savage, animal . . . barbaric', inflated, as it is, into hyperbole, is articulated in a tone of voice patently unrealistic. Consequently, since the audience's empathy is invoked on behalf of the protagonist and thus with the American 'objects' of this seemingly Chinese gaze, such epithets revert to the gazer. Thus inverted, the gaze remains that of the 'American'. This narrative technique of the objectification of the American, whereby the children appear incomprehensible to the Chinese aunt reverts, then, to the 'savage' person's inability to comprehend what, to the audience and the protagonist, would be the normal and everyday reality of American childhood.[9]

The protagonist's inability to plot a dialogue between or dialectic of the 'Chinese' and the 'American' voices/realities can thus be seen as a direct result of an inability to construct, much less to converge, two separate, independent gazes/subject positions, making any negotiations between alterities impossible. Although the overt structure seems to be one of 'interweaving gazes', this structure serves, rather, to conceal the reversed gaze evident throughout this chapter. Thus, other than in its construction as the normative audience/reader of the narrative, 'America' does not appear in any significant sense in the novel.

There are, however, a couple of places where the 'Chinese' and the 'American' share a potential line of suture. One of these occurs as Moon Orchid drives to her bigamous husband's office to reclaim him from his Chinese American wife and Brave Orchid reassures her sister with the statement 'a man's real partner is the hardest worker' (149). Coming in the context of the bigamous Chinese American husband and his Chinese passive/submissive wife, this curiously Communist sentiment (especially in the context of the Maoist liberation of women into the workforce) is also, at the same time, a very 'American' one. Here, I would argue, is a possible point of mediation. Questions of how this can be used to reformulate the abandoned first wife and reassess the position of the presumably more 'Americanised' second wife, if not actually the husband himself, form, instantaneously, a kind of penumbra of potential around this observation. This realisation could well serve as a point of suture, *of necessity ironic*, for these otherwise antithetical cultures/historical moments. This possibility hovers on the edges of the penumbra of a connection between the two wives which can, potentially, be constructed into a mediating space which would facilitate transition.

What Kingston does, however, is to distance the moment through recourse to the easily recognisable currency of the grotesque, B-grade film plot.[10] The obvious humour of Brave Orchid's melodramatic plans (as her son expresses his exasperation, rolling his eyes and trying to dissuade his mother: 'Mother, this is ridiculous. This whole thing is ridiculous.' 'Stop being silly,' his mother admonishes; 'you Americans don't take life seriously' (150)] could simply be there to emphasise the pathos of Moon Orchid's plight. What it succeeds in doing, however, is to reinstate the alienness of the Chinese Brave Orchid *at the very moment at which* she is most recognisably 'American' – in her insistence on justice and her rights, and in the courage with which she believes in them. Thus, the moment passes and the line of possible suture remains unexploited, parodied, dismissed.

In effect, then, there is no site that Maxine is willing to 'claim', whether 'Chinese' or 'American' or even 'Chinese American'. She wishes, finally, to escape the fate of the silent Chinese girl in her school whom the young Maxine torments in an attempt to get her to say something, anything. The process of finding her 'voice', as we have seen in her 'confrontation' with her mother, is highly problematic. Possibly recognising the inadequacy of this position, Maxine/Kingston ends with a semi-imaginative retelling of the myth of Tsai Yen. In her reading of this myth and its implications for the final position that Kingston wishes to occupy, Patricia P. Chu (2000) points out that the finding of Tsai Yen's voice is indistinguishable from the songs that she sings. Abducted by barbarians, Tsai Yen is inspired by the beauty of their music and begins to sing in words that they would understand. In so doing, she is accepted into their 'inner circle', the circle of barbarians sitting around the winter fire. For Chu, the implications of such a position run counter to the claims of homelessness that it makes on behalf of the protagonist. To my mind, the trope of the eternal wanderer is one which elides the spiritual implications of 'wandering' with the material. In other words, it is possible to see the final position of Tsai Yen (who has, at the end of the myth, been with the barbarians twelve years and has two children, heirs to the Han dynasty) as one of homecoming. Her material status is one of the inner circle, matriarch to dynastic rulers, while her spiritual state may be gauged by the songs that she sings. Not wholly in their language but in one that the barbarians understand and recognise as beautiful, her songs are such that 'the barbarians understood their sadness and anger. Sometimes they thought they could catch barbarian phrases about forever wandering. Her children did not laugh, but eventually sang along when she left her tent to sit by the winter campfires, ringed by barbarians' (209). The songs are about 'China and her family there' (209), and the implication seems to be that this is the 'song' and voice of the protagonist.

While I can understand that the myth is a metaphor for the text that Kingston has produced, such an interpretation would place her among the inner circle of her adopted homeland, singing with and for her audience. While the 'sadness and anger' are certainly evident, the nostalgia inherent in the story of Tsai Yen is missing in Kingston's narrative, even as the hatred and revulsion are missing from Tsai Yen's songs of 'China and her family'. It is difficult to see in what sense, then, either the protagonist or Tsai Yen are 'forever wandering'.

2 *The Joy Luck Club*

In many ways, *The Joy Luck Club* is a less dense text for the purposes of my enquiry. It differs from Kingston's novel in that it seems a more conventionally realist work. It has an overarching ideology that is comprehensive of a larger sense of reality. The fragments that are selected by the author signify a whole in the perspective it provides; the text is, thus, more heteroglossic in a Bakhtinian sense. The novel registers, also, some of the early Lukács's concerns regarding the relationship of the modern present with the epic past which is shown to be both desirable as well as not, but not wholly inaccessible. I will argue that Tan shows that the past can and must be owned, however selectively, in order to heal the divided selves of both the individual and the collective. In this sense, the novel can be said to be modernist.

The book opens with two compelling narratives: the story of the swan and its remnant feather, and the story of Suyuan's experiences during the invasion of China by the Japanese concluding with her fleeing the bombing of Kweilin. Together, these form the core of the process of identity formation with its critical positioning of the relationship of the daughters (in this case, Jing-mei) and their relationship with their mothers (in this context, Suyuan), inextricably bound with the constructions of 'America' and 'China'.

The 'old woman' who crosses 'an ocean many thousands of *li* wide' to get from Shanghai to America brings with her a swan that she will gift to her daughter: a symbol of the hope and a bond so essential between mother and daughter that the daughter 'will know [her mother's] meaning when she receives the swan – a creature that became much more than what was hoped for' (Tan, 1989: 3; all further quotes from this text are from this edition). 'But when she arrived in the new country, the immigration officials pulled her swan away from her, leaving the woman fluttering her arms with only one feather for a memory. And then she had to fill out so many forms she forgot why she had come and what she had left behind' (3). Even this remnant of the whole swan does not find its way to the daughter but remains a hope, a deferred desire, of the Chinese mother unable to speak the 'perfect American English' that her daughter will understand.

The story works to bind together several crucial ideas: the hope for freedom and emancipation that drives the immigrant out of her own land towards an alien place; the deep-seated desire to communicate this hope and desire to her daughters; the need to bring the home country to the American-born child in some form that would be both material and symbolic. Most compellingly, perhaps, the swan, reduced to a feather, gives the sense of the fragility of language and its ability to convey 'meaning', especially the kind of meaning that is the very blood and bones of the connection between mother and daughter. While the feather holds out the remote possibility of com-munication, the loss of the swan itself is a powerful notation of the loss of both significance as well as the means of signification. For the mother leaving her homeland, the immigration officer takes away her identity, her sense of herself, her connection with her homeland, the significance she derives from these and her means of communication when he takes away the swan. When the Chinese mother's means of signification are replaced by the 'forms' she must 'fill in', this new and alien means of signification both erases as well as overwrites the previous one. New 'meaning' is ascribed to prior information in the process of erasure and the immigrant mother is rendered mute until such time as she is able to master these new forms of signification (the 'perfect American English') and inhabit these new meanings. Thus, the feather becomes charged with both the hope as well as the futility of such a desire.

That the daughter is a native inhabitant of these new meanings and spaces, speaking in 'perfect American English' and has, in this sense, fulfilled the hope of her immigrant mother in being born in a world where 'her worth is [not] measured by the loudness of her husband's belch' (3) serves, in fact, to sever the connection between mother and daughter rather than strengthen it. The swan which would have ensured and been the material manifestation of this connection is lost in the act of immigration. Amy Tan's novel is an exercise in reforging that connection, a kind of literary and textual swan that will bring the stories of mother and daughter back to each other in something other than the pristine Chinese of the mothers or the 'perfect American English' of the daughters. More than the find-ing of a common language between Jing-mei and her dead mother

Suyuan, however (since much of the English text is actually translated Chinese, mostly in the speech of the mothers), the swan/novel
is constructed from the violence and urgencies of the home that
Suyuan was forced to flee. This is true in different ways of the other
three stories as well, but Tan begins her novel by twinning these two
narratives: the myth or folk tale of the swan (which serves as a pro-
logue to all four pairs of narratives) and the bombing of Kweilin
that immediately follows it. That Jing-mei had always thought of
this historical event as 'nothing but a Chinese fairy tale' underlines
the connection between these two narratives. In my reading of *The
Joy Luck Club* I will show the manner in which these two narratives
together function as the swan's feather, constructing between them
the sense of identity and home lost to both mothers and daughters
in the act of immigration.

The originary event of violence can clearly be identified as the
bombing of Kweilin from which Suyuan flees, leaving her two baby
girls on the road. It is to this experience that her daughter, Jing-mei,
must return, to experience both her participation as well as her
separation from the violence which expelled her mother from her
homeland. As the novel opens with the death of her mother, Jing-mei
hears this story as the narrative of the secret life or key to the life of
her mother; so powerful is its impact, that once the story is narrated,
it renders any understanding of her mother's identity impossible in
its absence. It becomes, in other words, the originary or foundational
narrative of her mother's life/identity. Narrated by the American-born
daughter, Jing-mei, the graphic description of the violence of World
War Two is distanced by the bracketing strategies of the opening
scene introducing the death of Suyuan and the introduction of her
first-person narrative as 'her Kweilin story', 'a story she would always
tell [Jing-mei] when she was bored' (7). This 'story' is briefly inter-
rupted in the middle by Jing-mei's voice which reiterates its nature
as 'nothing but a Chinese fairy tale' which was rendered all the more
unreal by the unstable narrative. 'The endings always changed . . . The
story always grew and grew' (12) until one day Suyuan tells her
daughter 'a completely different ending to the story' (13).

The end of Suyuan's 'story' is punctuated by a double displacement
of her daughter who finds that she has no place either in the story
of her sisters, or of her mother. 'Stunned to realize that the story had
been true all along', Jing-mei is told by her mother that she is 'not

those babies' who had been left by her by the roadside in the midst of the war. There is no way for Jing-mei to find herself in or through this story because this statement, Jing-mei says, '[makes] it clear that there was no more to the story' (15). The second displacement occurs immediately after in the following section of the Mah Jong game with the remaining three Chinese mothers where Jing-mei both expects as well as recognises the impossibility of these Chinese women ever accepting her in her mother's place. As she enters, Jing-mei thinks how 'they must wonder now how someone like me can take my mother's place.' She remembers her mother being insulted by some attributed similarities between the two, saying 'You don't even know little percent of me! How can you be me?' And this statement of irreconcilable difference is acknowledged by Jing-mei: 'and she's right. How can I be my mother at Joy Luck?' (15). This is a necessary admission of the chasm separating her from her mother and therefore from her past, from China, from her owning of a history which will give to her both a literal family as well as a sense of belonging and membership within a collective identity. Even before the Chinese mothers reveal to Jing-mei the existence of her half-sisters and send her on her journey of dis/recovery, she has already begun to assimilate the reality of the events at Kweilin. Even if she was 'not those babies', the feast at the Joy Luck Club is recognised as being 'just like...the Kweilin feasts' (20). But the reality of the violence that both separated her from her sisters as well as made her own existence possible remains bracketed off as 'story', and it is not until she dis/recovers these living sisters that Jing-mei will be reconciled with it and with her own identity. It is almost as if she, too, is abandoned by the roadside, 'screaming to be reclaimed'.

It is important, therefore, to recognise the graphic manner of the description of this violence in a text in which all violence is rendered obliquely. In her account of the Japanese invasion of China, Suyuan is, in fact, particularly attentive to the details of the effects of war in every conceivable aspect of city and human life. Thus, even before we see the Japanese or hear of their actual atrocities, we see the cities fill with refugees fleeing from them. Suyuan recounts with wonder the manner in which social and economic classes, among other divisions, are sundered and rendered meaningless by the violence of the war. 'Every day, every hour, thousands of people poured into the city... They came from the East, West, North and South' (8). The bizarre nature of this social upheaval is evident in Suyuan's account. 'We were a city of leftovers mixed together. If it hadn't been for the Japanese, there would have been plenty of reason for fighting to break out among these different people. Can you see it?' (8). Even the disease and homelessness and squalor did not make for tolerance or an acknowledgement of the shared human condition. As 'Kweilin [loses] its beauty' for Suyuan, the account turns to the manner in which the bombings turned the hills into hiding places for the Japanese, her home into a place of 'dark corners', the city a place of 'sirens [that] cried out to warn [them] of bombers' and the caves a place for the 'wild animals' that the people who hid there felt they had become (9). The human person, stripped of her social, economic, physical and even human attributes, is reduced to nothingness. Driven, symbolically, into the 'bowels of an ancient hill', these are people who can be seen as being pushed back into the womb, to a point of non- or pre-existence. 'Can you imagine how it is, to want to be neither inside nor outside, to want to be nowhere and disappear?' (9). Thus, when the sounds of bombing faded, they emerged like 'newborn kittens scratching' their way back to consciousness and the living (9).

The Joy Luck Club comes as a response to a very specific need. 'At all hours of the night and day [Suyuan can hear] screaming sounds. I didn't know if a peasant was slitting the throat of a runaway pig or an officer beating a half-dead peasant for lying in his way on the sidewalk...And that's when I thought I needed something to help me move on' (10). Even at the cost of being thought to be 'possessed by demons', the women of the Joy Luck Club fight their despair over the 'unbearable' loss of family and possessions with their weekly meetings (10). But along with this and perhaps more urgent is the visceral need to forget 'a home that burned down with your mother and father inside of it...[the] arms and legs hanging from telephone wires and starving dogs running down the street with half-chewed hands dangling from their jaws' (12). Thus, 'each week [they] could forget the past wrongs done to [them]' until the invasion of Kweilin forces Suyuan to flee and 'the news of the slaughter' materialises before her eyes in 'the streets of Kweilin...strewn with newspapers...and on top of these papers, like fresh fish from a butcher, [lie] rows of people – men, women and children who had never lost hope but had lost their lives instead' (13).

Suyuan recounts to her daughter, in minute detail, the stages of the loss of hope, the loss of tears, the loss of physical strength, of feeling. The loss of her two infant daughters is left unnarrated, a loss unaccounted for; one, in other words, for which there is no narrative, no 'account' possible. What is left 'lying on the side of the road... screaming to be reclaimed' (29), then, is all this and more: Suyuan's identity and that of her daughter. Even while registering that she 'was not those babies', Jing-mei recognises her place in this 'story': the part of her as much in need of reclamation as the babies with 'their red thumbs popped out of their mouths' (29). That this narrative is equally crucial to Jing-mei's understanding of herself is evident, also, in the level of her participation in it: 'and now I feel as if I were in Kweilin amidst the bombing' (29).

The narrative, once it is told, instantly establishes its own chronologies and teleologies: time becomes 'durational' – the event of violence is always in the present, coexistent with other realities of the present. The future cannot be imagined nor the collective constructed in its absence. It is not surprising then, to read almost immediately after of 'the east where things began' (32). Jing-mei's connection with her mother is also the connection with the violence of her mother's past and the severance of the link with her Chinese sisters. Thus, the split – or hyphenated – identity is seen as a consequence, not of the Chinese/American divide, but of the violence of the Chinese past of the mothers. In other words, the event of violence drives a wedge into the understanding of the collective's identity prior to and distinct from the experience of immigration. The rupture between mothers and daughters can be seen as a direct result of this event in that the mothers *fled from* the violence and thus brought with them to America experiences and memories, qualities and characteristics which the daughters neither know, remember nor honour. 'They are frightened,' Jing-mei says of the three mothers left alive. 'In me they see their own daughters, just as ignorant, just as unmindful of the hopes and truths they have brought to America' (31). If China is embodied forth and narrativised both through and by the mothers, then it is significant that this divide, which is a vital one, can be traced back to an event of violence in China, rather than to the cultural compulsions of growing up in America.

Tan's choice of the event of violence as a historical one distinguishes it in several significant ways from Kingston's choice of an imagined event. Kingston's fictional event functions as a generic type of the violence in and of China, thus effectively combining with the fantasy of the Fa Mu Lan legend to construct a far more essentialist picture of China as a place of violence. Such a place, as we have seen, then becomes able to assimilate all the sexism and classism in its feudal structure which Kingston demarcates as the many faces of its evil. This construction, as I have argued, can therefore only be exorcised; it can, and indeed, must never be accepted or accommodated in any vision of the narrator's personal understanding of her own or the collective's identity.

Tan's choice of a historical event rather than a fictional one focuses, instead, her sense of its inescapability: the mother who fled the bombs of Kweilin not only lived with/in the memory of these bombs all her life, but, on her death, bequeathed them to her daughter as a vital part of her inheritance. The notion of survivor guilt so often noted in Holocaust studies is not far from Jing-mei's sense of participation in and separation from this event: 'The babies in Kweilin, I think. *I was not those babies*' (29; italics added). Felman and Laub (1992) point out that the psychology of the survivor ensures that she feels not only guilt for having survived that which so many others did not, but also that her own death was enacted in the death of the victim. It is, perhaps, to escape this 'death' that Jing-mei must return to China in search of the sisters whom her mother had thought dead – the casualties of war.

Insofar as the identity of the collective is intimately connected with that of the individual's selfhood, it is significant that all the characters in Tan's novel construct their identities within the larger framework of their Chinese mothers. Such an emphasis on a selfhood emerging from the violence and suffering of both mothers and daughters establishes an equilibrium between collective identity and individual selfhood. (The structure of the novel is thus more akin to the heteroglossic structure of Alice Walker's *The Color Purple* in its interweaving stories which give voice to the community by recording the voices of individuals.)

Within this larger framework of the lives of the mothers, one of the most notable characteristics of the narration of violence in this text is the violence remembered but left unnarrated – also a characteristic of the narratives of the mothers. The overheard violence of the 'voices from the wall' becomes 'the nighttime life of [Lena's] imagination' (113). Available to her only in the form of sounds, Lena is transfixed by the absence of images that would make this violence accessible to her. From the 'scraping sounds, slamming, pushing and shouts and the *whack! Whack! Whack!*' she is lost in a sea of inferential information ('Someone was killing. Someone was being killed') which can be interpreted only within her own matrix of reference. Thus, the displaced 'screams and shouts' can only be translated within the already displaced/translated story of the imagined death of the beggar that this section opens with. And so, Lena imagines that 'a mother had a sword high above a girl's head and was starting to slice her life away, first a braid, then her scalp, an eyebrow, a toe, a thumb, the point of her cheek, the slant of her nose, until there was nothing left, no sounds' (114). Denied the chance to be a witness to her mother's trauma, or the occasion to bear witness to her own displaced one, Lena registers 'the horror of it all': of having 'witnessed with [her] ears and [her] imagination . . . [that] a girl had just been killed' (114).

   The story of the death of the beggar focuses this strand of imagined violence. What is 'the worst possible way' in which to be executed? Without the facts, without narrated details, without images with which to shape the horror of the killing, the young Lena St. Clair is left wondering. 'How was he killed? Did they slice off his skin first? Did they use a cleaver to chop up his bones? Did he scream and feel all one thousand cuts?' (105). Ying Ying St. Clair's response that the 'man has been dead for almost seventy years. What does it matter how he died?' (105) may seem to be the most rational one until Lena reveals the following:

> I always thought it mattered, to know what is the worst possible thing that can happen to you, to know how you can avoid it, to not be drawn by the magic of the unspeakable. Because even as a young child I could sense the unspoken terrors that surrounded our house, the ones that chased my mother until she hid in a secret dark corner of her mind. And still they found her. I watched, over the years, as they devoured her, piece by piece, until she disappeared and became a ghost. (105)

That 'the magic of the unspeakable' is as seductive as it is destructive is etched in the descent of Ying Ying into a kind of silent insanity in her obsession with an unacknowledged past. The basement in which Lena suspects her mother's 'dark side sprang from' beckons to the young child in its forbidden mysteriousness. When she 'falls headlong into this dark chasm...screaming' (105) the revelation of the evil man who 'had lived there for thousands of years', rapist, predatory, cannibalistic, serves to open up for Lena a kind of Chinese third eye. With this eye she is able to perceive and foresee all manner of horrors, especially those that could and would befall young girls. The dancing devils, the child-killing lightning, the child-faced beetle, the brain-splattering tether ball, all reveal themselves through her 'Chinese eyes, the part of [her she] got from [her] mother' (106).

If the narration of the violence in the past seems crucial to the identities of both the mothers and their daughters, then the schism endured by the mothers as a result of the violence must be healed – at least narratively – by the revelation of the violence to their daughters, and it is interesting to note the place Tan accords to incidents of violence in the lives of the daughters. As we have seen, violence in the lives of the daughters is never overtly revealed by Tan but always kept partially concealed, hinted at, gestured towards; revealed only when healing is most needed. Thus, although Lena's father claims to have 'saved' her mother 'from a terrible life' in China, that life is a 'tragedy' that her mother 'could not speak about' (106). Whatever this 'tragedy' may have been – or is, since Ying Ying continues to live it – direct access to it is denied to her daughter. Ying Ying herself is unable or unwilling to allow her family access to her past, leaving them to confront its trauma through a lens of displacement. Thus, father and daughter translate or interpret her moods and inexplicable actions within their own matrices of the 'normal'.

If Ying Ying St. Clair is a 'Displaced Person' (thus labelled by the Immigration Department which is unable to catalogue her in any of the available categories) then she is as much psychologically displaced by her trauma as she is geo-politically through the event of immigration. It is this psychological displacement that her daughter inherits from her and which she must acknowledge and heal. Lena's displacement, which lies also in her inability to access her mother's unnarrated trauma, is effected in the displacement of the violence she has only partial access to. Lena, herself, displaces acts of violence onto herself as well: thus, she is convinced that she 'was the one who had caused Arnold to die' through her enforced starvation that would, in her imagination, transfer the diseases of African children onto this unwanted suitor/tormentor. Propelled by her terror that Arnold was her destined husband, she is later as convinced that she has, indeed, met her fate – in not Arnold, but the equally unfit and similar sounding Harold. So powerful and deep-rooted is the hold of the 'witnessing' of such displaced violence that it is difficult for Lena – even many years later – to 'finally dismiss all this as ridiculous' (168).

In its position as imagined yet 'witnessed' violence, such a narrative of displacement slips out of the reach and control of the spectator: the real horror then becomes 'the terror of not knowing when it would stop' (114). This is the 'worst thing that could happen'. The book is full of such violence not narrated but remembered, overheard, imagined: whence Lena's determined resistance to 'the magic of the unspeakable'. For one whose mother becomes a 'ghost' devoured by the secret knowledge of such violence, the unspoken quickly becomes 'the unspeakable', and thus, control over this narrative – to be able to begin, recite and end it – becomes the only form of agency or power possible for the daughters to whom it is bequeathed. The killing of the other son, revealed without warning, is not fully 'witnessed' by either mother or daughter until Ying Ying decides to allow her daughter to bear witness to her mother's testimony as a means of healing her daughter. Until she recognises its healing functions, however, Ying Ying can only be seen as 'babbling' (116) hysterically, speaking in Chinese, mistranslated and misquoted by her daughter intentionally, just as her husband has misunderstood her much of her life, intentionally or unintentionally 'putting words in her mouth' for Lena's benefit. Surrounded by images of misshapenness and deformity, the hysterical climax ' "I had given no thought to killing my other son!"' (117) has no matrix within which it may be interpreted by Lena or translated for her father. Even after this revelation, therefore, that clearly lies at the heart of Ying Ying's trauma, Lena can only see her as 'crazy' – a revelation she refuses to inflict on her rational/'normal' father. 'I could not tell my father what she had said...How could I tell him she was crazy?' (117). Confronted with this narratorial silence that has extended now even to the narrator within the text, the reader must piece together whatever story can be constructed in the absence of any sort of narrative at all for it.

The connection here between violence and collective identity has, unlike Morrison's novels, little to do with the body and its signification and rather more with its psychological compulsions. The unfigured, unacknowledged violence is a similar but, perhaps in some ways, more terrible instance of the ubiquitous and unspoken violence upon which the narrative of selfhood must found itself. Built as they are upon this half-realised narrative of violence, all constructions of selfhood are necessarily left in a state of nascent becoming rather than complete realisation. The identities constructed are also, therefore, less decisive, less stable; founded as they are upon shifting memories traced back through at least one generation, they are distanced from the protagonists and narrators by geography, time and lack of proximity to the victims. In the case of Jing-mei and Suyuan, it is with the final episode of the unveiling of the story of Kweilin that the suturing of several schisms is effected: sister with sister, daughter with mother, immigrant with homeland. The complete story of the lost girls of Kweilin is finally made real for the daughter who has come to China in search of her sisters/Chinese self/identity. At a structural level, such a move bears certain similarities to Morrison's narrative structure; but at the level of identity formation, the final revelation of the facts of suffering and violence, which had existed only on the periphery of the narrative as imagined, remembered and overheard, is now graphically contextualised upon the reality of Chinese soil.

Tan's narrative, like Morrison's, seeks to open up spaces of healing and understanding upon which the self of the individual as well as the collective, rendered schismatic by violence, can be founded. Lena is eventually able to help her mother come to the realisation that she has 'already experienced the worst. After this, there is no worst possible thing', and thus to '[pull] her through the wall' (121) towards sanity. Although this is effected in a visionary rather than substantial manner, Lena is nevertheless able to knit together the separate strands of displaced violence into a fabric of significance, changing or perhaps translating the significations of each in the process. The imagined death of a thousand cuts becomes, in this new signification, a process of healing, while the pulling through the wall is no longer an act of murderous revenge but one of salvation. Through interpretation, translation, displacement and imagination, Lena constructs a 'perfect understanding' (121) with and for her mother without, at this point, being able to witness, or bear witness to, the trauma of her past in China.

Ying Ying decides to reveal the truth of her killed/aborted son to Lena in an effort to release her *chi*, and the tiger within her. She does this as a conscious act of healing and revelation, recognising the need to allow her daughter access to her mother's trauma. 'So this is what I will do. I will gather together my past and look. I will see a thing that has already happened. The pain that cut my spirit. I will hold that pain in my hand until it becomes hard and shiny, more clear. And then my fierceness can come back, my golden side, my black side. I will use this sharp pain to penetrate my daughter's tough skin and cut her tiger spirit loose' (284). Ying Ying recognises the loss of *chi* – spirit, or identity, sense of self – that she has suffered displaced onto her daughter in spite of her efforts to raise her differently. It is only in the act of bearing testimony to her own past that she is able to regain her own *chi* and provide her daughter with access to hers; 'the only way to penetrate her skin and pull her to where she can be saved' (274). The violence and its trauma, concealed or displaced, have been like a wall between the generations which mother and daughter fight to pull each other through. Revealed and testified to, it becomes a bridge between the two spaces of 'China' and 'America', mother and daughter, who have 'watched [each other] as from another shore' all their lives (274).

Jing-mei is the only one among the four daughters to actually travel to the other shore, to China, to the site of the past, in order to build this bridge, to reach through this wall between herself and her mother, and she is able to do so, not only when she knows the whole truth about the war and her mother's suffering, but when she is able to experience the 'China' that her mother left behind. The story of the bombing of Kweilin and the abandoning of the two girls as told to Jing-mei by her father does not really add any new information to what the reader and Jing-mei already know. The significance of this narrative comes, instead, from the site at which it is narrated. As Jing-mei approaches China from Hong Kong, the tingling forehead, the rushing blood, the 'bones aching with a familiar old pain [all make her] think [her] mother was right. [She is] becoming Chinese' (306). 'Once you are born Chinese, you cannot help but feel and think Chinese' (306). She sees 'a sectioned field of yellow green and brown, a narrow canal flanking the tracks, low rising hills, and three people in blue jackets riding an ox-driven cart on [an] early October morning' through 'misty eyes, as if [she] had seen this a long, long time ago and had almost forgotten' (307). Clearly, this confrontation of the past which is conflated with a meeting of sisters is a means of navigating both an individual identity (Jing-mei's as well as her mother's) towards a collective one.

Suyuan's position, when seen amidst the violence of the war, is one of a 'Chinese' victim oppressed by the Japanese. Jing-mei's father and his aunt discuss the event more in terms of the Japanese invasion and its political and actual veracity rather than as an experience undergone by Suyuan. This movement from the individual to the collective is one that is undertaken even in Canning's narrative of his wife's fleeing of Kweilin and the abandonment of the babies. The narrating and positioning of the event of violence draws several threads together into its fabric. The babies come to represent the mother herself, caught in her innocence in the senselessness of the bombing, and, as she divests herself of all her material belongings, she symbolically as well as literally becomes less and less a culture-specific individual and more and more an anonymous, innocent victim of war, much like the babies themselves. In a curious movement, this becomes a process of simultaneously divesting of as well as investing the mother with her Chinese-ness (she is a target of Japanese bombs by virtue of her nationality; differences of class and culture become increasingly irrelevant). In so doing, it becomes somewhat akin to an essentialist Chinese identity, but escapes becoming wholly so insofar as it remains grounded in its historical specificity. This seamless and 'natural' construction of a collective sense of Chinese identity, together with the historical event of violence, reflects the conflicted, but not unstable, nature of this identity. Indeed, the identity is all the more stable for being founded on an incident of such intense meaning. More importantly, this identity is also a specifically collective one in a novel which is largely taken up with the individual, rather than the collective, identities of the daughters.

The importance of this event for the establishing of a collective identity can be seen, in fact, throughout the text in the manner in which Tan retains the significance of the mothers' stories in the lives of the daughters as well as in the larger narrative. Thus, the novel consists of interweaving stories of not just many Chinese women, but of mothers and daughters, a strategy which indicates the acceptance of the mother in a way in which it is impossible for Kingston to do. Thus, while for Kingston the mother figure often becomes elided with 'Chinese oppression' which Kingston is so invested in exorcising, Tan's narrative makes the mothers and their acceptance by their daughters an organic part of her narrative and thus of her constructions of collectivity. Similarly, unlike Kingston's protagonist whose connection with a similar ancestor figure remains on the level of the nostalgic and sentimental (as is evident in the reference to the letters from the grandmother) the mother–daughter relationship, extending sometimes over three generations, is the narrative centre of Tan's text. Tan seems, consequently, less haunted by the stories of cruelty, oppression and violence the mothers necessarily bring with them, and, indeed, provides a much wider range of 'Chinas', thus negating the desire to or impulse towards exorcism and erasure. As my reading of both texts will have made clear, then, the stability of the collective identity is a function of the narratives of violence: the 'forever wandering' immigrant of Kingston's text, frozen in her flight from a China which cannot be lived in/with is as much a function of that narrative as Tan's more grounded, stable and integrated identity is a function of her narrative of the integration and acceptance of a violent history.

5
'An invisible country, a true Chile': the Body of Evidence in Isabel Allende's *House of Spirits*

In exile, Ariel Dorfman writes of the country he left behind as one which has not so much been destroyed as sent into hiding; one which is closely and carefully guarded by a bewildering cross-section of its people, from the anonymous person who paints a house red to the rebel who undergoes extreme torture at the hands of the state. All these people are part of a resistance movement whose task is not merely to thwart and oppose the functioning of the state, but, equally importantly, to sustain and preserve the cultural, political, spiritual and artistic pieces of a Chile which they see as being scattered and fragmented by a state bent upon destroying it.[1] This writing in of 'an invisible country, a true Chile'[2] requires objects and icons through and around which its 'invisibility' can be bodied forth, and which, at the same time, invest it with the validation and authentication which would mark it as the 'true country'. Along with cultural and political artifacts and practices which preserve/construct a sense of an older, pre-existing Chile, its current, beleaguered state as a country riven and divided with violence finds its icons, symbols and, indeed, material representation in the existence and images of the tortured rebels who resist the state. Because this process of 'country formation' is so integral a part of the resistance movement, so strongly identified with rebels, the captured, the tortured and the disappeared, these people and their images quickly provide a core around which the 'true Chile' crystallises.

Thus, the invisible and unbodied country is fed and sustained by both the rumours and stories as well as the actual photographs and bodies of victims of violence. The most fearsome are, thus, the 'disappeared', the ones upon whom the violence was so intense that it killed them; and also the ones upon whose bodies the violence, not available to the imagination or the consciousness of the survivors through images, generate more terror in their evocation of the unknown and uncontainable, unnameable horror. This 'invisible' and 'true' country, then, takes shape in the tension between the necessarily invisible and the compulsively embodied. A sense of territory – physical, tangible – is essential to the invisible, the unnamed, the silenced, the disappeared; its primary function of embodying the disembodied becomes, also, the means by which the dismembered and wounded body – of 'Chile', of the rebel – is made whole and re-membered.

It is clear from the edicts and proclamations of the Junta that the Pinochet regime, like most fascist regimes, recognised very early in its reign the importance of erasing, defacing and defaming any and all objects, persons and events which represent the country prior to the regime. Equally, when a fascist state imposes such a regime of violence upon a country, the hope of one day restoring peace and order and the fear of the existing disorder and repression force the oppressed to 'preserve' what they conceive of as the 'country' which has been destroyed. Although what is preserved may be only subjective memories, aspirations, ideologies and desires, these are given the name of country and are thought of as such because they are seen, in a more essential way, as a state of being and a way of life. Constructed piecemeal and in fragments, this form of resistance takes on all the passion and fervour of the forbidden. All things become, therefore, charged with the intensity of the violence which they resist, thus acquiring the stature of the political almost instantaneously, rather than having political meaning accrue to them over time. This, I would like to argue, is the Chile which is constructed by the end of the novel through the agency and persons of the main characters, most prominently, Alba and her uncle Jaime.

Allende sets up another Chile as well, which is constructed as pre- or always/already existing; the Chile which the text ends with is, I will argue, the result of a coming together, or at least of an uneasy truce between the two. The second Chile finds its articulation in the women: Rosa, Clara, Blanca and Alba. It is the Chile of magic, the Chile which cannot be created or destroyed, but which endures through all the changes wrought upon it; which seems to abdicate in the face of more powerful forces but which, in reality, bides its time, waiting for its moment to come again. It is a Chile which uses adaptability as a defence mechanism. This is the progression Allende traces in the line of descent from Rosa to Alba – even to Alba's unborn daughter.[3] In this mapping, Rosa is the least material, the most otherworldly: she seems, literally, to be from another world, a sea world, a 'creature' rather than a person. At the other extreme, Alba is very much a part of the material world, and she is the one whose body is reduced to 'raw meat' through torture. Rosa's body, too, is sought after and claimed by many, and this chapter will argue that, following the logical progression of the notion of Chile as Allende sets it up, Alba's body becomes the site of the struggle between two realities: the rebel's and the state's.

Clara is created, by Allende, as the medium through which the transcendent otherworldliness of Rosa and the more realistic, material, unmagical character of Alba coalesce and meet. She occupies, thus, the central position in the narrative, both in terms of sheer space and centrality (she occupies the 'centre' of the novel, literally) as well as in her symbolic status as the best possible meeting of the magical and the material – in other words, as the 'true Chile': both real – nurturer of the poor, shelter of the homeless, embodying compassion and non-judgmental goodness (unlike Rosa who seems to be more embodiment than body/person), as well as spirit, otherworldly, transcendental. That is how she survives longer than Rosa, who is only of the other world.[4]

The progression from Rosa through Clara, Blanca and Alba is, therefore, a significant one. Rosa's primary function seems to be that of the scapegoat – she dies in the place of her father, saving his life and, apparently, the rest of the family's as well. The event acquires a neo-originary status: the point from which – and through which – the family is defined. This is, therefore, heralded as 'the first of many acts of violence' which were to decide the fate of the family. Rosa's family is the prototype of the country through which we are to read the nature and future of Chile, and prophetically, her death brings together the violence and beauty, in the image and body of the dead, cut open, virgin bride, which are to characterise the country. The evocations of Christ bring out, also, in the curiously detached narration of her death, the subliminal invocation of the *felix culpa*. Her death is a necessary one which will facilitate the evolutionary process which will eventually lead to Alba and the painful birth of the new Chile.

Clara feels that she has killed Rosa and in a sense, Rosa must die for Clara to take her place; if both signify the spirit of Chile to some degree, then this makes narratorial sense. Further, Clara retreats into silence after witnessing the death of Rosa – not so much her literal death as the death of her magic at the hands of the doctor and his assistant – so that we know nothing of what her internal thought processes are; in a sense, she ceases to exist as a consciousness in the text and becomes merely a presence. When she speaks again, nine years later, it is to announce that she is getting married – significantly to Rosa's suitor. Thus, she literally takes her place. The act of marriage is significant in the context of their symbolic positions as spirits of Chile who are, of necessity, married to the feudal lord, and given into his care.

In the relationship which Trueba has with each of these women, Allende gestures towards the central conflicted space which the country occupies: the feudal system which was in the position of guardianship regarding all that was best and most beautiful – and, as such, most fragile – in the notion of Chile. Trueba's desire for both women is contrasted with their independence from him. There is no evidence of passion in either of the women's relationship to him. Even as Rosa's seemingly unconscious artistry evolves into Clara's sense of the magical and spiritual, her lack of agency is contrasted with Clara's prophetic gift. Clara expects everything, is therefore prepared for everything: she is never the passive receiver of any event. Her agency extends to manipulating even inanimate objects. In this sense, she is 'pure agency' and represents a power that can be used for good if put in the right context or the right hands. Her marriage to Trueba is the perfect coupling insofar as medium and inspiration can be brought together. Trueba's prodigious energy, willpower and ambition, his strong desire that manifests itself in all manner of sexual prowess is matched by Clara's own unique energies and powers of mind. Yet, even while Allende alludes several times to her evident pleasure in sex, in spite of Trueba's obvious and lasting desire for her, she remains curiously asexual in her beauty and this allows for her peculiar detachment from Trueba and, indeed, everything else normally considered 'real' or material. (She is described by Allende as being pampered in sensual, bodily ways, but never really referred to or described as being particularly beautiful herself.)

Clara's life, which Allende describes with an attention to detail almost indulgent, is like an enchanted utopia of sensual luxury, peace and innocence; but it is surrounded, supported and, indeed, created by ugliness and violence. This dependence renders it precarious and fragile, and the combination of this fragile innocence with the imminent violence which encircles it gives it the air of impending tragedy. Her early life as well as her years with Ferula during her marriage are invested with a deep nostalgia: each detailed description of the herbs used for making teas for the colour of her hair, of how she is bathed and powdered and dressed by Nana, renders her world enchanted on levels other than her magical and supernatural abilities.

The luxuriating sensuality and the sense of enchantment surrounding Clara and Rosa connect this nostalgia narratively to the Magic Realism permeating the story. This conjunction enables the writer to image forth the desire for the beauty and innocence of a lost age and culture even while registering its loss and impossibility and, in this sense, Magic Realism serves as the medium of this nostalgia. Allende's nostalgia, however, is never without an accompanying self-awareness which is registered in the gap between the otherworldliness, beauty and inaccessibility of the Magic Realist pre-torture section of the text and the physical, the gruesome and the constant presence of the wounded violenced body in the chapter titled 'Moment Of Truth' which deals with the torture perpetrated by the state. As my reading of the text will show, what torture dismembers, Magic Realism and nostalgia re-members.

What, then, is the nature of Allende's nostalgia? Does the Magic Realism contain it by rendering it self-aware and therefore useful for Allende's purposes? It is possible to argue, for instance, that, by interweaving the details of Clara's early life – where the bulk of the nostalgia is evident – with the details of her supernatural gifts, Allende bounds the nostalgia within the narrative of Magic Realism. Thus bracketed, the nostalgia inscribes the desire for a lost world even as it registers the awareness of its impossibility.

At the height of her magical powers, when she is most pampered by Nana and others, a portrait of Clara is commissioned: the painter paints, we are told, not under the influence of Chagall (whose style it apparently resembles), but what he 'physically saw'. The portrait – of a Clara floating above the ground – represented, Allende says, 'precisely the reality the painter witnessed'. 'That was the period when divine good humour and the hidden forces of human nature acted with impunity to provoke a state of emergency and upheaval in the laws of physics and logic' (306). The era for which the nostalgia yearns and of which it speaks in this section, then, is indistinguishable from the facility which magic enjoys in that environment. The two are inextricably intertwined: the magic is effective only in the context of 'divine good humour' and when Clara arrives to announce Alba's imminent trials, she admits to having no control over the events about to unfold. In other words, in the absence of 'divine good humour', magic, or even the 'hidden forces of human nature' cease to function. Such a dialectic works as a kind of definition of the world of Magic Realism. Her grand-daughter, Alba, is raised in this Magic Realist world 'completely ignorant of the boundary between the human and the divine, the possible and the impossible' (306). The function of this conjunction is two-fold: as a narrative strategy and as a political aesthetic.

One of the most interesting ways in which Allende's Magic Realism transforms her narrative is evident in the almost biblical system of typology she sets up, similar to the manner in which the New Testament decodes and fulfils the signs and prophecies of the Old Testament. The past, in this system, is revealed and made meaningful to the reader trapped in the present, by the predicted future. I call this Magic Realist insofar as it rests on the literal foretelling of the future in the manner of prophecy and soothsaying of non-realist texts such as the Bible, rather than the metaphoric foreshadowing of the novel. Characters achieve a transcendence of sorts over the normally material limitations within which characters in a realist narrative necessarily function by acquiring a knowledge of the future and an awareness of their own significance as well as the significance of symbolic objects and events and the functioning of 'signs' – usually a prerogative of the omniscient author. The characters' interpretive status and powers become similar to that of the readers', and the Magic Realist narrative can be said to depart from the realist in that it allows this symbiotic existence of characters, readers and author.[5]

In the preceding discussion of Allende's construction of a certain kind of Chile through the allegorical status accorded to the women, I have tried to detail, also, the way in which this allegorical construction participates in the quite distinct structures of her Magic Realism. Clearly, quite apart from this deployment of the strategic alliance between allegory and Magic Realism, Allende's Magic Realism is a profound component of the complex nexus of narratives that define 'Chile'. Thus, just as 'divine good humour' is symbiotically dependent upon the magical, the status of 'reality' within this narrative often seems, also, to bend with the demands of personal misery and persuasion. 'Reality seemed blurred to [Blanca]' we are told, of her stay in the Count's house. The sun had 'deformed the world…turned even the people into silent shadows' (291).[6] Similarly, Trueba explains the fatal flaw of Marxism to his anxious party members thus: 'Marxism doesn't stand a chance in Latin America. Don't you know it doesn't allow for the magical side of things? It's an atheistic, practical, functional doctrine. There's no way it can succeed here!' (350). Yet, neither Clara nor any of the other characters is ever really bound by their symbolic resonations; rather, they – especially Clara, who is the most 'magical' – seem to embody, in their easy straddling of real and non-real worlds, Allende's narrative strategy. Many of Allende's characters are invested with allegorical resonance, representing various aspects of 'Chile', its history/future or even the forces that shape this history/future. In itself, this is not necessarily associated with her use or understanding of Magic Realism: indeed, it can be understood as participating in some of the historical novel's conventional strategies to represent historical moments of transition in terms of influential forces and events.

Allende's Magic Realism has far-reaching implications for her construction of different Chiles, as I shall show later. In the present context, however, this aesthetic has significant political implications for Allende's position regarding feudalism, its responsibilities, its vices, its illusory beauty. While it is true that she underscores the dependence of the sensual beauty of Clara's early life on the ugliness and violence which support and surround it, that sensuality, in its very palpability, can also be seen as compromising her pro-democracy stance. At the centre of this ambiguity, however, stands, not Clara, but Trueba, her husband and the feudal lord of Tres Marias. Trueba personifies perhaps the central paradox of feudalism: love for the land and indifference and/or contempt for its people. Because the notion of 'country' so closely relates a love for both, Trueba's relationship to both is key to Allende's construction of feudalism, its faults and its responsibilities. When Trueba tells his sister that he is going to the family fiefdom, he says, in defence of his decision, 'Land is something one should never sell. It's the only thing left when everything else is gone' (60). Ferula's response, that 'land' is a romantic idea, underscores the feudal divide between 'country' and 'city'. Trueba reveals that he has always said that he would live in the country and that he 'hates the city' (60).

Trueba's love for the land and his country is often presented as the context within which Allende describes his acts of violence: first, against Clara and Pedro Tercero, and later, more indirectly, against the rebels. If Trueba's relationship with Clara is an index for the nature and history of the country, then it is significant that Trueba is sundered from both the women he loves through acts of violence: in Rosa's case, it is not his own; but in Clara's, it is his physical violence towards her which irrevocably separates her mind, and eventually her body, from him. Since the question of feudal violence is central to the understanding of the violence of the fascist regime, this love for/violence towards Clara acquires great significance in the context of the debate regarding the revolutionaries and their use/abuse of violence. The justificatory power of patriotism as a framing narrative for violence is recognised by every military regime, and the dangers of this usage lie in the use of the rhetoric of patriotism by state and rebel alike. If Trueba's love for Clara is a type for the love of the patriot for the country, then it is true that it can be applied, at least rhetorically, to the revolutionary as well as to the dictator.

Allende seeks to differentiate between these different categories through a few key episodes of violence. Primary among the incidents of violence in the pre-coup chapters is Trueba's attempt on Pedro Tercero's life. The extremity of the violence is matched by the intensity of Trueba's response to the land through which he travels on his way to Pedro Tercero's hiding place. At the moment of the only premeditated act of violence that he commits, Trueba recounts that he 'was overcome by the landscape, the forest, the silence' (238). His love for the land distracts him from his purpose, almost as if the beauty or even the sheer presence of the countryside or the land exercises a moral or corrective influence on his moral nature/violence. This almost Wordsworthian evocation of Nature as moral guide is double-edged for Trueba: he chooses this metaphor later in order to justify his methods and ideologies to Jaime who says he doesn't believe in Trueba's theory of the weak and the strong. 'That's the way it is in nature,' he says. 'We live in a jungle' (340).

The analogy of the jungle is more germane to the narrative Trueba provides for the actual act of violence: he lunges towards Pedro Tercero 'with a *wild* scream that rose *from [his] guts*'. 'I remained on *all fours, crouching* and gasping for breath' (239, italics added), he says, reinforcing the image of the animal; both of violence as an animal within the human, as well as that which makes an animal of the human. Violence, here, is seen as a spontaneous eruption, an act of primal instinct: literally another aspect or part of the human psyche – which seems to be inherent within the human being – albeit an animalistic part of it. This sense of violence being a separate instinct within the human psyche that takes over the civilised veneer is heightened by Allende's description of the act itself as something that *happens to* Trueba; something which has him in *its* grip, rather than something which he initiates. 'The axe gleamed in the air for a second and fell on Pedro Tercero Garcia. A shower of blood hit me in the face' (240). Trueba as agent seems erased out by the passive tense of this description. The axe gleams and falls and the blood hits Trueba in the face – seemingly by themselves, without his agency. The characteristic of violence, of acquiring a life of its own once it is unleashed, makes it capable of existing in and of itself, separate from, and independent of, the agent. 'The edge of the tool slice[s] off three fingers of his right hand' (240), almost as if the axe perpetrates the violence of its own accord. It is, moreover, a 'tool', now, to Trueba: the term carries with it the double sense of a means towards an end, thereby signifying an agent of which it is the instrument; but it also evokes – in its 'instrumentality' – a sense of the violence as an abstract act existing independent of the agent. 'The force of the blow thrust[s] [him] forward', almost as if Trueba has been hit by his own blow.

Once Pedro Tercero has run away, Trueba speaks of 'the violence that was suffocating [him]' (241), as he is sick to his stomach and retches, as if expelling an external influence from his body. Later, the tears that Trueba weeps are both an index to the externalisation of the force of violence that had him in its possession, as well as the exorcism of that possession. At the same time, they mark the distance between his violence and that of Esteban Garcia's – both weep but Garcia's tears flow from the thwarting of his very nature which is a violence more fundamental than that of Trueba's – which is a 'tool', a means towards an end. As Esteban Garcia gathers up the three cut fingers to his chest, the difference in the kinds of violent impulse driving both is chillingly clarified – the difference between motivated violence (the axe is a 'tool') and motiveless violence: violence for its own sake – as Garcia's seems to be – something that gives pleasure, an even more primal, if possible, instinct. Immeasurable, impossible, incommensurable with any human or known impulse, it becomes destructive of the boundaries of human experience, of limits, which define and contain reality.

Although Trueba, himself, sees Garcia as 'traitor' and refuses to reward him on those grounds, Allende does not allow the reader the luxury of such easy distinctions; the violence that distinguishes Trueba from Garcia is also the violence that binds them together. The 'terrifying scream' (240) with which Garcia leaves, echoing the scream with which Trueba flings the axe at him, ties the two together in a primal bond. The perpetrator and victim of violence share, according to several schools of thought,[7] a kind of contract which is as often seen as social, psychological, primal as well as sacred. In a ritual in which the perpetrator as well as the victim participate together, the violence engulfs and enfolds both. As they ride back together (as they must since they have arrived together, Trueba led by the boy) the journey back is not easy or smooth because nature seems hostile. The two figures are seen 'groping [their] way in the dark which fell quickly once the sun had set'. 'The trees made it difficult to advance; the horses tripped on the stone and brush,' Trueba recounts. 'Branches whipped *us* in the face' (241; italics added). Even as we see the difference between the two kinds of violence, we know that Esteban and Trueba are implicated in this together. Nature, thwarted and ignored, makes it difficult for them to simply slip back into the old reality. 'I was in another world. Terrified and confused at my own violence.' Trueba's sense of the two realities is reinforced by 'the cool evening air and the scent of the pine' which bring him 'back to reality' (241). Again, nature seems the moral or human norm/imperative. It is 'real' where the violence is a reality beyond the accepted one in which we live. The question is not really which is 'more real' than the other, but what it is that separates the one from the other. Violence defines that separation.

The larger implications for the origins and nature of state violence in this episode are ambiguous. On the one hand, Allende is clear as to

Trueba's fallibility in this context: Garcia is his bastard son and can, by extension, be seen as representing all those poor of the land who feel dispossessed of their true wealth, land and destinies. It would seem, then, that, for Allende, the feudal system with its endemic violence is responsible for the emergence of the kind of vengeance which Garcia is later to unleash. Yet, she is equally clear as to the difference which marks the two kinds of violence, separating them out so that the purity of Garcia's violence seems to exist in and for itself: *motiveless*, as it were. The implications for the nature of the pre-regime, feudal country, Trueba's and Clara's country, the country of Rosa, Clara, Blanca and Alba, are also deeply problematised. While acknowledging the place of feudal violence in Trueba, Allende succeeds in simultaneously isolating it in his figure. Clara has nothing to do with it and, indeed, as soon as it touches her, she isolates herself from Trueba permanently.

Images of violence are not, of course, restricted to either Trueba (before the coup) or Garcia (after the coup): images of violence of various kinds are woven into the fabric of the narrative of everyday life at almost every turn. Indeed, so deftly do they weave themselves into the pattern, so integral a part do they become, that they seem almost 'natural' to it. Several are surrounded by humour and irony which robs them of their ability to disturb and destroy. For some clusters of images there is, however, an evident pattern, even meaning. For instance, it seems no coincidence that the earliest images of violence to appear are the religious. Father Restrepo's graphic description of the wounds of Saint Sebastien suggests an originary or original violence. The obvious narrative of religion which encompasses these images and makes them comprehensible within that discourse is intended to contrast with the violence to which Alba and other rebels are subjected by the state at the end of the novel, which destroys existing discourses and demands new ones. Perhaps this is why the subtext of martyrdom in Father Restrepo's narrative of Saint Sebastien is not exploited by Allende but rather played down with the large dose of irony administered by the young Clara. But the fact of violence is so closely interwoven with the religious and the political that it is hard to separate the two, and when Rosa dies instead of her father, the sub-text of sacrifice, scapegoat and martyrdom surface in a much more serious manner.

Father Restrepo's graphic images of hell and suffering – also heavily ironised – do, however, perform the function of presenting violence as a defining of limits (Life/Death, Heaven/Hell, Saints/Sinners). It is in this connection, therefore, that Allende introduces what appears to be a working definition of Magic Realism. She seems to define it, initially, as a strategy that allows her to ask 'questions without answers' and to record a sphere that 'transcends reality' (14). Rosa is presented, almost immediately thereafter, as a kind of personifica-tion of Magic Realism (15). Allende's attention to the mapping of her exterior, rather than her inner consciousness, the emphasis on her as a figure of otherworldly beauty which serves rather to inspire men than to function as any aspect of her vision of herself, all become markers of Allende's use of Rosa as, at least in part, a personification of an artistic/literary device. It is most significant, then, that Rosa's only individual expression is her art. Her embroidery recalls literary ances-tors ranging from Homer's Penelope to Tennyson's Lady of Shallott, from the ancient Greek Fates to Hawthorne's scarlet woman embroi-dering new and wonderful meanings out of the letter 'A'. These figures attest, also, to the innately amoral nature of their art, and it is no surprise that, in creating Rosa as otherworldly, Allende does not, therefore, mean her to be heavenly: her 'nightmare menagerie', or her 'monsters', as Allende refers to them, are witness to the neutral nature of her creations. They represent, not so much, even, the world of her imagination, as another world altogether. This is the guise in which Rosa can be seen as a personification of Allende's notion of Magic Realism as a system. But the definition of Magic Realism as a literary strategy comes in her characterisation of Clara, both as char-acter as well as chronicler, a role which Alba inherits later. The novel, then, takes upon itself as its first task the mapping of the sphere of Magic Realism. This mapping, embedded in the context of religious rhetoric, sets it up as an alternative vision or mode of access towards transcendence of the material world, at the same time as it reveals its connections with religion, especially, as being implicated in some of the same 'mythology', rhetoric and images.

For the moment, however, Allende is interested in providing a sort of 'fundamental' vision of violence: I will show later that she then distinguishes sharply between feudal and state violence and enters into a discussion of the complex implications embedded in these alliances and distinctions. For the moment, however, what this connection reveals is the tenuous offering of violence as the bedrock which both religion (as belief in another world) as well as Magic Realism (as literary device) struggle to comprehend and eventually transcend. Violence is shown, simultaneously, as being both deeply ingrained in the very fabric of religion, as well as being a neutral, amoral force, beyond good and evil (17); a force that blurs the boundaries between good and bad – indeed, any such easy categorisation – even while participating within a rhetoric designed to create such divisions (good/bad, heaven/hell, sacred/profane). The embalming of Rosa's body (42) reflects this uneasy conjunction of narratives; the body of magic, innocence, purity and beauty poisoned and dissected is a body defiled both within and without. Yet, in this ultimate juxtaposition of beauty and death, she remains Rosa the virgin, Rosa the pure. (It is typical of Allende's rigorous realism, however, that this remains true even as any nostalgia invested with the impossible beauty of Rosa is stripped from her in the graphic description of her dissection.) She is pure body as Alba is to be 'raw meat' later, and the two images circumscribe the ends of the spectrum of this collision of magic and materiality. The issue at stake, among others, is the question of agency. Rosa, who never seemed to have any, other than in her art, is now stripped of any vestige of it. She is helpless to object to or prevent even the assistant's necrophiliac desire, just as Alba is impotent against Esteban Garcia's perverse desire/violence. Thus, Clara, who is to be her successor, is deprived of speech after witnessing Rosa's dissection, and does not speak until the day she acquires agency through her decision to marry Rosa's suitor.

The incident of Rosa's death and dissection seems to mark a point in the text at which sexual, religious and physical violence begin to cohere almost inseparably into single images. Ferula's confessions to the priest, for instance, are as explicit in their graphic description as the hair-raising account of Barrabas's gory death on the occasion of Clara's marriage. From this point onwards, the text begins to proliferate with seemingly inconsequential details which are startling in their varied and casual imagery of violence. Thus, Jaime and Nicholas are born 'under the gaze of their grandmother staring open eyed at them from the bureau' (147) (the head is the decapitated head of Clara's mother, and while the image can be seen as signalling the threat of death and violence which looms over both their lives later in the book, its primary function still seems to be one of casual shock).

The startling reference to the 'Communist priest [who was] shot between the eyes' (163) provides an intense image of religion, politics and violence fused together.[8] Soon after, there is the mention of cannibals in fairy tales (167), and the 'immense, bloody Christ' (196) in the office of the Mother Superior in Blanca's school. The offhand image of 'the table which had served as Rosa's bier' (253) transforms itself into the 'butcher's table that had been used to slaughter calves' upon which Nicholas starts doing the flamenco, and turns up again as a signifier of death when Amanda recognises in the operating table the 'materialisation of death' which had, until then, been 'an abstraction' (276). Later, Jaime's instruments of surgery become the 'instruments of torture' (278). Alba's birth, as witnessed by Miguel, becomes, also, an event of great, implicit violence as he sees the 'vision of a huge balloon of veins crowned with an enormous navel, from which [the] bruised creature emerge[s], wrapped in a hideous blue membrane' (302). It is mentioned, incidentally, of Blanca's Jewish suitor, that Trueba managed to frighten him off even though he had 'survived a concentration camp, poverty and exile' (317). Almost immediately after, Alba decides that if she lost her mother she would plunge her head into a bucket of water and drown herself 'just as the cook did with little kittens the cat gave birth to every four months or so' (318). The only notable contrasting image is of Nicholas's trip to India in search of non-violence (311). Alba inherits, along with the violence, the skills and strength to withstand it, and his teachings become useful later when Alba is taken to the torture chambers.

The seeming casualness of these images is, I think, the point: they are meant to be seen as so much a part of the very fabric of life that their mention should excite no more comment than any other material detail of daily living. It can be argued, indeed, that, other than Alba's birth being seen, prophetically/symbolically by Miguel as an event of great violence, these images are, in fact, buried in the woof and warp of daily life. The question here is whether, therefore, this violence is different from the violence that Allende so clearly denounces later; and if so, in what way. If violence is present in such a fundamental, even organic, sense, before the coup, then in what sense can this society be said to have either changed, or contributed to the violence unleashed by the state? Is this society, in other words, in some sense, complicit in the culture of violence perpetrated by the state? I would like to argue that, although Allende

is very careful to record, even meticulously map, the kinds of violence present in Chile prior to the coup, and to trace the ways in
which certain social systems encouraged and enabled the coup, she
is also very careful, at the same time, to distinguish between the kinds
of violence. As the early episode of Trueba's violence towards Pedro
Tercero has shown, Allende wishes to make this distinction as early as
possible – at its very origin, in fact. The child Esteban Garcia is shown,
even in extreme youth, to contain within himself an impulse towards
violence which cannot be comprehended within any given narrative
for violence. None of the ways of understanding or containing the
fact of daily, casual or necessary violence is sufficient to explain or
encompass Esteban Garcia's betrayal of Pedro Tercero, his clutching
of the dismembered fingers, or the indifference with which he turns
from the driving of nails into chickens' eyes to trying to drive them
through his dead grandfather's.

This is not to say that Allende condones or justifies the violence
of feudal Chile: she does, however, mark it as 'comprehensible'.
In other words, there are existing narratives within which feudal
violence can and, indeed, has, elsewhere, been explained, and this
serves to contain it. For instance, historical and literary accounts
have, traditionally, provided various recognisable narratives for the
clash of classes in the forbidden love of members of the ruling
family and peasants. Some of this recognisability is evident in the
account of the relationship between Blanca, the feudal lord's (that
is, Esteban Trueba's and Clara's) daughter and Pedro Tercero, the
peasant. Allende surrounds their meetings with images of potential,
imminent violence (184).[9]

What, I think, is unique to this account, however, is the idea that
this pairing forms the second alternative to the marriage which will
signify Chile in the future (the first being Clara and Trueba's). An
alliance across social classes and in defiance of them is a revolutionary
vision of Chile for its time and is, at first, invested with all the fervour
of its rebellion (187). This is what accounts for the images and events
of natural violence which accompany it: the eruption of the volcano,
the earthquake and the subsequent fire and disease, the plague of
ants, all give to the event the status almost of the biblical plagues
(190). The atmosphere is intended, it seems, to achieve epic, even
apocalyptic proportions, such is the revolution inherent in the act of
the coming together of classes in this deeply riven society. The sense

of the end of the world is not unintentional, then, in that it precedes the coming of a new order.

That Blanca and Pedro Tercero are not this new order but merely the necessary catalysts of it is clear. Theirs is not the final vision of Chile, and, as Alba and Miguel take over this function, it is significant that the intensity and urgency of the love of Blanca and Pedro Tercero pales into middle age. The passion does not disappear but is rather tamed into control so that it is no longer powerful enough to dictate their destinies, even as the revolutionary Pedro Tercero lapses into a comfortable middle age, having forged a lucrative career out of his passionate and revolutionary ideals/songs. The couple and their relationship come to represent, not the Chile of the future, but the complacency and smugness, even among the young and idealistic, which allowed Pinochet to come to power.[10]

The earthquake, therefore, causes 'the house of Trueba' to fall, literally, about his ears, as it crushes Trueba and almost kills him. As an ironic counterpoint, Nana – the symbol, support and mainstay of the aristocracy – dies almost unnoticed, and we know that the days of the aristocratic old order are numbered. Clara provides the link between old and new as she divines the death of Nana and locates her, holding a poignant funeral for the woman who had looked after generations of the family and who had 'died alone' (200). The aftermath of this upheaval in 'nature' is, however, more ambiguous than one would expect. The socialist preacher is ironically referred to as the 'false priest' (223), as if he, too, is guilty of leading on the people according to his own beliefs and desires, and this casts a small but nagging doubt over Allende's position regarding socialism. Meanwhile, both Clara as well as Blanca succumb to Trueba's wrath and the 'slicing' of what is described as the 'almost human flesh' of the Venus and Adonis wedding cake signals, not so much a tragic end, as an unhappy compromise. It is an anti-climactic end to a revolution that began with a heaving of the earth and fire from heaven. Evidently, the true resolution of this conflict will be found later, elsewhere, in another forbidden union, initiated by another Trueba woman.

Meanwhile, the vision of the Chile of Rosa, Clara, Blanca and Alba continues to develop, sometimes independently of, and sometimes in response to, natural and social changes. It is possible, I think, to see that the women become increasingly part of the material world and, perhaps as a consequence, more rebellious, as they move away from the luxury and protection of the aristocratic seclusion of Rosa in the evolution of this Chile from Rosa, through Clara and Blanca, down to Alba. That is, they are increasingly able to act in the real/material world (rather than only in the magic world in which Clara exists and acts so much of the time) and thus to realise their dreams, imagination and vision.[11] However, although the men (Trueba is the only significant male character who can be said to represent anything as large as a historical era) look to and depend upon the women (first Rosa and then Clara, and finally, even Alba), for their vision, dreams and aspirations, the women are characterised by their independence from the men. Rosa is too otherworldly to have material ambitions, but it is significant that her fantastical animals finally find a material articulation in Blanca's crèches, rather than in any man's actions. Similarly, Clara's earthly ambitions must be fulfilled by herself – she cannot depend upon Trueba to carry out her very modest and material aspirations for the villagers of Tres Marias – and she goes out into the heat and the dust and educates the children and women and even the men herself. While she can be seen as the human face of Trueba's ambitions for his property and tenants, he certainly does not share her political and social views and, in fact, actively militates against them. Clara finds her place in Tres Marias; she throws herself into welfare activities and, as befits the 'spirit of Chile', has clear socialist ideals (127). She has some success in reforming Trueba, for what it is worth. In some sense, Clara can be seen as being worldly enough to create that beauty in the social and human sphere that Rosa could only personify and imagine forth as art.

In a Chile that is pronounced 'that country of catastrophes' (188), Clara awakes as from a long childhood where she had been protected and pampered – 'the earthquake had brought her face to face with violence, death and vulgarity' (194). She, herself, fills the gap between herself and the country when she observes that 'it's not [she] who's changed, it's the world' (197). She is rewarded by Pedro Segundo's undying loyalty and devotion to her. Father of the rebellious Pedro Tercero, Pedro Segundo is the silent 'son-of-the-soil' kind of peasant who takes over the duties of Trueba once he is crippled by the earthquake.[12] His fantasies of giving up his life for her confirm Clara as a kind of spirit of the country, which inspires patriotism in its people. Clara's breaking away from the norms and rules of Trueba's feudalism is heralded by the 'din' of birdsong in her garden which becomes 'a jungle', in a house which she transforms into 'a labyrinth' (259). The unstructured and chaotic succeeds the predetermined and uniform mindset of Trueba in a confusion that is seen as happy and healthy. The implication is one of the more natural growth process of a wild plant rather than the clearly drawn lines and categories of a rigidly programmed and overseen development. Of course, it is also clearly 'feminine' as opposed to the more 'masculine' system of Trueba.

Once Blanca's rebellion has cleared the way, it is Alba who is seen as the true inheritor of the past. It is an inheritance of violence as well as of grace – her grandmother thinks that she is favoured by the gods and fate, and this could mean that the violence she (and the country) undergoes later is a kind of baptism into a higher state of being. While she does not inherit Clara's magical powers, she is nurtured by and around them. She does, however, inherit Rosa's green hair, which places her firmly within the line of descent of magical creatures. The past is available to her, also, in the material form of objects – the basement is her hideout, filled with the family's relics and history, including Barrabas. And finally, she inherits, also, the skill of artistic representation; as a child she paints, an art form closer to Blanca's sculptures and Rosa's embroidery. As an adult, she uses Clara's gift of writing as an act of testimony.

From early childhood, Alba is destined and groomed to shoulder the burden of 'Chile'. Some of her experiences and personality are prophetic/symbolic: for instance, the 'lifelong horror' she acquires of enclosed spaces, cages and bars from her visits to the zoo with her mother's suitors foreshadows the solitary confinement to which she will be subjected later. The empathy she feels for the caged animals is thus transformed into a childhood expression of her later compassion for her fellow prisoners. At the same time, the experience marks her out as one fated to a similar confinement even as it prepares her for it. Alba's early years are, therefore, full of this double-edged symbolism: the events, at once prophetic and representative of the violence both existing and to come, both present her as a marked person as well as prepare her to withstand the fate she is marked for. Sudden mention is made, for instance, of the emblematic death of Neruda and Alba's march holding 'bloody carnations between rows of machine guns' (323). She is fated, as is Chile, for violence, and to live in violent times. She is trained for violence, to withstand it, to suffer it, to understand it, to transcend it, to transform it into something good and beautiful and positive, and this is the only clue we have to the ultimately forward-looking nature of the end of the novel.

Significantly, then, Alba's coming of age is heralded by the onset of menstruation, which occurs during her first real involvement in a revolutionary and potentially violent event/act. The use of the symbol here is ambiguous; it could indicate that this – the student's strike – was the beginning of a 'natural' phenomenon, the revolution. It could also mean that this strike indicates the ability or the power of the resistance to produce a real and living change (just as menstruation indicates the ability of the womb to produce life), signifying, also, the pain and violence that accompany such a birth. This is why Esteban Garcia calls the blood evidence of an 'abortion' (368–74): as far as he's concerned the strike is an aborted attempt at a revolution and the 'life' has been ejected/evicted from the movement. It foreshadows, also, Alba's own pain, humiliation and physical suffering later at the hands of Garcia, as a result of the revolution; her blood can then be seen as a kind of baptism into a higher being and new purpose.

The onset of menstruation is accompanied by the revelation of Garcia's sexual abuse of Alba when she was a little girl, and again when she was fourteen. That the culmination of assault will be her rape at his hands in the prison and the bearing of his child at the end of the book is a reminder that, in the socio-historical context in which the Truebas live, they can have no offspring/create nothing that is not tainted with violence, ugliness and the mark of the crimes committed by their class and kind. It is useful to remember here that the classic metaphor for an emerging or dying collective is wrought through the parentage of the symbolic/historical figure. Hence, when Esteban Garcia is molesting her, 'she smelled... his violence' (373). Garcia is 'the beast' – both within (as in Trueba) as well as the created one. 'Alba discovered that the nightmare had been crouched inside her all these years and that Garcia was still the beast waiting for her in the shadows, ready to jump on top of her at any turn of life' (374). It is not so surprising, then, that Garcia should be seen by Alba as a part of herself: he, too, is the grandchild of her grandfather. But he is not seen as an inheritor in any sense. It is Alba who is seen as '[Trueba's] only heir' (454), and he, too, is her past and her inheritance. The feudal history that is responsible for so much of the violence of the present is her personal and political past. She inherits, also, from him, his passionate love of, and belief in, his country. Of all the so-called patriots, Allende tells us that only Trueba was willing to give his life to his cause. Ironically, in this, he is akin to both Pedro Segundo as well as Miguel, Jaime and Alba: all the rebels and 'Marxists' he rails against. In spite of being instrumental in enabling the coup, his faith in the innate strength of the country is not shaken. 'Believe me, gentlemen,' he tells his fellow politicians, 'I know this country. They'll never do away with freedom of the press' (391). His connection to the land is a fundamental, almost elemental bond; an older but different kind of love for the land. Allende resists romanticising it and exposes the violence of the legacy he bequeaths to his descendants. This is the love and faith that is also Alba's heritage.

While she is paired with the revolutionary, Miguel, she does not depend upon him to realise her vision of Chile. She renders her vision real upon her own body when the 'moment of truth' arrives. Similarly, it is her child – not her's *and Miguel's* – who is the result of her rape by the state torturer, possibly Esteban Garcia, who is the future of Chile. Alba is, thus, transformed into a Lukácsian historical protagonist who is not so much the initiator or agent of action as a 'hub of events',[13] to whom everything that is relevant in that particular historical moment happens. She thus becomes a kind of personification of the country, signifying its essential as well as its historically specific nature.

So far I have tried to focus the ways in which Rosa, Clara, Blanca and Alba construct, between them, a certain vision of Chile and the place of violence within this construction. I will concentrate now on Allende's interrogation and exploration of violence: feudal, revolutionary and state. After the coup, Alba loses the agency that characterises Clara and becomes more this 'hub of events' than an initiator of action and Esteban Garcia begins to define the times in which he reigns. His personification – both literally as well as symbolically – of state violence stretches into an embodiment of pure evil (221): violence in its purest form. This seems to be a process of essentialising, and perhaps is even though Allende does map the psychological process by which he is created. However, we do not see him progressing from stage to stage through a process of becoming: rather we see him in a state of being, and that is why he seems to personify pure evil/violence. The psychological 'explanation' sits uneasily next to this essentialising impulse and the only narrative possible seems to be that although he is a creation of certain social and psychological forces, he functions as a pure, essential force himself. It is no coincidence, then, that Esteban Garcia is driving nails into the dead Pedro Garcia, the personification of the good forces of nature, wisdom and compassion. The act prefigures the coup: it is a dethroning of one set of forces and a usurpation of rule, replacing old values with a new credo. In this, in spite of the many ways in which he is descended from and a product of these forces, he makes a clean break from them and establishes a new reality.

In the creation of a kind of alterity, the violence that is the only reality in Garcia's reign, creates its alter-ego: the violence of revolution (364). Of course, change is always violent, according to the structure set up by Allende, in terms of class conflict; the apocalyptic vision of natural upheaval at the site/event of Blanca and Pedro Tercero Garcia's union makes this abundantly clear. The vexed issue of major and fundamental change, which is violent in its very nature, being accomplished without physical violence is one that Allende discusses at length. Miguel, the militant rebel, constantly voices the view that the 'violence of the system need[s] to be answered by the violence of revolution' (374), and that 'radical change is never brought about willingly and without violence' (380). As Alba defends his ideology to Jaime she points out that 'you cannot make a revolution at the ballot box but only with the people's blood. The idea of a peaceful, democratic revolution with complete freedom of expression was a contradiction in terms' (383). Until this point, Allende tells us, Jaime, the pacifist, had 'always managed to avoid Miguel. He did not wish to know him.' Miguel is 'one of those fatal men possessed by a dangerous idealism and an intransigent purity that colour everything they touch with disaster'. Yet, even Jaime admires 'the strength of his convictions, his natural gaiety, his capacity for tenderness, and the generosity that made him willing to give his life for ideals that Jaime shared but lacked the courage to take to their ultimate conclusion' (404).

However, Allende does not create Jaime to be merely a foil to Miguel. Jaime has 'helped bring Alba into this world', watched her grow and been instrumental in her growth; he cannot, now, 'accept that she needed another man more than she needed him' (383). If Alba is the new nation, then the surrogate father figures as well as her sexual partners are organic parts of the symbol. Hence, Jaime's ideology does not want to acknowledge the validity of violence and revolution and he cannot bear to think that his beloved country needs this revolution more than it needs his humanitarianism. Amanda, the woman of his youth and passion (who can be seen, in this context, as the 'country' Jaime spent his youth being in love with) is now dying through neglect and indifference and if she is to be raised to life once more 'she is going to go through hell' (386). The unlawful desire Jaime feels for Alba after he has ceased to love Amanda is indicative, perhaps, of this sense of being 'out of joint' with 'the time'.[14] Ironically, Amanda, the gypsy-like blithe spirit whom Jaime loved, who was so akin to his mother, Clara, is also the mother of Miguel. The politics of this symbolism renders the image of Amanda ultimately weak and disease-ridden – a kind of 'false ideal' or illusion fostered by men like Jaime. At the same time, it makes the violence of rebellion almost inevitable, even imminent. Allende resists romanticising Miguel and the rebels (in the way that, for instance, Neruda is valorised as 'The Poet'); yet, in her upholding of the resistance and in Alba's heroism, is implicit an authentication of revolution, if not the rebel's violence. For all the heroism of Alba and the women of Chile this ambiguity is maintained in Alba's ultimate stance of 'waiting for Miguel', which reminds us of the lack of agency of the one and the sphere of action of the other.

The nature of resistance Allende maps in Alba and the women of Chile is one which re/constructs the country from the pieces into which they see it as being fragmented. They are the ones left behind, silenced and forced into the seclusion and fragile security of their besieged houses. How these women become both the literal as well as the symbolic figuration of Chile is apparent at the close of Allende's narrative and follows an increasingly intense mapping of the torture perpetrated upon Alba's body. Before this can be done, however, it is important to see how the duality of feudal lord–local people is replaced by that of the state–rebel one in the context of the relationship of the feudal or old Chile and violence.

As the news of the coup is revealed, Jaime is killed at the hands of the military. The state appears for the first time, and it is significant that it appears in its most impersonal guise – as 'they' (402). The manner of his death binds this impersonal state indelibly with the fact of tate violence: specifically, torture. Immediately after, however, it is revealed that Trueba, who believes that only a military coup can overthrow the Marxist regime, has a cache of arms that Allende calls the 'perfect instruments of death' (400). At this point, the casual metaphors and instances of violence that were presented as part of the fabric of Chilean life have materialised into actual weaponry. If Allende is invested in interrogating the origins and nature of the violence of the Pinochet regime, then Trueba's house is revealed as the foundation of that violence. He and his class supported the regime, but more than that, it is a violence that already exists which is condoned and justified by that class.

The full impact of this connection, however, is mitigated by Allende's seemingly indulgent attitude towards the role in which Trueba is now cast. She refers to him as 'the old man' and later Alba and Jaime laugh as they 'raise a toast to the face old Trueba would make when he discovered he had been robbed, laughing till the tears rolled down their cheeks' (402). This gentle, indulgent picture of the hoarder of the weapons, transforms him into an old, helpless and, most importantly, harmless, man whose little schemes can be laughed at and undone before they harm anyone. Soon after, the reconciliation of Pedro Tercero and Trueba implies that this conflict is anachronistic, healed; that the violence does not flow from here, from this conflict which is so old that, although for each of them, 'the other was the very incarnation of everything most hateful in the world, [they were] unable to find the old fire of hatred in their hearts' (411). As Pedro Tercero, the peasant rebel, rescues Trueba, the feudal landlord, from the wrath of his tenants,[15] Allende's mapping of the origins and base of the violence of the Pinochet regime becomes deeply complicated. When Trueba sees Pedro Tercero, he recognises the three fingers he had cut off and this recognition indicates to him that 'this was the end of the nightmare in which he had been immersed', and this cycle of violence seems to have come to a natural close. The violence of Esteban Garcia seems almost an arbitrary offshoot of the violence that marked the relationship and near-fatal encounter between Pedro Tercero and Trueba. It is not, in other words, seen as part of the cycle of violence brought to its conclusion here. While it is true that in fact the violence Trueba intends is not the vicious form of torture that it becomes, it seems as if the politics of Allende's aesthetics, here, seek to exonerate him as harmless. While this is clearly troubling and problematic, leaving several unresolved questions, it is true that the violence that the rest of the text describes is certainly different in kind.

Later, in the telling of Trueba's (and not the cook's: she is not the subject of this revelation – or at least, seemingly not the subject) trauma, the fact of the cook's husband's killing at the hands of the state, as well as her son 'who had been hanged from a post with his guts wrapped around his neck, the people's revenge for his having carried out the orders of his superiors', is mentioned almost incidentally, accidentally. We are told that 'the poor woman had lost her mind soon afterward, and Trueba lost his patience, fed up with finding in his food the hairs she had torn from her head in her unending grief' (449). The casual images of violence here become chilling in their very casualness, as this casualness becomes an index to the ubiquitous and random nature of the violence perpetrated by the regime. While the violence inflicted by Trueba upon his tenants could also be said to be similarly ubiquitous and random, Allende is very careful to have Trueba mention that he never actually killed anyone as all the stories claim he did.[16] Thus she portrays the violence of the totalitarian state as differing in kind rather than simply in numbers. Whether or not this is true is clearly debatable; the very existence of some form of resistance, evident in the presence of the Marxists in such strength prior to the coup, is an indication of the degree of oppression suffered at the hands of feudal lords. More to the point, however, Allende shows the intimacy which informs the feudal violence. The raped women are kept in the house and their bastard children looked after. The entire village knows of their parentage. While Allende certainly does not condone the rapes on these grounds, she does provide the fleeting image of the young girl who knows she is to take the place of Pancha Garcia in the master's bed and kitchen and gives to her the knowledge and agency of a grown woman. The image is at once disturbing as well as infinitely sad: a girl of fourteen with knowledge not just of sex and its power beyond her years but also one who sees such a relationship – if it can be called that – as a desirable and liberating alternative to the life she would otherwise live. The ambiguity which thus surrounds the act of rape is Leda-esque in its subliminal message of the transference of power from the violating god to the willingly ravished, perhaps even seducing, victim. While such a scenario may well be more statistically accurate than a post-feudal sensibility is willing to admit, the politics of Allende's narrative distinguish this rape and violence from that of the rape of Alba and the other women and the torture of the rebels at the hands of the state both in kind as well as in degree.

The important difference between violence as torture and violence as force lies in the fact that the one is intimate and symbolic while the other is impersonal and begs the question of degree. Several ethical debates regarding means and ends surround it, reinforcing the fact that it is a 'tool' – even as Trueba describes the axe he threw at Pedro Tercero as a 'tool'. Torture renders violence an end unto itself. It *is* the message, it *is* the end; thus it functions both materially as well as metaphorically, and the gap between signifier and signified is closed.[17]

The two kinds of violence are differently represented as well. The violence of the pre-coup chapters is metaphorical, oblique, narrativised – part of the fabric of imagination as well as of the lived experience of the community. The violence of the prisons is significantly different in that it is torture: intimate,[18] with something akin to the personal investment that resonates in the violence of slavery and ethnic violence. Here, the body is tortured *in and for itself*, in order to mutilate, to induce pain and, most importantly, to mark it as a body which has undergone pain. Even though the mutilation of the body is intended to signify the mutilation of the spirit, and the breaking of the physical body is meant to achieve and embody the breaking of the spirit, it is the body that is of vital importance here, not the manner or symbolic import of its marking. State violence is unique in that it attains the seemingly paradoxical stage of violence in which the violence is at once intimate as well as wholly impersonal. This is distinct from the violence of the war as discussed in *Sula* because the violence there, while being impersonal, is not at all intimate. It is almost always a wholly mechanised and depersonalised violence which horrifies in its very mechanisation and depersonalisation.

It is in the course of the more intimate and personal violence of torture that the metaphoricity that separates the 'rape of the land' from the rape of Alba is destroyed; that 'poetic justice' ceases to be a linguistic and ideological trope and becomes the three missing fingers on Alba's hand. It is the fact of torture, which, indeed, brings Ana Diaz and Alba together not under the umbrella of some ideology but through the experience of the extreme physical pain suffered in the course of torture. This coming together is understood in ideological terms by Alba in solitary confinement when she begins to narrativise the violence in her mind, and again, in the prison of women in which she discovers both healing as well as community. Thus, another narrative emerges from this fundamental community of tortured bodies; a different, more ideological bond, which is that of the rebel's dream/ideal. The violence is a part of the sacrifice that the true believer is called upon to make and which, indeed, she sees as her true calling. The bond between the perpetrator and the victim, then, becomes the ritualistic bond between the sacrificer and the scapegoat/sacrificee.[19] It is, from the point of view of the victim, an almost holy bond, at once desired and resisted. For the rebel, and equally for the state – whomever, indeed, is the initiator of violence on either side – 'killing erodes stability' according to J. Bowyer Bell, in *The Dynamics of the Armed Struggle*.[20] 'Anybody will do, any body will do ... The dream assures absolute truth' (33). In the case of the state, the 'dream' is more often the ideology of repression, but in either case it is treated as the 'absolute truth'. For both, the body – the depersonalised physical entity – is the site of the conflict. For the rebel, it is offered in sacrifice, and for the state, it is the physical destruction of the body which will destroy the spirit and thereby, literally as well as symbolically, the resistance. It is this duality which essentialises the nature of the state for the rebel. Thus, Esteban Garcia, the director and often the perpetrator of the violence of the state, becomes the personification of pure violence: he represents the essence of the notion and function of torture. This elision of Esteban Garcia with a form of violence serves, however, to complicate the nature of torture insofar as Esteban Garcia represents, also, violence which is carried out in and for itself: an impersonal, motiveless malice that luxuriates in the pleasure of the violence itself.

In the balance, in this ritualised struggle, hangs the status and ownership of 'reality'. Where the state wields ownership of reality through the deployment of legitimate – or legitimised – authority, the rebel, through his or her sacrifice, can '[turn] legitimate authority into oppression, reason into ruin. Reality, for [the state], for most of those threatened by rebels, is not as tangible as imagined, not an asset held by the powerful' (Bell, 1998: 38). This intangible reality, then, is what both state and rebel must wrench from the other. This is what is at stake in the struggle, what, one may go so far as to say, is always at stake in the ritualised enactment – or enforcement – of sacrifice.[21] For the rebel, the 'dream' as 'revealed truth' is an attainable vision of the future, a 'reasoned goal', a desire for a reality which, 'like the messiah, [is] ever sought, never found' (Bell, 1998: 39). The gap between desire/dream and reality is bridged by the faith of the believer. It is neither a reasoned nor a practical foundation, but a gap bridged by a leap; a leap of faith. Hence, the dream which is merely another term for the deferred reality of the future which the rebel envisions, is not recognised, acknowledged or intellectualised as dream – that is, unreal – by the rebel. It is their only reality; like the messiah, it is merely deferred.

Thus, in the encounter of torture between the state and the rebel, the rebel attempts to render the dream real – to 'real-ise' it, if you like – and this is why every mark on the tortured body and every bit of pain suffered by the rebel brings that deferred reality one step closer to realisation. It is also one step closer to bridging the gap between the dream and the reality. The state, meanwhile, invests in this encounter its efforts to enforce its own notion of 'reality' – state or military authority and power – in the act of taking control of the body of the rebel. The victor enforces his or her own 'reality': whether the rebellion is crushed, its 'reality' destroyed or discredited, and the 'reality' of state power consequently publicly displayed and established as the only existent reality, or the rebellion is successful, and the dream realised in practical terms.

Of course it is true that methods other than torture are also employed in order to enforce (in the case of the state, or construct/create, in the case of the rebellion) their own version of reality – social, economic, cultural, psychological. However, the case of the rebel is different from that of any other opposing faction that challenges the state. The battle between the totalitarian state and the almost inevitable resistance movement is always marked by the loss of negotiation: that space is replaced by the torture chamber, even as the conflict is characterised by violence. This is what makes torture a unique form of violence in the context of collective identities. (Which is to say that it does not take into account the use of torture to conquer crime, for instance, although the argument can be made that this, too, is a version of the conflict between the more inflexible arm of the state and the more inflexibly violent of the threats that face it.) The state, in its perpetuation of the discourse of Order, will almost always portray its use of force as an attempt to maintain 'law and order' or even simply to bring order to a chaotic situation such as a riot. The state thus projects itself as the instrument of desirable order in conflict with a naturally unruly, unpredictable, potentially or actually violent populace: thus its demonstrations and other, even peaceful challenges to state authority and figures are recorded and described even by the press as riots, chaotic, mob action, madness etc. These incidents are in turn seen as 'ancient' and 'innate' and even 'tribal' or 'savage' conflicts which are 'natural' to that populace.

Thus, the struggle between Alba and Esteban Garcia is both violent as well as inevitable, and the status of 'reality', at stake. In order to signal a clear demarcation between the violence of the old Chile and that of the new, Allende indicates the limits of the spirit realm which had presided over the old Chile; this gives us, also, the limits of Magic Realism as a narrative device. Luisa Mora and Clara appear to Trueba to announce their vision of 'a terrible sequence of events, bringing blood, pain and death . . . [and of the] terrible times [which] lie ahead'. 'There will be so many dead they will be impossible to count,' Clara tells Trueba, almost in accusation. The blood of the 'piles of corpses', it is implied, will be on his hands. Among these might well be the blood of his grand-daughter, Alba. 'Death is at your heels' (415), she tells Alba, and advises her to go across the ocean where she will be safe – as Blanca does later. Thus begins the final section of the novel which, I will argue, functions as a detailed mapping of the process and nature of violence as torture, and the means by which the collective is constructed from the narratives this process produces.

Magic Realism deserts the narrative at the point of extreme and explicit violence just as the magic and spirits leave Alba when she enters the prison, leaving her 'blind for the first time' (458). This, the entering into the torture prisons, Alba recognises as her 'destiny':

> Then she knew her destiny. She invoked the spirits of the days of the three-legged table and her grandmother's restless sugar bowl, and all the spirits capable of bending the course of events, but they appeared to have abandoned her, for the van continued on its way . . . It was then that Alba entered the nightmare that her grandmother had apparently not seen on her astrological chart

when she was born and that Luisa Mora had seen in a fleeting premonition. (459)

This is a clear break in the narrative which signifies the break between the old and 'true' Chile, the Chile of Clara and her magic and her spirits, and the new Chile – the Chile of Esteban Garcia. Although there is a clear break in the nature of these two countries, Allende underlines the connection between them. As Alba is introduced, not as Miguel's lover – which is the reason she is there – but as 'Senator Trueba's granddaughter', the link between the past and the present, or, as Allende would have it, the past and its 'destiny', is firmly established. Thus, 'Alba recognised the voice of Esteban Garcia. At that moment she understood that he had been waiting for her ever since that distant day when he had sat her on his knees, when she was just a child' (459).

The connection is a deeply fraught one. The evocation of the innocence of Alba who was 'just a child' overlies the guilt of Trueba, with whom Esteban Garcia's connection and quarrel is. It is true that, as Trueba's grandchildren, it is Alba's and his destinies, which are comparable, and it is her destiny, which is the possible material alternative to his own. But in bringing the innocence of the one to the knees of the almost pure evil of the other, the grey of the beleaguered space of the conflict between Trueba and Esteban Garcia is rendered black and white, the differences sharply drawn, the boundaries and limits of good and evil clearly defined. Thus, even while violence has been shown to be a system whereby the neat divisions that make life comprehensible are blurred and obscured, in the course of this incident and especially through the clearly defined 'evil' of Esteban Garcia, a line is drawn demarcating the limits of historically, socially and morally comprehensible violence and evil itself. Violence as defined through Esteban Garcia does not allow for any narrative other than itself or any raison d'être other than itself.

Esteban Garcia wrests control over 'destiny' from the 'spirits capable of bending the course of events' by violence: literal, physical violence. Therefore, his narrative must necessarily lie outside the purview, also, of the world of spirits and magic. This is a realist, material narrative, in sharp contrast to the Magic Realism of the pre-regime chapters. The presence of extreme violence marks the Pinochet regime as different in kind from that of earlier political or social upheavals, which were characterised more by natural phenomena. Hence, the abdication of Magic Realism as a narrative form is also an abandoning of it as a means of comprehending the world – both for the protagonists as well as for the author.

Allende does not refer to the onset of the violence of the fascist regime as injustice, or fear, or violence – she refers to it as 'the terror'. The term is deprived of all meanings that may accrue to it through ideological meta-narratives such as 'justice'. It is stripped down to the starkest essence of human emotions, a mindless and abject surrender of self-possession and composure. At the same time, the term refers both to *the thing itself*, as well as that which inspires terror. Thus, it signifies both perpetrator as well as victim simultaneously. This 'terror' is contrasted with Alba's 'serenity' (456). Her serenity at the moment of her imprisonment is significant because it gives the sense of a destiny at the moment of its fulfilment. The entire incident takes on the ceremonial force of the ritual – almost, the Greek tragedy. It is a tragedy foreseen and foretold. The sense of a destiny fulfilled is an index to Allende's political thrust.

In perhaps the only use of even mildly metaphoric language in this final section, Jaime is called away in the middle of the night 'dressed like a sleepwalker' (417). Bowyer Bell points out that the rebel goes from the revolution to the point of utopia like a sleepwalker, and later, when Jaime is led into the boiler room by the soldiers he is again said to be standing 'erect as if he had been sleepwalking' (421). Bell's point is germane here in that Jaime bears out the image of the single-minded pursuit of one's truth or goal that must, necessarily, be oblivious to all obstacles. For Allende's purposes, however, Jaime is a 'sleepwalker' in that he is caught in a situation in which his humanitarianism is helpless against the violence: a man out of his time. Although Jaime may carry some of the marks of the sacrificial lamb, it is President Salvador Allende who is set up as the first and primary sacrificee. His farewell speech to the nation is suffused in the language of ritual sacrifice: significantly, this is also the rhetoric of the revolution. This speech, far more than that of Miguel's idealism, serves as the focal point – as well as the point of origin – of all the 'sacrifice' (419) which follows.

In a chapter notable for its grim realism, the figure of Salvador Allende appears glorified, romanticised into heroic proportions. Any wrongdoing or fallibility is erased from him so that he may acquire the purity necessary for the scapegoat. Whatever the historical truth regarding the facts that Allende provides or contests, this cleansing appears on the textual level as a compromise. Allende goes out of her way to explain how the economic collapse during the President's tenure was not his own doing, but rather a conspiracy waged against him by Pinochet's party. Interestingly, this is the very image that Salvador Allende had for the rebels – his – real or constructed – innocence and purity made him a focal point around which the resistance movement organised itself and its ideological idealism.The 'other' side is, therefore, correspondingly essentialised. The soldiers who take over the President's headquarters are the first people to be described in the state of violence: Allende portrays them as people who have 'lost their senses' and seem 'possessed' (420). Jaime's disbelief and incomprehension are an index to the beginning of the 'madness' – the process by which violence breaks down all barriers and limits which define sanity, rationality and civilisation, moving into the unknown, uncharted territory carved by violence. Thus, the very language of the military is transformed. 'The military was a breed apart, brothers who spoke a different dialect from the civilians and one with whom any attempt at a dialogue would be a conversation of the deaf, because the slightest dissent was considered treason in their strict honour code. Trueba realised that they had messianic plans' (443). Allende's language here is a bit ambiguous. They are 'a breed apart', yet they are 'brothers'; they speak a different dialect, not entirely a different language; and conversation with them would be a conversation *of* the deaf, not *with* the deaf. This would imply that the civilians are not the only ones who would not understand the military: the military would not understand the civilians either.

More significantly, they, too, have 'messianic plans' – much like the rebels who wait for a second coming, a leader/messiah who will lead them, Moses-like, to freedom by destroying the enemy. (Bell's notion of the messianic dreams of the rebel as always sought, never gained, is pertinent here.) Therefore, although it seems as if the military are a breed apart, they are, in fact, a part of the citizenry of the country. However, violence makes dialogue or dialectic impossible, thus making violence itself immutable, unchangeable. Thus, it can only destroy. It cannot change. The guerrilla's immutability is seen in the depersonalisation of Miguel into 'a guerrilla' through disguise. His acceptance of the torture of people in order to discover his whereabouts as simply part of the 'horror of war' (450) seems to be part of this process. His becoming a guerrilla is seen by Allende as 'fulfilling his destiny' which he had been moving towards since he was a teenager. This, too, is 'messianic'. The fact that Miguel's predictions of the future have all been realised, as Alba points out to him (451), seems at least for the moment to justify his philosophy that 'the violence of the rich must be met by the violence of the people' (450).

This process of the construction of dualities/alterities is buttressed by Allende's somewhat ingenuous reference to the 'possession [of the soldiers] by a new hatred that had just been invented and that had bloomed in the space of a few hours' (420). The ambiguity surrounding the irony of Jaime's partial recognition of Esteban Garcia (as he lies on the road waiting for the tank to roll over him and another man) makes the intentionality hard to read. Is it just in Jaime's mind that the 'boy he used to play with in Tres Marias' seems not to connect with Trueba? Is it simply Jaime's state of 'sleepwalking' that prevents him from connecting Esteban Garcia's violence with the violence and social injustice that was part of Trueba's feudal reign at Tres Marias? Even if Allende herself means to make this connection later, the lack of it at this first, and highly charged, instance of state torture serves to underscore the idea that the difference in the two instances of violence is one of kind rather than degree. This difference serves to break the easy continuity of what would otherwise be seen as a chain of violence, connecting the violence of the old Chile with that of the 'new'.

Thus, the personal, passionate, intimate violence of Trueba, shown to be so unnatural to him – an offshoot of his naturally passionate nature and his social conditioning which forced him to view the union of his daughter and a peasant as apocalyptic – becomes very different from the premeditated, cold-blooded violence of Esteban Garcia. Garcia's violence is innate to him in a way in which Trueba's is not shown to be. More than that, Garcia's earlier sexual and casual violence – his molestation of the fourteen-year-old Alba, the attempt to poke out the eyes of old Pedro Garcia as casually as he had poked out the eyes of the chickens, his gathering up of Pedro Tercero's fingers – is shown to be compulsive and perverted, as if he were an aberration of nature – a monster.

Jaime's death becomes iconic of both the tortured and killed, as well as the disappeared; Alba and Amanda refuse to believe the reports of his death until they have physical proof and keep him alive in their 'dry-eyed yearning' (432). Tracking down the disappeared – to bring alive again, to resurrect, to give flesh to memory and desire – becomes a way of retaining/regaining sanity after violence has destroyed it. The disappeared become the physical symbols of the loss or destruction of a world, an order, a way of being, thinking and understanding the cosmos. The search for them, in the belief that they exist, physically, and can be brought back, made material again, becomes a quest to bring back a lost world of safety, security and order. The desire for the lost person and the desire for the lost world/life become intertwined and inseparable. This desire is lent intensity from the physical pain suffered by the people who 'reappear' – come back from prison and torture – and of the sheer proximity of the pain made material in the form of their wounds and deformities.

The people now become focused around iconic symbols of the tortured and the disappeared: Amanda helps find food for 'the families of prisoners, the disappeared and the dead [who] have nothing to eat'. 'The unemployed . . . and the children' (432) are included in this list. These are the categories around which the notion of the suffering 'people' crystallises. In contrast, the state – whose position here is championed by Trueba and 'everyone else in his class' – '[denies] the existence of hunger just as vehemently as he [denies] that of the prisoners and the torture' (433). Later, even 'a large part of the middle class' which also supported the regime, finds that 'there was someone to mourn in every family, and [they] could no longer say, as they had in the beginning, that if he was imprisoned, dead, or exiled it was because he deserved it. Nor could they go on denying the use of torture' (438). Even Trueba, confronted by the violence of the state, feels that 'his hour of truth was finally upon him' (457). While for Trueba it is not a question of physical endurance, as it is for Alba, for both it is a test of one's courage and integrity. The situation demands, in a very essential sense, a redefinition of identity, and this is why it is such a powerful metaphor for the moment of truth of a nation; a point of time in which a nation's true identity reveals itself or is formed.

One of the most powerful of the symbols around which this collective identity was formed was Neruda – called, almost biblically, 'The Poet'. His death is the first real demonstration of this ability of the people to formulate 'Chile' around the figure of a fallen hero, killed, as the funeral procession believes, by the excesses and at the hands of the military. Thus, in the chanting of the mourners, his name bleeds seamlessly into that of the President's. The destruction the state effects is not just of the poet of the people but also the literal destruction of the possessions which surround and define him, as well as what he comes to stand for: the resistance movement (440–1). It is the destruction of everything which hints at the 'old Chile' – words are banned, history and geography are rewritten, buildings and colours changed. Anything which hinted at, not only the resistance movement and other politically threatening ideas, people or events, but in fact anything which had a connection to Chilean cultural or historical icons around which the resistance could form itself, is effaced or destroyed. In a process which is, perhaps, dialectical, this destruction produces (as it is produced by) a crystallising of the notion of the 'Chilean people': thus, The Poet's funeral inspires people to join in from the streets with the chant of 'the people united will never be defeated' (435–6).

It is from this sense of unity that the resistance is forged, and it takes many forms. In order to make it more recognisable to the people in her rescue organisation, Alba paints big, bright sunflowers 'with the brightest yellow paint she could find' (431) on Jaime's car that had survived exactly where he had parked it. Given the context of Amanda's 'dry-eyed yearning' and Alba's sorrow at his disappearance, the survival of the car, intact and at the same site, would have invested it with the resonance of a memorial. However, Alba's act transforms the poignant *memento mori* quality of the car into a signifier of the life-giving energy that the saving of rebels enacts. In other words, life is wrested physically from death, and images of death are transformed into images of life and vitality. Other images are more ambiguous and less amenable to material transformation. 'The great house' of Alba and Trueba, the house of resistance and love for the country, the house which is the home of the old Chile, 'pant[s] with the laboured breath of an old woman' with 'the ghosts of all those unknown dead...and [Alba] [feels] noises in her bones: a distant screeching of brakes, the slam of a door, gunfire, the crush of boots, a muffled scream' (422).[22] The power of these images derives its intensity both from the vast numbers of the disappeared, as well as from the violence of the disappearance and the terror of the process: the knock at midnight, the torture, the taking away. As much marked by the unseen as those who disappear, this process of disappearance intensifies the need for witnessing.[23] The inability to bear witness to the disappeared or even to the process of disappearance prevents the narrativising that is such an important part of the process of healing.

Jaime's death is also the first instance of the torture and death the state is capable of meting out to those who resist it; it is, as such, the first case of torture in the narrative and the change in Allende's style is evident. The narrative voice seeks distance from the event, trying to describe it in the sparest prose, without dwelling on the details or luxuriating in the pain. The fact that his death is a part of the deaths of many anonymous people also serves to distance it: yet this double distancing is precisely what gives the account its power and magnitude.[24] Where before the text had sought to give an extra-ordinary dimension to the mundane, natural details of daily life, by connecting them to the not-normal and not-natural, here, that added dimension comes from the association of one detail with other, identical and anonymous ones. The magnitude of Jaime's death lies in its *reduction* into anonymity, in the character and person being reduced to *thing*[25] a *corpse*, one among nameless others. It is the beginning of the state's attempt to prove that the most powerful force opposing the ideal is the material: that idealism is met with death, and the hero can be transformed into 'thing'. This is the 'reality' which the state is invested in imposing upon the rebel.

This process of reduction affects Alba well before she is physically taken to the torture chambers. It begins with the destruction of every-thing that is personal to her as well as to Jaime, as Miguel calls asking her not to call or try to contact him, not to speak of him or to him to anyone, nor even to contact any of her friends (424). This severance from her loved ones and the destruction of all her personal things is the beginning of the dehumanisation the state imposes. However, it is also the *depersonalisation* required of the rebel and, as such, one of the first conflicts the rebel must resolve: how to depersonalise her-self and her cause without dehumanising either. For Alba, therefore, the process of destroying her personal effects is also the process of divesting herself of all that marks her as a unique person; so that by the time she is tortured, she is reduced to 'rebel'. The process is a crucial one in that therein lies the danger of being objectified into 'body' – or 'thing', as Alba's own perception of herself as 'raw meat', after the torture, shows. At the same time, the state requires a similar dehumanisation of its own functionaries. Thus, the soldiers, also, are dehumanised into killing machines, characterised by 'the blind obedience, the use of arms and other skills that soldiers can master once they silence the scruples of their hearts' (436). Indeed, Allende invests great poignancy in the few instances of those who resist this dehumanisation, such as the soldier who offers Jaime a cigarette, claiming Jaime had saved his mother's life, or the few who show some kindness to Alba and the other prisoners later.

This destruction of the personal effects of individuals is also part of the state's attempt to destroy any trace of the Chile of the rebels – whether it be cultural, political or merely traditional. Anything which the rebels or even the average citizenry could use as symbols of the old Chile, a Chile prior to the regime, around which they could formulate a Chile alternative to the one being constructed by the new regime, is destroyed. This destruction is effected, characteristically, through violence, which destroys not just materials, but, more importantly, significance and meaning. It is here that the almost epic list of books burnt, foretold several times in the course of the book so far, appears. Even here, it is described in historical terms as 'an infamous pyre' (456) (where 'pyre' carries the weight both of barbaric ritual as well as of the death and ceremonious ending of a living, almost sacred thing) and 'a scandalous bonfire' so that its historical resonance and importance is given in no uncertain terms. All that was good and valuable about the old Chile and the old culture – all that the regime seeks to destroy – is signified by these books of magic, medicine and philosophy, and of course, 'a leather bound set of the complete works of Marx'; works of art, 'bibelots' and even Trueba's 'opera scores', and 'his classical records' (456). Thus, even the landowning and self-sufficient Trueba is put in a position where he must maintain a 'precarious stability' after the violence of the regime has brought into being a world in which 'the line between what was good and what was bad had been blurred' (453–4).[26]

The success of this destruction of material and meaning is seen as Alba tries to remember a world and a time 'before the hurricane of events had turned the world upside down, when things were still called by familiar names and words, had a single meaning' (460). She thinks of Miguel, their love making and the feeling of security and timelessness, but the sounds of people being tortured, 'the screams, the long moans', destroy not only her reverie but even her ability to remember the life before the violence. 'The woods, Miguel and love were lost in the deep well of her terror and she resigned herself to facing her fate without subterfuge' (461). Violence changes and destroys reality as we know it. Even before the violence is visited upon her own body, Alba has felt its ability to rearrange and reorganise the boundaries and limits of human experience and life. 'After that terrible Tuesday, Alba had to rearrange her feelings in order to continue living...She felt that everything was made of glass, as fragile as a sigh, and that the machine-gun fire and bombs of that unforgettable Tuesday had destroyed most of what she knew, and that all the rest had been smashed to pieces and spattered with blood' (430).

Denial, the natural response to the destruction of the old as well as the presence of the new reality, signals the next stage. As the guards beat and rape her, Alba is reduced to 'a monumental *no*...until she could no longer think, could only say *no, no* and *no*' (462). At this stage, she can still 'calculate how much longer she could resist before her strength gave out' but this is only because the full enormity of her situation has not hit her and she does 'not [know] that this [is] only the beginning' (462). Denial is followed by withdrawal, and 'tortured by the pain...and the terror' she 'curls up like a fetus' (463). Such withdrawal can be seen as an extreme form of denial, but nevertheless, it seems to be the end of the phase which began with the destruction of everything that made her an individual (her books, personal things, anything which would betray her thoughts or life): of the divesting herself of her self-hood.

As the violence begins to destroy not only the past but also her sense of the present, 'her loneliness, the darkness and her fear distorted her sense of time and space. She thought she saw caves filled with monsters...She decided to forget everything she knew, even Miguel's name' (463–4). At this point, the violence has seeped through her body into her mind, her sense of her material self is being steadily eroded along with her idealism. Thus, 'the third time they took her in to Esteban Garcia...she had no illusions. She did not even try to evoke the woods where she had shared the joy of love' (464). The loss of illusions about her ability to resist (she does not, in fact, know Miguel's whereabouts, so she cannot buy her way out of this even if she wanted to), about her fate, brings her then to the depths of despair. The loss of illusion is next only to the loss of hope, which is then inevitable. Thus, the only power she has now is 'the strength of hatred'. This is not an incentive to live, and so she reaches the logical conclusion of this phase, which is despair: when Garcia lets her go for a little while 'she [uses] [the short break] to invoke the understanding spirits of her grandmother, so that they would help her die. But no-one answered her call for help' (464).

It is at this point that the person becomes what, according to Ledbetter, she is always in danger of: she becomes 'thing'. Once Alba is given electric shocks, she becomes pure body. Not in the way in which pleasure induces the body to celebrate its sensuality, but in the manner in which only pain can reduce it to pure materiality. 'Then she felt the atrocious pain that coursed through her body, filling it completely, and that she would never forget as long as she lived. She sank into darkness' (465). When she awakes, she is, therefore, naked. She has no memory. 'She could not move, recalled nothing, had no idea where she was or what had caused the intense pain which had *reduced her to a heap of raw meat*' (465; italics mine).

This is, then, the lowest point to which the human spirit can sink, and it is here, therefore, that we hear a muted but clear reference to Christ on the Cross: 'she felt the thirst of the Sahara and called out for water' (466).[27] Christ's 'I thirst' after the thirty-nine lashes is at a similar moment of despair. In Allende's hands, this subdued but unmistakable reference provides a subtle sub-text of the rebel's sacrifice and martyrdom to an otherwise spare and literal description of torture. Thus, it is not surprising that after hitting the nadir of despair and pain, Alba is put into the care of Ana Diaz ('of God', or 'of Light'); the appearance of Ana in the midst of Alba's torture is the turning point in her mental and psychological state. Because Allende distinguishes the violence of state torture from all other kinds (both feudal and the 'casual' violence embedded in the fabric of everyday living) as well as from all other narratives, it is important, here, to consider whether Allende is not resorting to pre-existing narratives for the violenced body in her invocation of the religious symbol of Christ on the Cross. Appearing at the point at which the body/person loses all meaning, this is a traditional and relatively simple way of reinvesting the body with signification and the person with relevance. The answer is not simple. It is, of course, clear that the narrative of the violenced body as sacred and the person as martyr or sacrificial lamb is pivotal to Alba's survival and understanding of self and community.

That this is a pre-existing narrative is also beyond doubt. However, a few things need, I think, to be taken into account here. One, the rebel's ideology is, as we have seen, suffused with this vision; it is, necessarily, a quasi-religious one. Two, the power of the violenced body emanates precisely from its loss of meaning, and its ability to signify both 'nothingness' as well as *anything*, and the religious is not the only meaning it acquires in the text. For Esteban Garcia, for instance, the seduction of torture comes precisely from the violenced body's ability to lend itself to any number of contexts. The inventiveness of his techniques and methods derive their inspiration from everything: from revenge (literally stripping Alba of all that signifies her social class and dignity, such as her clothes), the perversion of desire (molesting her when she was a child, and later raping her), revulsion of the senses (plunging her head into a bucket of excrement), simple pain (the electric shocks), and the sheer expression of power (the beatings). It is important to remember this violence is carried out either by Esteban Garcia, or under his supervision, and that violence, in his context, has already been defined by its meaninglessness (the clutching of the three fingers and the knocking of nails into the chickens' and his grandfather's eyes). For the purposes of the state, the violenced body is an index to the loss of power and validity of the rebel and her vision. Simultaneously, it is a validation and imposition of the reality of the state as against that of the rebel. For the resistance movement, as we shall see, each wound, mutilation, dismemberment, is a realisation of a vision; each disappeared body or person, its valorisation. Upon this realisation and valorisation, the resistance constructs its notion of the country.

Finally, it is important to note the specific process through which the body acquires this religious narrative, and how this narrative is modified by it. The electric shock episode underscores the suggestion that the body has its own memory and therefore the marking of the body in acts of violence – especially torture – has a peculiarly potent power. Thus, although she cannot see him, the memory of 'the howl' of the man whose legs are run over by a truck as punishment '[stays] in her memory forever' (465), and it is precisely this sharing in the pain of others which marks the movement up and out of the depths of despair for her mind, and redeems her body from its 'thingness'. The process of 'redemption', then, is effected largely through the feeling of community, of unity with fellow sufferers.[28] Thus, Ana Diaz is the first to call Alba *companero*. Moreover, the language of religion is not employed by Allende, herself, other than the oblique reference to Christ on the Cross. Rather, it springs as analogy to the reader's mind in a section which is noteworthy for its lack of metaphorical language.

The complete loss of hope, then (there is no escape for her, because Garcia has no motive and no goal other than to torture her; it is an end in itself), brings Alba to the rock bottom of despair, and she can either surrender or find a way out. It is through empathy with the pain of her fellow prisoners that her salvation lies. It is, of course, possible to state it the other way around and say that it is her upward movement that allows her to feel compassion. At any rate, the two are inseparable from each other. When Garcia plunges Alba's face into a bucket of excrement until she faints from disgust, 'Alba [understands] that he was not trying to learn Miguel's whereabouts, but to avenge himself for injuries that had been inflicted upon him from birth and that nothing she could confess would have any effect on her fate as the private prisoner of Colonel Garcia. This allowed her to slowly venture out of the private circle of her terror. Her fear began to ebb and she began to feel compassion for others' (467). While the logic here is somewhat ambiguous (why should this knowledge not, for instance, serve to terrify her the more?), this 'compassion' allows Alba to move into the next phase – out of her involvement with herself (or her 'self') and into a community of pain. In this process, Alba is helped by Ana Diaz, who is clearly at this point herself. Thus, she is able to help Alba through her pain even while undergoing so much herself.

This is the beginning of the formation of a collective in Alba's mind, and its nascent form is of a shared resistance. 'Ana Diaz helped her to resist when they were together' (467), marking the point at which it becomes possible for Alba to acquire agency through her sense of collectivity with other sufferers. Although the nature of this community/collectivity is often no more than an animal comfort (when Ana comes back after losing her baby, she and Alba '[huddle] together like two small animals' [468]), the movement from selfhood through pain and compassion towards resistance and a common cause/enemy is complete. From here, what remains is to construct an abiding sense of a larger collectivity. It is at this point that Alba joins the group of singing women. Singing is an ancient and traditional form of expressing community-hood, with a deeply embedded religious context as well as folk and cultural roots. In the context of the prisons, it becomes, also, a means of including the men who are physically separated from the women.

The test of the strength and potency of this collectivity comes when Alba must draw upon its support even when she is physically separated from it. At this stage there is no meta-narrative from which to seek as collective identity and sustenance. When Garcia has her thrown into the 'doghouse', Alba is left to her own resources as well as whatever reserves of strength her new-found sense of community has given her. Trying to 'stave off madness...now that she was alone, she realised how much she needed Ana Diaz. Despairing, she began eagerly waiting for death' (469). The physical isolation marks another, more potent kind of despair, because it threatens the means by which Alba had regained signification earlier: the community. It is significant, therefore, that this time, she must *construct it* herself – or rather, *re-construct* it through artifice. It is when she almost succeeds in starving herself to death that the Magic Realism enters once again in the shape of Clara. Alba's grandmother appears to her 'with the novel idea that the point was not to die, since death would come anyway, but to survive, which would be a miracle...She suggested that she write a testimony' (469–70). In itself not a meta-narrative, such a testimony becomes one in the significance of its very existence. The mere presence of a testimonial document acquires a materiality and authority that the act of sharing of pain cannot have. Moreover, the importance of not merely testifying to the truth of one's reality through suffering, but of recording the suffering of others *for* others, becomes crucial to the *construction* of the collective. Testifying does not construct an artifice: writing a testimony does. Thus, in this investing of an artifice with life, for the first time since Alba is taken away, the magical reappears in the novel; in a chapter bereft of all metaphoricity, the spirit of Clara appears.

Significantly, this spirit is described in acute material detail. How she looked and how she smelled, these details make Clara 'real' – as real as Alba's isolation and wish for death. Only thus can she be an effective foil to the desire for death. Only thus, also, can Allende help to render 'real' the vision of the rebel rather than that of the state, aesthetically weighing in on their side, as it were. The politics of Allende's aesthetics is evident, equally, in depicting the torture on

Alba's body as well as on the other prisoners' bodies – and in show-ing their minds and integrity to escape whole – in the most material and graphic terms. By doing so, Allende is, I think, rendering the suf-fering, as well as what it stands for, for the rebel dream, 'real'. For her, the rebel's reality is uppermost, victorious, even though political change is yet to be achieved, and it is possible to see the inscription of this vision as mediating between its realisation and its deferment.

Such a tactic – the 'arbitrary' reappearance of Magic Realism – indicates Allende's agenda of pointing a way out, a path for hope. This can, according to the politics of her aesthetics, only be done through a connection with the spirit or essence of that Chile which the rebel seeks to reanimate and which the state seeks to destroy. That life-giving animus is Clara, both as spirit of 'Chile' which must be preserved as well as of a Chile which must be constructed. The act and idea of testimony, moreover, is historically, as well as psycho-logically, accurate.[29] Fittingly, then, this is the process by which the violenced body is seen as evidence rather than merely as a signifier of pain. Thus, although at first Alba's 'intention to compose a documen-tary' is thwarted by the sheer number and urgency of the thousands of characters and stories which press upon her mind, eventually her desire and ability to remember everything 'over[comes] all her varied agonies' (470). Thus it is that Alba reaches the stage that finally lifts her 'beyond [Garcia's] power' (471).

The importance of the act of bearing witness or providing testi-mony lies largely in the fact that it initiates the process of healing by investing the violenced body with meaning. 'These people bore their suffering thus for this cause.' Even if the act of testimony is carried without a political cause in mind, there is always a purpose behind the act of testimony. In the case of the Holocaust, for instance, it may simply be that such suffering must never go unremembered: if not for the explicit purpose of avoiding such suffering in the future, then at the very least – and perhaps at its most powerful – it is undergone as an act of faith, an act of commemoration, an act of valorisation. 'Such suffering must not go unacknowledged.' The acknowledgement, the recognition renders it always real and always present; accords to it a status and stature beyond the individual, investing it with a meaning which endures beyond and separate from the event itself.

In the act of bearing witness, or providing testimony, the body is, of course, the most material evidence. Both sides – the state as well as the resistance – use it as a sort of living palimpsest where the proof and mark of the reality of the torturer can be written and overlaid upon the living, innocent and unmarked body of the victim. These marks are, of course, read quite differently by the victim, who sees in them the struggle to make the rebel's vision a reality. In this context, the indisputable, material presence of the body and its wounds is translated into the indisputable and material presence of the visionary future for which the rebel undergoes the torture. Thus, the violenced body becomes the site of conflicting narratives.

The body as 'thing' is invoked by the 'pile of corpses' with which the narrative of torture begins: although they are somewhere else, the name of the city of Djakarta becomes almost iconic. By transforming the individual rebel into pure object (the 'raw meat' which Alba's body and, indeed, Alba herself, becomes) the torturer seeks to divest the victim of all individuality and her body of all meaning. If the body means nothing, it also means 'nothing': in other words, it signifies 'nothingness', the indifference and meaningless at the heart of all things which serves to render the quest and cause of the rebel null and void. The vision which the rebel seeks to render real through her body can no longer be attached to the body; this disjunction prohibits the possibility of either one investing the other with meaning. The vision can no longer give meaning to the violenced body, nor can the violenced body render the vision real upon itself. This, then, is the purpose of the torturer, and it is the possibility of this happening that creates the fear beyond pain which is the most potent and the most destructive to the rebel's will for survival.

At the same time as the body becomes capable of signifying nothingness, and for that reason, it resonates with the suddenly endless possible means and manner of pain to which the body can be subjected. Historically, narratives of several kinds have been provided for the body, comprehending it within sacred, secular, sexual or other ideologies. I would go so far as to say that the overwhelming need to provide such narratives for the body springs from the subconscious recognition that certain narratives need to be kept out. Among these is the possibility that all narratives are constructs and that the body, in and of itself, is mere 'thing'. Hence, in the invalidation of certain narratives, others, feared and unknown, become possibilities. With the outer layer of skin, the boundaries/barriers and limits are also breached and broken, and the shell of acceptable security within which the person must necessarily live is violated and shattered to the same degree in which the body's inviolability is destroyed. This is the paralysing fear beyond pain which Alba confronts in the dog-house. Only the act of reinvesting her own as well as other bodies with significance can, therefore, counter the nullifying effect of the violence inflicted upon them.

The revelation of the three chopped-off fingers in Trueba's trau-matised account to Transito Soto comes as a dramatic climax to this nexus of narratives and narrative possibilities woven around the tor-tured body of Alba. It comes, also, at a point when Allende has slowed down and deintensified the account of torture in the prison: when Trueba begins his narrative, it appears as though all that remains is the denouement – the manner of Alba's release and her homecom-ing. As it happens, it is, indeed, an account of the manner of her homecoming, but premeditatively deceptive. There are three reasons why this event should not have been included in the description of her torture. First, this act of violence is different from the other torture inflicted upon her body and its peculiar symbolic resonance would have confused the issue of the sheer physical torture and pain which the 'Moment Of Truth' chapter seeks to focus on. Second, the symbolic significance has to be allowed to reverberate long after the initial shock of the act has passed. The manner of its narration – as part of the long, frenzied monologue by Trueba, at a point when the reader thinks that the worst is over and all that remains now is to discover the means by which Alba is freed – is calculated to deliver the most powerful impact possible; and, of course, it succeeds. Third, the revelation must come at a point when Alba has moved beyond despair and into a sense of healing and community; beyond hate and pain. Only then can the reader fully appreciate that she is the instrument through which the debt of violence is paid; she is the sac-rificial lamb, the scapegoat, who is to pay, with her body, the price which will signal the beginning of the end of this violence. Finally, to have described the event in the present tense would have put too great a burden of awareness on the part of Esteban Garcia and Alba: as it is, the questions remain but are not integral to the narrative. Does Garcia's ordering the amputation of the three fingers indicate an awareness of the larger significance of this act in terms of the chain of events which brought him to where he is? Does Alba know about the three fingers cut off by her grandfather in the feudal feud between him and Pedro Tercero Garcia? Clearly, Garcia's posting the fingers to Trueba is a reminder both of their complicity in the violence inflicted upon Trueba as well as revenge for his 'bastard peasant fate'.

Trueba's narrative to Transito Soto asserts Alba's innocence, thereby merely reinforcing the connection: 'A macabre joke that brings back memories, but memories that have nothing to do with Alba, my granddaughter wasn't even born then, I'm sure I have a lot of enemies, all of us politicians have enemies, it's not surprising there's some maniac out there who wants to torture me by sending me fingers through the mail' (478). Trueba sees himself as 'just a poor, destroyed old man' (478), and possibly at this point, is not able to see his responsibility or the chain that links him to Esteban Garcia. But the memory of the three fingers lingers in Esteban Garcia's mind and comes to its own 'natural' conclusion with the ritual cutting off of Alba's fingers.[30] This act is never portrayed but rather presented to the reader almost casually – it is all but concealed within Trueba's traumatised ravings as he breaks down in front of Transito Soto when he begs her for her help. Even then, it is left unclear whether Trueba is speaking of his fear of some such thing happening or whether it has, indeed, happened; and if it has, then which part of Alba's body was sent to him remains hidden. The fact of the three missing fingers is revealed only upon Alba's return and then it is not dwelt upon too much. Trueba weeps and Alba consoles him but it is almost as if the trope has served its purpose and its revelation is merely the occasion for the reconciliation – of Trueba with the truth of his failure, and with his grand-daughter.

At this point also, of course, Allende is invested in rehabilitating Trueba, a task that is easier since the more demonised Garcia gets in the course of the 'Moment Of Truth' chapter, the more disparate Trueba and he become. Thus, in his monologue to Soto, he says: 'I was present for the Te Deum in the cathedral, and precisely because I was I can't accept that this sort of thing should happen in my country.' Earlier, he rails against an order where, 'if people like us can be arrested then nobody is safe' (475).

The epilogue functions both as a record of the process of healing through bearing testimony as well as – at least in part – the testimony itself. Trueba moots the idea that the act of writing down everything is a means of '[taking] [her] roots with [her]'. Thus, the testimony that Alba records is, in fact, her 'country'. Of course, the entire book is the testimony itself, but the epilogue bears witness specifically to the tortured and the survivors. Thus, there is the detailed description of Rojas the doctor. Even non-Chileans will recognise the name of Rojas Rodriguez, the nineteen-year-old photographer who burned to death as part of the extermination campaign of the Pinochet regime. The Rojas of the novel, 'who had already cared for an interminable procession of unlucky souls . . . kept an exact tally of everyone who entered and left and he could recite their names, dates of entry and departure, and their circumstances without hesitation' (482).

The 'Epilogue' is also the first point at which Alba speaks of herself in the first person, indicating, perhaps, that she has reached the final stage of a selfhood that is part of a collective identity. Thus, she, Trueba and her unborn child, who emerge at the end as the survivors and true inheritors of Chile, spend their first few days cleaning up the house and making it livable again, for the first time after the death of Clara. At this point, also, Alba is reinforced as symbolic of the country itself: Miguel and Trueba join forces to rescue her, just as Trueba had earlier made his peace with Pedro Tercero who rescued him because of his daughter, Blanca. Alba, in her direct confrontation with Esteban also, signifies the country ('Chile') that must be saved, preserved, salvaged. In her lies the past of the magic world of Rosa, Clara and even Blanca's revolutionary love, from whom she inherits each of their rebellious characteristics: Rosa's green hair, Clara's care and concern for the people of her land, and Blanca's tragic, demanding and absolute love for a revolutionary. Where each of these women failed, faltered or was only semi-successful, Alba succeeds, completes and perseveres. In her is also the past of Trueba; his conviction, his love of the land, his strength and fortitude. She is the only person with whom he truly connects, with whom he can have a reciprocated relationship of love and mutual understanding. His sins are her burden, his past her present. In all of this lineage of inheritance and accumulated sins and joys, the future rests squarely on Alba's shoulders. The future is hers: hers and Esteban Trueba's – Trueba's legacy of good-and-evil. She is, thus, the future of Chile, and the best hope of its present. It is, then, a grim but fitting truth that her child – the child who, by the logic of this lineage, will be the future 'Chile', the inheritor of the conflict or pact between Alba and Esteban Garcia – could well be the child of incest and rape (if he is the product of Esteban Garcia's rape of Alba) or simply the product of Alba's rape at the hands of several faceless torturers. In other words, her child, the new Chile, will necessarily be the product of the rape of the old Chile by the new, even while it is also the natural descendant (and consequence) of the old Chile.

Finally, the epilogue gives an account of the process of healing for Alba, which is also the process of bearing witness, and testimonial recording. As the conclusion of a book of testimony, also, this is a fitting conclusion: the book ends with a vision of collective harmony and caring, hope for the country and the future. The 'Ode To Joy' is a poem about the equality of all men, and in the act of singing it, the women in the prison project both a vision of future equality as well as the joy which springs from and in spite of suffering. The vision of the country is given in the women in the concentration camp, and exemplified in the woman who shelters Alba for her first night outside:

> She was one of those stoical, practical women of our country, the kind of woman who has a child with every man who passes through her life and, on top of that, takes in other people's aban-doned children, her own poor relatives, and anybody else who needs a mother, a sister, or an aunt; the kind of woman who's the pillar of many lives, who raises her children to grow up and leave her and lets her men leave her too, without a word of reproach, because she has more pressing things to worry about. She looked like so many others I had met in the soup kitchens, in my Uncle Jaime's clinic, at the church office where they would go for infor-mation on their disappeared, and in the morgue where they would go to find their dead ... The days of Colonel Garcia ... are num-bered, because they have not been able to destroy the spirit of these women. (487)

Thus, unlike the collective of women in *Beloved*, this is not so much a collective as a vision of the unique place of women in the resistance against a power which threatens to destroy the culture of which they are the symbols and bearers.

In this text it seems clear, as I have shown, that Allende sets up a sense (and history) of 'the women' (484) as the survivors, the nar-rators, the regenerators, the reservoirs of memory and the source of future life and hope.[31] They are the bearers of stories, songs and crafts that carry the culture on and preserve it. In prison, Alba feels that Adriana's children will carry on these songs and gestures to their children. Adriana is reminiscent of Morrison's Sethe in her attempt to kill her (Sethe's) children in order to save them from the slave hunters. The place of women is also deeply implicated with that of mothers: protection becomes of the utmost importance in a culture where all people, including children, are in danger of their lives. Thus, women also become the mourners, the lamenters, the bearers of sorrow, the mater dolorosas who weep for their lost and killed sons. Thus, Alba bears testimony on behalf of 'mother[s] who had gone mad...unfamiliar mothers who had not lost their voices for lullabies', and '[she wonders as she writes] how Adriana's children would be able to return the songs and the gestures to the children and grandchildren of the women who were rocking them to sleep' (485). This notion of repeating the gesture is startling when Allende mentions it in the context of the cycle of history in which, as Alba says, 'afterward the grandson of the woman who was raped repeats the gesture with the granddaughter of the rapist' (490). Both gestures are part, Alba implies, of 'an unending tale of sorrow, blood and love' (490). This curiously sanguine tone seems out of place and incongruous as an ending to the novel, coming, as it does, almost too soon after the harrowing details of torture and pain. What it does do, however, in distancing itself from the action and giving a sense of the ongoing-ness of history, of history itself as a meta-narrative encompassing the particular life and narrative of the individual, is to give the story the philosophical status of an epic saga.[32] It also deftly avoids the options of either projecting a future which might prove too utopian to be realistic, or to focus on the pain and torture which would not be an adequate conclusion.

Thus, Allende gives to Alba the transcendence she needs to 'break that terrible chain'. 'It would be very difficult for me to avenge all those who should be avenged,' she says, 'because my revenge would be just another part of the same inexorable rite.' She does not wish to 'prolong hatred' (490).[33] The limitation of self-growth that such hatred demands requires, also, that the victim remain within the stasis of the past – the process that Felman and Laub call 'durational time'. Such a positioning excludes the possibility of the breaking out of the binary of oppressor/victim that is essential for the formation of any collective more fundamental or lasting than that of shared victimhood. Thus, the selfhood and love for the country that is imperative for the process/act of owning is never allowed to be put into place. It is this process which is necessary for Alba to undergo in order to be able to 'own' the country as her own in spite of the suffering inflicted upon her. Thus, rather than carry out revenge, she breaks the chain in order to write while she 'waits for Miguel' (an act of faith and hope) and to 'carry this child in my womb, the daughter of so many rapes or perhaps of Miguel, but above all, my own daughter' (491).

This transcendent viewpoint is akin to the epic in its rising above and beyond individual enmities and hatreds in order to give a larger, fuller picture. This epic stance merges seamlessly with the individual figure of Alba, positing the country's/collective's past and future in her person; freezing it in a present whose stillness defies stasis. The intensity of past pain and the intangibility of hope for the future are held in tremulous tension in the act of waiting. As such, it is a syncretic act and the only resolution that the narrative can reach towards.

Notes

1 The Mystery of Violence

1. While there is not the space here to discuss her theorisation in this regard, I think that it is significant that she distinguishes between pain and emotions such as fear or love. The answer to the question of why pain is a separate category is, perhaps, implicit in much of her work in this book but Scarry addresses it directly only briefly. Her explicit explanation bases itself on her observation that pain 'takes no object' and therefore, is impossible to objectify. In other words, while other emotions such as fear and admiration are always necessarily fear 'of' or admiration 'of' someone or something, pain attaches to nothing other than itself. Although she does not explicitly make the distinction between emotion and bodily sensation herself, she goes on to argue that pain is different from pleasure in that articulations of love may be found in *Romeo and Juliet* or the poetry of Keats, while no such text exists for pain. It can be argued, however, that pain, too, is attached to something: the cut, the scrape, the burn; or the pain *in* the arm, the head, the broken bone. One could even say that the object of pain is more immediate, more intimate than the object of respect or admiration, a proximity that renders it rather more attached to its object than less. The idea that *Romeo and Juliet* or the poetry of Keats is any more an articulation of love than *Titus Andronicus* or *Beloved* is of pain and violence I find hard to defend. Indeed, it could be argued that while pain and violence may be audibly, if non-verbally, articulated in several ways on stage at least (the scream, the cry, the groan; even the expression of agony is easily effected on stage), love and pleasure have comparatively fewer audible expressions. Even facial representations of the emotion of love are harder to convey than those of pain.
2. This interrogation of the structure of faith in general and Christian doctrine in particular is undertaken, not in order to reflect upon the individual author's adherence to this or any other religious narrative, but rather to offer an alternative understanding of the status of the violenced body as being both mysterious as well as having absolute agency to create or destroy. Within certain kinds of Christian narratives, faith has the power to imbue all things with significance while violence destroys all signification.

2 'To witness . . . these wrongs unspeakable': the Metaphorical, the Material and the Violenced Body

1. The two are closely connected and I will distinguish or conflate them as the context demands. Similarly, notions of suffering and death also carry a great deal of slippage and I shall clarify my meaning in context.

2. I use this term to indicate the body to which violence has been done and for which there is no narrative: the violence beyond 'comprehension'. I find it necessary to reject other available terms such as 'violated' and 'wounded' since both of these imply certain assumptions which I wish to avoid. Both terms – the notion of being 'violated' or 'wounded' – assume a narrative of wholeness, sanctity or purity that is invaded, injured and/or destroyed, and both can be subsumed within familiar and different narratives.

3. William Shakespeare, *Titus Andronicus* (London and New York: Routledge, 1991). All further references will be from this edition (ed. J. C. Maxwell); Act, Scene and line references will be included in the text.

4. Stephen Owen, *Mi-Lou: Poetry and the Labyrinth of Desire*, in Ledbetter (1996: 1).

5. I use the notion of the Church, in spite of its anachronicity, to indicate the institutionality of the religious system within which Titus is placed.

6. A similar movement occurs in *Hamlet* when, after defending his life from an attack at sea, Hamlet abandons his previous cogitations on the soldier's/son's ethic of unthinking action in defence of his murdered father, and gives himself over to the codes of revenge and the action it demands from him.

7. For which reason Marcus is able, at the end of the scene, to pity Titus because 'he takes false shadows for true substances' (III, ii, 80) without realising that, for Titus, the gap between the two no longer exists: all is 'substance'.

8. Dori Laub, in his chapter titled 'An Event Without a Witness' (in Felman and Laub, 1992: 79), points to a different kind of silence surrounding the Holocaust. 'The imperative to tell the story,' he says, 'is inhabited by the impossibility of telling.' But this is not to say that there exist no narratives of the Holocaust or even that there was a time – perhaps earlier, closer to the event – at which there was a complete silence, comparable to that surrounding the Partition. There have, indeed, been accounts, but 'even those who have talked incessantly feel that they managed to say very little that was heard' (Laub, in Caruth, 1995: 64). In other words, the Holocaust shares the psychological impossibility of speech with the Partition, but not the literal and absolute absence of it.

9. Laub points to an eerily similar phenomenon in the efficacy of the Nazi system of indoctrination of 'otherness'. 'The Nazi system,' he says, was foolproof...in the sense that it convinced its victims...that what was affirmed about their "otherness" and their inhumanity was correct and that their experiences were no longer communicable even to themselves, and therefore perhaps never took place' (in Felman and Laub, 1992: 82).

10. In Manto's short story, 'Open', Sakina has been abducted during the Partition: her father's desperate search for her ends when he finds her in a hospital. The doctor who greets him warns the father that Sakina has probably undergone repeated beating and rape at the hands of her abductors and he is not sure whether she is even alive. The distraught father watches through a window as the doctor commands that the door to the

room be opened. As he calls 'Open!' to the orderly waiting inside, the seemingly lifeless body of Sakina begins to undo the cord of her pyjamas. Even as the significance of her gesture sinks in, her father shouts out in joy: 'She's alive!' The story ends there.

11. The national identity of people who were in the process of moving from India to Pakistan or vice versa is physically implicated in the long caravans of entire populations moving in either direction across the newly created boundaries from one nation to another. Thus, the actual nationality of each person was literally in a fluid state, vulnerable to violent appropriation. Each woman abducted by either side and assimilated into the abductor's family was one less citizen of the other nation.

12. Laub's case, that the Holocaust was made a holocaust precisely because 'of the unique way in which, during its historical occurrence, *the event produced no witnesses*' (in Felman and Laub, 1992: 80, original emphasis) is an interesting one which can, I think, be extended into an understanding of other violent conflicts as well. Laub's argument that 'not only, in effect, did the Nazis try to eliminate the physical witnesses of their crime; but the inherently incomprehensible *and* deceptive psychological structure of the event precluded its own witnessing, even by its very victims' (in Felman and Laub, 1992: 80). Recent global history has shown us that most ethnic violence has within it structural, if not psychological impulses towards 'cleansing'.

13. 'Writing as an Act of Hope' (in Zinsser, 1989).

14. In this context, Allende's own response to interpretations of her novels seems intriguing: on being presented with differing readings of the death of Barrabas in *House of Spirits*, she replies, 'well, really, Barrabas was just the dog I had at home. And he was killed as it was told in the book. But, of course, it sounds better to answer that Barrabas symbolizes the innocence of Clara, so that's the explanation I give when somebody asks' (45). After she has been at such pains to emphasise the fluidity of the real and the non-real in her fictional work as well as in her actual life, and to register the importance of every part of the text as a symbolic force, this resistance to the very act of interpretation and her insistence on the verisimilitude of her work seems odd. The 'reality' of her representation of life in Chile does not, elsewhere in her theorisation of her writing practices, exclude the possibility of multiple significations. Indeed, it would appear to establish this very aspect of her narrative strategies.

3   Remembering and Dismembering: Toni Morrison's *Beloved* and *Sula*

1. In the context of my reading of the Book of Daniel dealing with the story of Shadrach, Meshach and Abednego, the Shadrack of *Sula* reacts in a significantly divergent manner. While the experience of being thrown into the furnace by Nebuchadnezzar seems not to touch the biblical Shadrach at all (or, at least, as I have pointed out in Chapter 2, the event is not narrated at all, and we are told nothing of what he feels during or after his

experience in the furnace), Morrison's Shadrack is spiritually destroyed, rather than avenged by his experience in the war. In the context of my reading of *Sula* it is significant, perhaps, that Shadrack is alone, without his companions in suffering, Meshach and Abednego, from whom he is not differentiated at all in the Book of Daniel. This sense of total isolation is foundational to his post-war psyche and instrumental in his formulation of the 'community' of the dead on National Suicide Day. There are no war veterans in the Bottom, no one who has shared his experiences of the war – returned alive from the furnace, as it were.

2. And this is why, in this context, the opposite of 'remember' is not to forget, but to 'dis-member'.

3. In theorising this area, I owe a great debt to my conversations with Madhu Dubey: many of the formulations and nuances of my argument here surfaced in the course of stimulating and provocative discussions.

4. Controversial as the notion of realism in the novel is, I wish only to clarify that I refer, at this point, to the impulse sustained from the earliest British novel towards demystification, on the one hand, and towards foregrounding the scaffolding of its own structures on the other.

5. For an excellent, detailed discussion of the generic implications of this tension as well as the contradictions and complexities of Morrison's own position regarding this issue, see Dubey (1999).

4 Immigration and Identity: Maxine Hong Kingston's *The Woman Warrior* and Amy Tan's *The Joy Luck Club*

1. For the sake of clarity (since the text identifies itself as a 'memoir', indicating that the author and her persona within the text are one and the same person) I will refer to the protagonist and narrator as 'Maxine' and the author as Kingston.

2. I do not wish to join the debate regarding the genre of this text. Much has been written about the circumstances under which it was first published as an autobiography, and Kingston herself chooses not to consider it a novel, citing its usage of many forms and genres. In my understanding of this debate, I do not see anything that seriously controverts my view of it as a novel.

3. See, for instance, the telling of stories in the laundry: Maxine's mother tells her children the legends of ancient Chinese heroes Kao Chung, Chou Yi-han, Chen Luan-feng, Wei Pang and the 'anonymous scholar' who were 'big eaters' and ate the ghosts who confronted them. Immediately after this catalogue Maxine recounts the times that her 'mother has cooked for [them]: raccoons, skunks, hawks, city pigeons, wild ducks, wild geese, black-skinned bantams, snakes, garden snail, turtles that crawled about the pantry floor and sometimes escaped under refrigerator or stove, catfish that swam in the bathtub.' 'I have seen revulsion on the faces of visitors who've caught us at meals,' she says, establishing the 'American-normal' perspective. 'I would rather live on plastic' (88–92).

4. Wendy Ho, *In Her Mother's House: the Politics of Asian American Mother-Daughter Writing* (Walnut Creek, Oxford: AltaMira Press, 1999).
5. 'The Intellectual Physiognomy in Characterization' in *Lukács: Writer and Critic*, ed. and trans. Professor Arthur Kahn (London: Merlin Press, rep. 1978).
6. Although, in response to criticism that she presents too negative a view of China, Kingston has reiterated in several interviews that she intended only to represent her own family and her own, personal experiences, in the light of my reading of this novel I find this view less than persuasive. For Kingston's articulation of her position, see Paul Skenazy and Tera Martin (eds), *Conversations with Maxine Hong Kingston* (Jackson: University Press of Mississippi, 1998), p. 67. At other times she seems to support the notion that her family was seen by her as being representative. See, for instance, *Conversations* (91): 'My whole family was in that book. All those faces, with the complete physiognomy of that first generation of Chinese American chaotic families.'
7. It should be said that Kingston's own understanding of the realist novel is quite different from the one that I have briefly alluded to here. She sees her one 'craft [to be] ... so revolutionary' because 'God in the nineteenth century was a white man'. Her statement that '[she is saying that] that's not so anymore' (89) gestures towards a far more monolithic and far less complicated vision of realism and the nineteenth-century realist novel.
8. This dilution of the term from something malevolent to something merely insubstantial is seen as soft pedalling the degree of racism Chinese immigrants face in America.
9. Moon Orchid follows Maxine and her siblings around the house 'narrating' their every action. 'She followed her nieces and nephews about. She bent over them "Now she is taking a machine off the shelf. She attaches two metal spiders to it. She plugs in the cord. She cracks an egg against the rim and pours the yolk and white out of the shell into the bowl. She presses a button, and the spiders spin the eggs"' (140).
10. Kingston mentions in an interview that she chose this episode to experiment with different forms and decided to use the form of the melodramatic Chinese movie.

5   'An invisible country, a true Chile': the Body of Evidence in Isabel Allende's *House of Spirits*

1. Elizabeth Lira and Isabel Castillo (researchers for the Latin American Institute for Mental Health and Human Rights [ILAS]), document some of the edicts of the Junta: 'The regime remodels the very perception of social reality, changing names of towns and streets that recall forbidden ideas ... A community born of a land occupation during the Popular Unity government was named "New Havana". The military rulers renamed the place "Nuevo Amanecer" (New Dawn). In Temuco, the

low-income community of "Lenin" became "Lanin", the name of a volcano which exists on the Argentine-Chilean border. In Tarapaca, the new
officials forbade residents to paint their houses red.'

Lira and Castillo also speak of the official language employed by the
military rulers, particularly the use of the verb 'to clean', to describe military operations: 'Public walls are cleaned. With black or white paint,
slogans and murals of the past are erased. Public offices are "cleansed",
and everyone who brought dirt into the workplace is out of a job... In one
clean-up operation thousands of books, magazines, phonograph records
and posters [were] confiscated from the San Borja high-rise apartment
complex (in Santiago) and burned in public bonfires.'

2. Ariel Dorfman. See also the documentary on Che Guevara's body (PBS,
   21 September 1999, 10.30 p.m.).
3. Although allegorical figuration (especially that in which women are
   used to represent collective identities) is – and has historically been –
   compatible with realist narratives, it seems allied, in this novel, with the
   more non-realist strategies of Allende's Magic Realism. Such an alliance is
   especially facilitated by the fact that the women are also the main media
   of this magic world.
4. It is not surprising, then, that Clara is seen, very early in the novel, as the
   voice of realism when the child Clara speaks out against Father Restrepo's
   rhetoric of heaven and hell (17). Insofar as she eschews the rhetoric of
   extremes, the language of religious fervour which invests so much of the
   writing regarding the 'true Chile' by exiles and revolutionaries, this voice
   of reason is an index to Allende's far more even-handed recognition of the
   larger nexus of forces which are responsible for the evil of the Pinochet
   regime.
5. After Clara's death Alba starts having (prophetic) nightmares where she
   sees the future – everyone dying, the house deserted, herself alone (346).
6. The ancient, overwhelmingly beautiful pottery of ancient Indian origin is seen as native, original and real as against the 'monsters' from
   Blanca's crèche, which are reminiscent of Rosa's nightmarish menagerie
   (292–3). This is one of the few times that the past is uncomplicatedly
   valorised, beautiful and seemingly simple as against the monstrous and
   complex present. Yet even this picture is complicated by the presence of
   the 'Indians' who seem so unchangingly ancient and decadent.
7. See René Girard (1979), Felman and Laub (1992), Kleinman, Das and Lock
   (1997, 2000) and Scarry (1985).
8. The complex nexus between religion and politics is particularly pertinent to Chile's resistance movement under the Pinochet regime. On
   18 September 1973, Spanish priest Joan Alsina was arrested, beaten and
   shot ten times in the back: he was both head of personnel as well as
   involved with the Workers Movement for Catholic Action (MOAC). Two
   other priests, Miguel Woodward of Valparaiso and Gerardo Poblete of
   Iquique, were killed before Alsino. Alsina, Woodward and Poblete were
   only the first of the many priests who were intimately involved in the
   resistance movement. Several religious organisations were also formed

for the active rehabilitation and/or help for tortured or disappeared people, as well as for the purpose of advancing the legal representations of these people or their families and documenting human rights violations. These include the Vicaria de la Solidaridad, a church-run organisation dedicated to the defence of human rights under the dictatorship which now runs archives. After Sebastian Acavedo's self-immolation in protest against the arrest and torture of his children (11 November 1983), priest Jose Aldunate became the head of the Sebastian Acavedo Anti-Torture Movement which quickly grew into a broad-based organisation that challenged the practice of torture. On 10 December 1983, the Catholic Church confirmed its earlier resolution to deny torturers communion. The bishops unanimously approved the resolution at the Chilean Episcopal Conference, headed by Bishop Bernardino Pinero. The resolution states: 'torturers, their accomplices, and those who have the power to prevent torture, but fail to do so cannot receive the holy communion unless they sincerely repent … the fundamental reform of security forces and the CNI in particular is absolutely indispensable and urgent so that they act within the confines of morality and just laws that should govern a country'.

Historical data has been taken from *Piscologia de la Amenaza Politicia y del Miedo*, compiled by Elizabeth Lira and Maria Isabel Castillo (ILAS, 1991 – Lira and Castillo), unless otherwise specified.

9. Blanca and Pedro Tercero are evocative of Catherine and Heathcliff in the socio-sexual conflict that crystallises in their relationship (320). Their bond is at once earthy and material in its social context and implications, as well as dreamlike and idyllic; 'the realist, pragmatic' count is confronted by what, even he, sees as a 'meeting of body and soul' (231).

10. For a contextualisation of Pedro Tercero's survivor guilt, see Felman and Laub (1992) and their accounts of this syndrome with regard to Holocaust victims. 'He began to be obsessed by the idea that he was a coward and a traitor for not having shared the fate of so many others and felt that it would be more honourable to surrender and meet his fate.' One of the first acts of the Pinochet regime was the torturing and killing of the world-renowned folk singer, Victor Jara, at the Chile Stadium on 16 September 1973. Allende's rewriting of Jara's 'fate' in Pedro Tercero's exile is at once cynical, ironical, realistic and sad. In an arena where 'honour' entails torture and death, exile is the only 'honourable' means of survival. While it is not known exactly how many people were exiled, 'thousands' were allowed to re-enter Chile when the Pinochet regime ended their forced exile on 10 August 1988; about 177 persons continued to be denied re-entry at this time. As a token or representative of the thousands who fled, or were forced into exile by the state, it is significant that Pedro Tercero has given up his revolutionary activities even before the regime takes over: in effect, the regime is not really required to force him to surrender. While this may or may not have been the average profile of the Chilean exile, in the account of the exile of Pedro Tercero and Blanca – both of whom live in relative comfort and complacency on

Trueba's money in Canada – Allende strips the act and nature of exile of its romance.

11. This is an interesting progression insofar as the traditional (European, novel) narrative of this vision/action binary is usually personified in the visionary woman and the active man. The clearest example of this binary which springs to mind is the pairing of Charles and Emily Taylor in Conrad's *Nostromo*; others can be seen in the Kitty-Levin and Anna-Levin couples in Tolstoy's *Anna Karenina*, Paul's pairing with both Miriam and Clara in D. H. Lawrence's *Sons and Lovers*, Jim and Jewel in Conrad's *Lord Jim*, and Margaret and Henry in E. M. Forster's *Howard's End*. The earlier part of the nineteenth century is full of such pairs: Fanny and Edmund in Austen's *Mansfield Park*, David and Agnes in Dickens's *David Copperfield*, Elizabeth and Farfrae in Hardy's *The Mayor of Casterbridge*, and Dorothy and Casaubon as well as Will in George Elliot's *Middlemarch*. Similar examples can also be found in Russian and American literature of the period.

12. Pedro Segundo is the bridge between his father, Old Pedro Garcia, who functions as a kind of 'ancestor figure' (his wisdom, natural cures, almost magical understanding of animals and nature etc. mark him as closer to nature and goodness), and the rebel, Pedro Tercero. Old Garcia is, of course, also the natural ancestor of Esteban Garcia, who 'sits at his grandfather's feet hating Trueba and his destiny as a peasant' (220); as ready to drive nails through his grandfather's dead eyes as through the eyes of chickens.

13. Georg Lukács, *The Historical Novel* (London: Merlin, 1962).

14. William Shakespeare, *Hamlet*; the phrase is echoed, also, in Macbeth's 'frame of things disjoint'. It suggests both the characters' sense of reality being slightly askew, a sense which speaks to Jaime's asynchromicism. At a time when he could have functioned as the male guardian of the spirit of Chile, he was enamoured of an image of the country which could not survive the political and social changes forced upon it. When he does recognise where and what the true spirit of Chile is, he is no longer the kind of guardian it requires. Hence, the emaciation of Amanda and the illicit desire of uncle for niece.

15. The exchange between them is like the formal ritualistic closure of the mass – an inversion of the beginning: in an inversion of the incident in which Pedro Tercero rescued Trueba, Trueba rescues Pedro Tercero, and says, 'I've come to get you.' Pedro (instead of Trueba) says, 'Go to hell.' And finally Trueba says 'Fine. That's where we're going, and you're coming with me.' When 'They both [smile] simultaneously' (447), we know that the old enmity/binary is finally laid to rest. They are both united before the common enemy of the regime. Thus, also, the violence and injustice of pre-regime Chile is distinguished from the violence and injustice of the regime.

16. Trueba's violence is once again described as similar to that of the regime's, as well as distinguished from it: he is remorseful and is said to have a conscience. His 'love' for the land is once again mentioned and it is clear

that he wreaks havoc on the land, the cattle and the people out of some strong – if misplaced – sense of revenge (439–40). Again, when Trueba realises that he has made a mistake and weeps we are told that 'He was not crying because he had lost. He was crying for his country' (443). Once again, Trueba is seen as mistaken and wrong-headed but patriotic and right-hearted. If the military are a breed apart then this statement is made at this point precisely in order to distinguish their power, violence and totalitarianism from Trueba's violence and his authoritarianism.

17. See the discussion of *Titus Andronicus* in Chapter 2.
18. I use the term 'intimate' in order to indicate the difference between the totally impersonal violence of war (especially the world wars, as my discussion of *Sula* shows) and the prolonged familiarity and investment engendered by the one-on-one process of torture. The context of ethnic or racial hatred that often attends acts of torture (where slavery would be a special case) compounds the degree of personal investment and knowledge that informs forms of violence I would classify as 'intimate'. (It may be useful to point out that documentation and commentary regarding domestic violence often use the notion of 'intimate violence' to distinguish it from other kinds of abuse. My usage of the term, while similar, is, of course, not identical to this usage but is nuanced by the context in which I use it.)
19. See Girard (1979).
20. (London: Frank Cass, 1998).
21. 'The pile of corpses in the streets of [the] distant city [of Djakarta]' (413) invokes this city in the name of all similarly beleaguered spaces, echoing Neruda's famous refrain: 'come and see the blood in the streets' in 'I Would Like To Explain A Few Things'. The name appears on the walls of Buenos Aires like an omen of the violence to come. At the same time, it is a portent of the sacrifice that will be demanded of the rebels: a reminder that death is the ultimate price that the rebel is required to pay for her dream.
22. This exception to the absence of metaphor in this section is interesting in its evocation of the ghost of Clara who, in her allegorical representation of Chile, would, indeed, be an old woman slowly dying.
23. The psychology of fear employed by the regime played upon the terror induced both by the overt display of military power as well as the more subtle – and therefore, more intimidating – power of the unseen and the unspoken. 'Heavily armed military forces are visible in the streets; helicopters fly over major cities at night. Arrests are made in the light of day, and people are taken away in Armed Forces vehicles. The press and mass media relay extensive information about military operations.' 'One hears the silence of fear in the subway stations and other places where many people congregate and which were always noisy in the past ... No one whistles, no one hums a tune, no arguments are heard. One sees the fear in the fleeting glances, in the controlled gestures ... in exaggerated courtesy' (Lira and Castillo).

24. The Rettig Report and the National Corporation for Reconciliation and Reparation, established on 3 January 1992 to continue the work of the Rettig Commission, concluded in 1996 that: 'A total of 3,197 people died or went missing between September 11, 1973 and March 11, 1990 as a result of human rights violations at the hands of the state agents of repression. Of these 1,102 classify as disappeared and 2,095 as deaths.'

      The Rettig Report and the National Corporation for Reconciliation and Reparation only investigated those cases which concluded in death or disappearance. They did not take into account the thousands of cases of torture and imprisonment which took place during the period of military rule. (See Padilla, 1995.)
25. 'We live in peril of the body becoming thing'. See Mark Ledbetter (1996).
26. I wish to distinguish Trueba's sense of the blurring of the lines between good and evil from my own observation as to the role of violence in establishing a demarcation between the two. In the story of Trueba's own, personal growth, this blurring can be seen as progress insofar as his otherwise rigidly defined world is now opening itself up to alternative modes of understanding. In other words, Trueba is beginning to see the grey in his black and white worldview.
27. Similar invocations can be found throughout Western literature: see Major Barbara's 'my God, my God, why hast thou forsaken me?' in Shaw's *Major Barbara*, at a similar point of despair.
28. Sartre's idea that it is only through our feeling for and with others that we establish a sense of ourselves is borne out here, in Alba's ability to feel compassion for others. This process is evident, also, in much of Western literature, most famously, perhaps, in Lear's 'wits begin[ing] to turn' on the heath as he realises his shared status as part of 'unaccommodated mankind'. William Shakespeare, *King Lear*.
29. See Felman and Laub (1992).
30. Reports from Sierra Leone and Liberia of the cutting off of hands in the ethnic cleansing are especially germane to this context. In response to Charles Taylor's campaign slogan that proclaimed that 'the future is in your hands', rebels retaliated by cutting off the hands of his supporters. (See Chris Allen, 'Warfare, Endemic Violence and State Collapse in Africa', *Review of African Political Economy*, Vol. 26, No. 81, Violence and Conflict Resolution in Africa [Sept. 1999], pp. 367–84.) Apart from the literalisation of the metaphorical that is such a potent aspect of ethnic violence, the significance of hands seems to be a new phenomenon in some ways. Ethnic cleansing and warfare usually focuses (especially for women) on rape, breasts, faces, hair and sometimes backs. It is possible that in terms of the symbolic resonance of certain kinds of violence, hands do have special significance of agency which is literally and symbolically in the process of being wrested from one's opponent (see the place of hands in *Titus Andronicus*). If the question of agency is the important one here, then for the rebel it is a kind of 'unmanning', a destroying of the ability to fight or defend: in an activist, even militant confrontation, this would become an especially potent symbol.

31. I wish to distinguish the desirability of such a construction from my own position. The history of such constructions has shown us that, regardless of its social context (in which, oftentimes, women are, indeed, the ones who remember the stories, songs, gestures etc. that characterise certain kinds of culture) women are consigned to a status of vulnerability and weakness, placing them in the category of second-class citizens. Thus, while I map out Allende's own construction here, I do not endorse it.

32. Allende's Chilean readers (at least, if not others also) will recognise this text as being immersed in the history of the Pinochet regime and, as such, in the history of Chile itself. The characters and plot of the novel, therefore, carry the weight of historically resonant figures and events, much in the same way that the epic does (or did). It is in this sense that I think the historical novel – in structure and agenda – participates in or coincides with the epic.

33. This is also Morrison's idea of the limits of hatred, which is clear from her portrayal of the death of Baby Suggs and the life-sapping effect that Beloved's insistence on the remembrance of past suffering has on Sethe.

Select Bibliography

Ahmad, Aijaz. 'Jameson's Rhetoric of Otherness and the "National Allegory"', in *Theory: Classes, Nations, Literatures* (London: Verso, 1992).

Allende, Isabel. *The House of Spirits* (New York: A. A. Knopf, 1985).

Amin, Shahid. *Event, Metaphor, Memory: Chauri Chaura, 1922–1992* (Delhi: Oxford University Press, 1995).

Anderson, Benedict. 'Cultural Roots', in *Imagined Communities: Reflections on the Origin and Growth of Nationalism* (London: Verso, 1993).

Arendt, Hannah. *On Violence* (New York: Harcourt Brace and World, 1969).

Armitt, Lucie. *Contemporary Women's Fiction and the Fantastic* (New York: St. Martin's Press, 2000).

Auerbach, Erich (c. 1953, trans. Willard Trask). 'Odysseus's Scar', *Mimesis: Representation of Reality in Western Literature* (New York: Doubleday, 1957).

Bakhtin, Mikhail M. (trans. Caryl Emerson and Michael Holquist). *The Dialogic Imagination* (Texas: University of Texas Press, 1981).

Bell, J. Bowyer. *The Dynamics of the Armed Struggle* (London: Frank Cass, 1998).

Benjamin, Walter (trans. Harry Zohn). 'The Storyteller', in *Illuminations* (New York: Schocken, 1969).

Benjamin, Walter. 'A Critique of Violence', in *Reflections: Aphorisms, Essays and Autobiographical Writings*, ed. Peter Demets, trans. Edmund Jephcott (New York and London: Harcourt Brace Jovanovitch, 1978).

Bhabha, Homi, K. (ed.). *Nation and Narration* (London: Routledge, 1990).

Bloom, Harold (ed.). *Modern Critical Interpretations: Beloved* (Philadelphia: Chelsea House Publishers, 1999).

Bloom, Harold (ed.). *Modern Critical Interpretations: Toni Morrison's Sula* (Philadelphia: Chelsea House Publishers, 1999).

Bouson, Brooks J. *Quiet as it's kept: Shame, Trauma, and Race in the Novels of Toni Morrison* (New York: State University of New York Press, 2000).

Caruth, Cathy (ed.). *Trauma: Explorations in Memory* (Baltimore: Johns Hopkins University Press, 1995).

Cavell, Stanley. 'Comments on Veena Das's Essay "Language and Body: Transactions in the Construction of Pain"', in Kleinman et al. (eds), *Social Suffering* (Berkeley: University of California Press, 1997).

Chambers, E. K. (ed.). *Poems of John Donne*. Vol. I (London: Lawrence & Bullen, 1896).

Chang, Joan Chiung-huei. *Transforming Chinese American Literature: a Study of History, Sexuality, and Ethnicity* (New York: Peter Lang, 2000).

Chin, Frank. *Bulletproof Buddhists and Other Essays* (Honolulu: University of Hawaii Press, 1998).

Chin, Frank et al. (eds). *The Big Aiiieeeee! An Anthology of Chinese American and Japanese American Literature* (New York: Penguin, 1991).

Chu, Patricia P. *Assimilating Asians: Gendered Strategies of Authorship in Asian America* (Durham: Duke University Press, 2000).

Clastres, Pierre. *Society against the State: Essays in Political Anthropology* (New York: Zone Books, 1987).

Conner, Mark C. (ed.). *The Aesthetics of Toni Morrison: Speaking the Unspeakable* (Jackson: University of Mississippi Press, 2000).

Das, Veena (ed.). *The Word and the World: Fantasy, Symbol and Record* (Beverley Hills: Sage Publications, 1986).

Das, Veena (ed.). *Mirrors of Violence: Communities, Riots, Survivors in South Asia* (Delhi: Oxford University Press, 1990).

Das, Veena. 'Time, Self and Community: Features of the Sikh Militant Discourse', in *Critical Events: an Anthropological Perspective on Contemporary India* (Delhi: Oxford University Press, 1995).

Das, Veena. 'Language and Body: Transactions in the Construction of Pain', *Daedalus*, Vol. 125 (1996).

DeKoven, Marianne. 'Postmodernism and Post-Utopian Desire in Toni Morrison and E. L. Doctorow', in N. J. Peterson (ed.), *Toni Morrison: Critical and Theoretical Approaches* (Baltimore: Johns Hopkins University Press, 1997).

Dubey, Madhu. 'The Politics of Genre in *Beloved*', *Novel*, Spring 1999.

Duvall, John N. *The Identifying Fictions of Toni Morrison: Modernist Authenticity and Postmodern Blackness* (New York: Palgrave Macmillan, 2000).

Fanon, Frantz. 'On Violence', in *The Wretched of the Earth* (New York: Grove Press, 1968).

Felman, Shoshana and Dori Laub. *Testimony: Crisis of Witnessing in Literature, Psychoanalysis and History* (New York: Routledge, 1992).

Foucault, Michel (trans A. Sheridan). *Discipline and Punish* (New York: Vintage, 1977).

Frye, Northrop. *Anatomy of Criticism* (New York: Atheneum, 1957).

Frye, Northrop. *Fables of Identity* (New York: Harcourt, 1963).

Frye, Northrop. *The Secular Scripture* (Harvard, 1976).

Gao, Yan. *The Art of Parody: Maxine Hong Kingston's Use of Chinese Sources* (New York: Peter Lang, 1996).

Girard, René. *Violence and the Scared* (Baltimore: Johns Hopkins University Press, 1979).

Grewal, Gurleen. *Circles of Sorrow, Lines of Struggle: the Novels of Toni Morrison* (Baton Rouge: Louisiana State University Press, 1998).

Ho, Wendy. *In Her Mother's House: the Politics of Asian American Mother–Daughter Writing* (Oxford: AltaMira, 1999).

Huntley, E. D. *Maxine Hong Kingston: a Critical Companion* (London: Greenwood Press, 2001).

Jameson, Fredric. 'On Interpretation: Literature as a Socially Symbolic Act', in *The Political Unconscious: Narrative as a Socially Symbolic Act* (Ithaca: Cornell University Press, 1981).

Jameson, Fredric. 'Third World Literature in the Era of Multinational Capital', *Social Text*, Fall 1986, pp. 65–8.

King, Jeanette. *Women and the Word: Contemporary Women Novelists and the Bible* (New York: St. Martin's Press, 2000).

Kingston, Maxine Hong. *The Woman Warrior: Memoirs of a Girlhood Among Ghosts* (New York: Vintage International Edition, 1989).

Kleinman, Arthur, Veena Das and Margaret Lock (eds). *Social Suffering* (Berkeley: University of California Press, 1997).

Kleinman, Arthur, Veena Das and Margaret Lock (eds). *Violence and Subjectivity* (Berkeley: University of California Press, 2000).

Ledbetter, Mark. *Victims and the Postmodern Narrative, or, Doing Violence to the Body* (New York: St. Martin's Press, 1996).

Lévi-Strauss, Claude. *The Savage Mind* (Chicago, 1966).

Lévi-Strauss, Claude (trans. Monique Layton). *How Myths Die* (New York: Basic Books, 1976).

Li, David Leiwei. *Imagining the Nation: Asian American Literature and Cultural Consent* (Stanford: Stanford University Press, 1998).

Ling, Amy. *Between Worlds: Women Writers of Chinese Ancestry* (New York: Pergamon Press, 1990).

Lukács, Georg (trans. Hannah and Stanley Mitchell). *The Historical Novel* (London: Merlin, 1962).

Lukács, Georg (ed. and trans. Professor Arthur Kahn). *Writer and Critic and Other Essays* (London: Merlin Press, rep. 1978).

Manto, Saadat Hasan (trans. Khalid Hasan). *Mottled Dawn* (New Delhi: Penguin, 1997).

McKeon, Michael. 'Political Poetry', in Dennis Todd and Cynthia Wall (eds), *Eighteenth-Century Genre and Culture: Serious Reflections on Occasional Forms: Essays in Honor of J. Paul Hunter* (Newark, DE: University of Delaware Press, 2001).

Moretti, Franco. *The Modern Epic* (London: Verso, 1996).

Morrison, Toni. *Sula* (New York: Knopf, 1974).

Morrison, Toni. *Person to Person* (London: Blackwell, 1980).

Morrison, Toni. *City Limits, Village Values: Concepts of the Neighborhood in Black Fiction* (New Brunswick: Rutgers University Press, 1981).

Morrison, Toni. 'Memory, Creation, and Writing', *Thought*, Vol. 59, No. 235, pp. 385–90 (Bronx, NY, 1984, December).

Morrison, Toni. *Faulkner and Women* (Jackson: University of Mississippi Press, 1986).

Morrison, Toni. *Beloved* (London: Picador, 1988).

Morrison, Toni. 'On Behalf of Henry Dumas', *Black American Literature Forum*, Vol. 22, No. 2, pp. 310–12 (Terre, 1988, Summer).

Morrison, Toni. 'Unspeakable Things Unspoken: the Afro-American Presence in American Literature', *Michigan Quarterly Review*, Vol. 28, No. 1, pp. 1–34 (Ann Arbor, 1989, Winter).

Morrison, Toni. 'Black Matter(s)', *Grand Street*, Vol. 10, No. 4 (40), pp. 205–25 (Denville, NJ, 1991).

Morrison, Toni and Lacour, Claudia Brodsky (eds). *Birth of a Nation'hood: Gaze, Script, and Spectacle in the O. J. Simpson Case* (New York: Pantheon Books, 1997).

Morrison, Toni and Naylor, Gloria. 'A Conversation', *Southern Review*, Vol. 21, No. 3, pp. 567–93 (Baton Rouge, LA, 1985 Summer).

Padilla, Elias. *La memoria y el olvido: Detenidos Desaparecidos en Chile* (Ediciones Origenes, 1995).

Redding, Arthur F. *Raids on Human Consciousness: Writing, Anarchism, and Violence* (Columbia: University of South Carolina Press, 1998).

Rosenberg, Eva. *Gender-Voice-Vernacular: the Formation of Female Subjectivity in Zora Neale Hurston, Toni Morrison and Alice Walker* (Heidelberg: Universitatsverlag, 1999).

Scarry, Elaine. *The Body in Pain* (New York: Oxford University Press, 1985).

Shakespeare, William. *Titus Andronicus* (London and New York: Routledge, 1991).

Sharpe, Jenny. *Allegories of Empire: the Figure of the Woman in the Colonial Text* (Minneapolis: University of Minnesota Press, 1993).

Skenazy, Paul and Martin, Tera (eds). *Conversations with Maxine Hong Kingston* (Jackson: University of Mississippi Press, 1998).

Solomon, Barbara H. (ed.). *Critical Essays on Toni Morrison's Beloved* (New York: Palgrave Macmillan, 1998).

Tan, Amy. *The Joy Luck Club* (New York: Ivy Books, 1989).

Vidal, Denis. *Violence and Truth: a Rajasthani Kingdom Confronts Colonial Authority* (Delhi: Oxford University Press, 1997).

Zinsser, William (ed.). *Paths of Resistance: the Art and Craft of the Political Novel* (Boston: Houghton Mifflin, 1989).

Index